D1198629

HOOKED
Hardwired Trilogy Book 1

DeAnna Browne

This is a work of fiction. Names, places, characters and incidents are either the product of the author's imagination or are used fictitiously, and any resemblance to any actual persons, living or dead, businesses, organizations, registered trademarks, and registered service marks are the property of their respective owners and are used herein for identification purposes only.

HOOKED
Copyright © 2018 DeAnna Browne
Cover Art by Bukovero
All cover art copyright © 2018
All rights reserved.

ISBN-13: 978-1-948884-01-3
ISBN-10: 1-948884-01-1

All rights reserved under the International and Pan-American Copyright Conventions. No part of this book may be reproduced or transmitted in any form or by any means, electronic or mechanical, including photocopying, recording, or by any information storage and retrieval system, without permission in writing from the author.

DEDICATION

To my critique partners,
for their never-ending support and
motivation to brush off the dust
and publish this story.

CHAPTER 1

This isn't real.

Ari stood on a nearby hill above the familiar carnival with her brother, Marco. Rides spun endlessly in the distance, and neon lights flashed, illuminating the dark night. It stole her back to a time when the world was a different place, a place full of laughter. An uneasy sensation crawled along Ari's skin as she thought of her body tucked back in reality with wires streaming from the port in her neck.

"Remember how you puked on the Spinning Hammers?" A wide smile lit up Marco's face. Marco and Ari both took after their mother with their tanned skin, dark wavy hair, and chocolate eyes. Except for the smile—Marco wore their father's smile.

She couldn't figure out how her brother always appeared so put together, in and out of the virtual realm. Ari wore a flannel shirt and beat up jeans, and not on purpose. The VR program let people change their clothes, but Ari never stuck around long enough to bother with fashion.

She turned back to the carnival, the rides antiquated and shedding their paint even in this computerized replica.

The carnival had come around every spring when they were little. People lined up all day and night for rides, an event so popular someone made it into a VR.

"Please, Marco, I feel like I'm about to lose it." She dug her nails deep into her palms and welcomed the pain as it grounded her in reality.

"What? You don't like it?" Marco acted surprised. "I had to ask them to dig into their storage to find this virtual for you. Come on."

Marco grabbed Ari's hand and pulled her down the hill towards the rides. The cool night air brushed against her face as they raced down the grassy path, and she fought to keep her fear from bubbling over. She had never lasted more than two minutes in one of these programs, but today she needed to. Her future depended on it. Assignments for their continued education were coming soon, and if she couldn't pass the VR simulation, she might as well sign up for a life of kitchen duty.

Her breath came in rapid pants as they reached the entrance. A disfigured clown face with exaggerated eyes and teeth welcomed them, his mechanical voice scratchy. Her throat tightened as she tried to breathe. She panicked at the idea of being stuck here forever, trapped in this virtual world, spiraling into a VR coma like her father. The government limited the hours kids could be inside a VR, but people, young and old, still slipped, which left their family paying the bill in hopes they would return.

The clown image frizzed momentarily into a dark void with specks of light replacing the creepy face. "Marco, what's going on?" She pointed at the distorted image. There had to be some sort of glitch.

Marco glanced at the clown. "What are you talking about, Ariana?" He tugged on her arm. "Snap out of it. I told Mom we would have fun." He yanked her toward the Tilt-a-Whirl.

An elderly man worked the empty ride, or so her brain told her. He wore a plain blue uniform and a smile that was a touch bigger than necessary. Holding the gate open, he welcomed them inside.

The virtual showed its age as the computerized character blinked constantly and tilted his head every three seconds like clockwork, but they couldn't afford anything more sophisticated. Ari wasn't sure if it was the uncomfortable memory of wires hooked into her unconscious body or this man's creepy behavior that made her want to run away.

She froze with fear at the gate. "I can't do this."

"Yes, you can." Marco's dark eyes locked onto her with a firmness that didn't suit him. "You don't have a choice. Get used to VRs or get used to cleaning toilets while Mom tries to marry you off. Is that what you want?"

Normally she would have smacked her older brother for talking like that, but the truth hit its mark. Biting her lip, she stepped toward the small compartment built for two. Marco climbed in and slid across the faded blue vinyl bench. She squeezed in beside him and fastened the thick black strap.

"I thought you loved being here. I always did."

Every spring, her father would empty the jar of coins on top of the fridge and treat Ari and Marco to a fun day at the carnival. They would fill up on fried bread and cheese curls, watching the night descend into a blur of neon lights. But, unlike her brother, this reminded Ari of what they didn't have anymore: a father and a jar full of savings. In a VR coma, their dad was more dead than alive, and the chipped jar now sat empty on top of a rundown fridge.

Chest tightening, she pushed back the memories. "I'm sorry. I can't, Marco. I gotta go." She clawed at the thick black safety belt as the ride surged forward.

"Are you really going to waste Mom's money? You know this is your last chance before your tests." If he saw the fear in her eyes, he ignored it. "Whatever. Go. I'm staying and getting my money's worth."

She bit her lip and faced forward, holding back her rising hysteria. The cart picked up speed and pushed her against Marco, who screamed in delight, arms raised high in the air. She wanted this so badly, wanted to let go of reality, to let go of the gnawing sensation in the back of her neck. As the cart continued to spin, Ari closed her eyes, hoping to endure. By the time her cart approached the aged man a second time, she was gone.

Her eyes opened to a water-stained ceiling. The stench of old cigarettes and filthy bodies welcomed her back to reality. She strained to turn her head. Her neck pinched from the cords in her port. Disgust tasted sour as she clawed the base of her neck, pulling at the thick cable.

"Hey, girlie. You're going to tear your port, and I don't have the stuff to fix it." A man's thick hands turned the cable until a click sounded, and then he gently pulled the wires out. She wanted to scratch at the insertion site, to tear away the mechanical feeling that lingered inside of her. Instead she undid her ponytail and covered the port site with hair, smoothing it down.

Her brother lay next to her in a reclined chair, a smile pasted on his handsome face. His wavy, thick hair, often kept short, curled around his temple. He always appeared more innocent while unconscious.

Glad to see he's enjoying himself. She pushed back the bitterness boiling inside. He had been trying to help.

The large man, covered in old tattoos and smelling of yesterday's beer, winked at her. Revulsion rolled around in her gut. Before he could speak, she rushed out of the room. She detested this shop as much as the virtuals themselves. The VR center stood only a few blocks from her house, a permanent fixture in her rundown neighborhood.

Ari hurried through the metal doors, squinting as she welcomed the sun. The real sun.

Her sun.

"Missy, want to catch a trip with a real guy?" A

withered man sat outside, his dirty clothes hanging off his body. "Trust me. I look a hell of a lot better on the inside."

She snapped her head back to the road in front of her, ignoring him.

"Don't be like that," the man said.

Someone reached for her, grabbing at her arm, but she swatted it away, quickening her step. *Please just leave me alone.*

The jeers of the strung-out VR addicts followed her for the rest of the block.

She tried not to imagine how her father had used to be there, hanging out with the bums to catch a free VR. She tried, but it didn't work.

CHAPTER 2

The next day, Ari's final exams approached faster than she expected. Leaning back in the vinyl chair, Ari flinched as the examiner slid the cable into her port. She closed her eyes, trying to block out the image of metal claws burrowing in her mind. The cable clicked shut, and she was drawn into another world.

The empty white room gave off a sterile feel. A lone light in the ceiling illuminated the square space with not a dust mite to be found. In the center of the room, a simple table held three objects. As she moved closer, they each took a distinct and unique shape: a silver pyramid, a black oval, and a red square. They must represent some type of puzzle, like the chains of knots she'd often played with as a child.

Ari drew a deep breath. *I can do this.* She had spent hours at home repurposing and reprogramming tech. This wasn't much different. She reached for the pyramid, or what looked like it could be a pyramid. Yet instead of only flat surfaces, portions were twisted and inverted. It took several minutes for her to solve the puzzle, but eventually she snapped the last piece in place.

As she completed the puzzle, the image flashed. She

jumped, surprised by the bright light. The puzzle slipped through her nervous and clammy fingers. The silver pyramid now morphed into something black with numbers scattered along the surface. An uneasy feeling prickled the hairs on her neck, and her pulse picked up. Was this part of the test? It felt ... off.

Three doors hissed open in front of her. Three separate voids of darkness, each door standing at a different height. Some psychological reason probably loomed behind this choice, but she couldn't seem to care. Her purple sneakers felt as heavy as lead. She picked at a cuticle as she inched her way toward the nearest door. Every step pushed her closer to the unknown, not only in the VR but in life. Her eyes burned as she blinked back the tears. Dread and terror snaked up her spine and landed in her weighted limbs. Which step was too far? Which step would push her towards something that she could never escape?

With a tortured gasp, she snapped back to reality. Ari swiped away at the river of tears on her face. Intentionally or not, she'd done what she always did. She'd fled.

7 minutes 42 seconds. Yes, a measly 7 minutes and freaking 42 seconds.

That was how long she'd lasted in the VR final, instead of the normal hour or two. Back in the examiner's office, Ari tried to explain to the woman that she knew the information, that she'd studied the text just not in the VR. Her perfect grades must count for something.

Instead the stern examiner just stared at Ari like she was a freak, and then, after checking the computer, the woman offered to allow her to try the VR again. A second chance, something Ari had never heard of before. She declined. Her hands shook just thinking about it.

By the time lunch was over, the results were in, and the students lined up in the cafeteria-turned-auditorium, awaiting their assignments. The principal stood at the front, along with two testing authorities from the education department. The lone school security guard stood beside them with the usual tired expression on his face. Backed up against the wall, metal chairs were lined up for family members and friends.

Ari's mother slipped in late through the side door to join the other families. Her hair wrapped up in a bun, she donned the familiar factory uniform. With two jobs, she had to work through the three-day weekend.

Clamping down on her emotions, Ari stared at the worn brick wall at the back of the room. The cafeteria had once been a factory, remodeled years ago as a school. They threw white paint on the old brick walls, but the smell of oil and metal still lingered. Ari tried to maintain her composure, not wanting others to see the fragile hold on her control. How could she be the only one troubled with all of this? Their future decided by a machine, controlled by people they didn't even know.

The computer announced the first assignment: mechanics. A collective sigh spread through the audience, followed by enthusiastic clapping. Everyone took it as a good sign when the first announcement was non-military. The Never-Ending War took more than its share of young men.

The assignments continued: health, food management, and avionics, always followed by applause. Someone was assigned to a technical school, and they clapped. Many to military. They still clapped. The announcement could be for obituary sciences, and they would clap. Frustration and anxiety boiled inside of Ari. She wanted to scream at these clapping mindless drones. This was a sentence not a future.

The principal, old and stoic, made fleeting remarks between assignments, giving congratulations or nods of agreement. Yet, what never came out of his mouth was the truth. He never said, "I'm sorry you guys are all too poor to choose your own assignment." Instead, he regurgitated the blessings they received from the government:

education, the lack of unemployment, and the gift of technology to enhance society.

Ari's friend, Taidem, stepped up to receive her assignment, her blonde hair pinned up to perfection. How could Ari be so close to the front already?

"Education," the machine announced.

The crowd applauded, including Ari. Education usually involved plugging kids in or tending the young ones. It was a steady job with decent pay, but not Ari's first choice. She wanted to go into electro-engineering, a job where she could create and build something worthwhile, something more than the old gears and bots around her house.

As Ari moved up another space, she tensed and tried to prepare herself for anything, for everything. A life headed towards what the government deemed she was talented for.

Four more people until her turn.

She twisted the HUB on her wrist, or as she called it, her electronic brain. It held all her contacts, ID, books ... her life. Too bad it didn't have the answer for what came next.

Three students left.

A gnawing sense of fear climbed up her throat. In the distance stood Marco and his best friend, Reed. Great, more people to witness her humiliation. As much as she loved having her brother around, she wished he didn't have off school right now.

Two students left.

What did it matter anymore? She'd failed her test and would receive a life of janitorial duty either way. Before the rising panic inside of her exploded into something unimaginable, she took off.

Tears blurred her vision as she shoved through the door of the cafeteria. Shouts rang out behind her, but she couldn't stop. The hot summer wind warmed her but didn't relieve the pressure in her chest. She kept running down the corridors, past the concrete sidewalks.

Finally reaching a group of trees, she stopped. With one hand on a tree, she sucked in mouthfuls of air and tried to calm down. She sank onto the ground, leaning against the trunk. A wave of self-loathing disappointment settled uncomfortably in her stomach.

The sun beat down on her and warmed her bone-deep chill. She tried her hardest not to think of what she'd just done. The tremors in her hands slowly stopped, and she wiped away the last of her tears. She turned on an audiobook loaded on her HUB, hoping to lose herself in the drama of another life for a few minutes.

Her solitude didn't last long. Marco slumped down next to her and clicked off her book. "Thought I'd find you out here."

She stared out at the track field, not wanting to talk.

"I have your assignment."

Ari pulled back to look at him. "What? How did you do that?"

Marco gave one of his winning smiles, the kind that had wooed more than enough girls and now apparently even the principal. "Mom and I talked to the authorities. They let her receive the assignment, but you'll have to talk to the principal later about accepting it."

"Who says that I will?"

Marco raised an eyebrow. "You really want to stay here, work in the factory, and end up like Mom? No offense to Mom."

"Of course not. Doesn't mean I don't like the illusion of choice." She held her hand out for the paper, her gut twisting in response.

"This one even surprised the principal. I never thought I'd see such shock on that old plastic's face." He handed her the paper. "The plus side is you'll be at the same campus as your endearing brother. I can harass you all year round."

She unfolded the crisp white paper. Skimming the

small print, she found her assignment:
Virtual Reality Programming.

CHAPTER 3

She shuddered and shoved the paper back at Marco. They would never place her in a VR program. "Nice joke. I knew the principal wouldn't let you accept for me."

Marco's smile waned, as sadness spotted his eyes. The paper remained in a crumpled heap between them. "Sorry, sis. It's true. The principal wants your personal confirmation by tomorrow." He stood and walked off.

A cold numbness poured over Ari's body as she realized her brother wasn't joking. She grabbed at the paper again. How could this be right? She could barely stand being inside VRs, much less designing them. Marco would be great at this. Why not him? She knew computers and coding, but only from this side of reality. She'd much rather read a book and picture her own world than have one provided for her.

"Marco," she called for her brother, but he was already gone. She needed to talk to someone. This had to be a mistake.

When she walked back into the cafeteria, a mass of people encompassed her. Classmates congratulated each other, making plans. Families hugged—a bittersweet reminder of the upcoming farewells. People congratulated her on her assignment, but most had a wary look in their eye. Ari's fear was known through school—sort of like the girl who was deathly allergic to peanuts. Technology was a coveted position and often led to high-paying jobs with the government. It also wasn't awarded often, especially to scholarship kids. Ari pushed her way through the mass of bodies and ended up in front of her mom and Marco.

"Mom, you made it."

With her mom here, maybe they could straighten this out. Her mom pulled her into a tight hug. Ari squeezed her mom's thin frame under the stiff blue uniform. Her long hair streaked with silver was wound up into a bun for work.

"You don't have to go," her mom whispered in her ear.

Ari pulled back. "They made a mistake. They must have."

"No, sweetie. I talked to your principal, but you don't have to go. You can stay here with me."

Ari wasn't surprised. Her mother could be self-sacrificing to a fault. This assignment could lead to a career and money that her family desperately needed. An opportunity she could never have working in the factories. Ari tried to paste a smile on her face. "It might not be that bad." She attempted the lie, though her eyes swam with tears.

"Look at the bright side," Marco interjected nearby. "You can hook me up with VRs for free."

Ari turned to glare at her brother. "Really?"

"You'll fit right in with all those geeked-out kissups." Marco slugged her lightly in the arm.

Ari tried to return the hit, but he skirted out of the way.

"Marco," Mom chided him, while holding tight onto Ari's hand.

"Maybe you are smarter than we thought," Marco

13

shrugged. "They say some of the best programmers can never quite enjoy the VR themselves. They complain about how artificial it is. Not being able to see past the program."

Maybe, but it didn't change her predicament. Before she could reply, Taidem came barreling into their conversation. "Congratulations." She gave a weak smile. "I guess. You okay?" She leaned in and hugged Ari.

"Yeah," Ari said. "I'll be fine. Congratulations on teaching. You'll be great."

"Thanks." She flashed a smile in Marco's direction. "Graduation. Crazy, huh?" She tucked a curl behind her ear, giving a nervous laugh. Taidem had been crushing on Marco for years, despite Ari's warnings that her brother was a huge flirt.

"You'll be a great teacher, Taidem." He leaned in closer to Ari's friend.

Taidem was one of few people that put up with Ari's phobia and enjoyed hanging out in the real world, getting coffee and listening to music. With her blonde hair and tall curvy figure, boys were often attracted to Taidem. Ari had more of the stick figure look going for her with the dark hair and skin that was common in the Southwest.

Taidem gave another encouraging smile to Marco. "Going to celebrate?"

"Of course." Marco never missed a good party. He was usually in the middle of most of them.

"Great," she said with enthusiasm, then turned to Ari. "We're all headed downtown."

"I'm going home, but have fun." Ari needed time to wrap her brain around her assignment and figure out what came next.

"No way." Taidem's eyes narrowed into her familiar stubborn gaze. "We only graduate once."

"I just—"

"Go." Her mother squeezed Ari's hand. "Be with your friends tonight."

Ari wanted to refuse, but her mother couldn't hide the

emotion in her eyes. There was no good answer for Ari's future. Going to school, fitting in, these were things her mom wanted for Ari. Maybe ignoring responsibility for a night would help? She had the rest of her life to work.

Star, another classmate, appeared. "Ready to go?" On her arm was Marco's best friend, Reed. He didn't look quite as enthusiastic as Star with her bright red lips pulled up in a smile.

Taidem grabbed Ari's hand. "We're coming."

And with little left to say, Ari was dragged into the throngs of celebration.

The club was a horde of bodies dancing, moving, drinking as if they were all one collective organism, thriving on the energy and sensual excitement in the air. Ari shied away from the sweaty bodies for the most part and drank soda at the bar.

Taidem and Marco were close by, too close really. Taidem bit a cherry out of his mouth, and Marco cheered with excitement. Ari turned her head. She couldn't quite match their enthusiasm. At least they weren't going to the same school next year. Marco went through girls like games, and Ari didn't want him to hurt her friend.

A cute guy approached, taking the seat next to Ari, looking vaguely familiar. He was probably from a neighboring school. His gaze flickered around the room for a moment, and the metallic glint told Ari he must have the new contacts. She grimaced at the idea.

He gave one final blink and then turned his attention to Ari. His dark hair was slicked back with more hair product than Ari used in a month. He wasn't bad looking, just not her type. He lifted a brow in her direction. "Wanna tab?"

Ari had already had a drink in front of her, a dark cola. A tab would turn her drink into something more. In the olden days, kids used alcohol or drugs, but after countless people were killed by overdoses or strung-out with addiction, tabs were created. The clear small pebble-like pills dissolved in any drink or even under your tongue—all the high without killing yourself. Unfortunately, throwing up or hangovers were still a reality. The government wanted some negative effects to keep the kids from getting wasted all the time.

"No thanks." Ari had been of age since she'd turned sixteen the previous month but had no desire to act like an idiot.

He shrugged and turned to the bar. His eyes darted erratically around as if watching something she couldn't see.

Ari stood up, ready to leave. She'd tried to have fun—she'd even danced one song with Taidem—but her future loomed over her, mocking her like the twisted clown from the virtual carnival.

Star stumbled towards the bar with Reed in hand. "You're not leaving, are you?" Star leaned slightly towards Ari, the sickly-sweet smell of drink overpowering. "The fun is just starting."

Ari gave her a thin smile. "Lots to get ready for."

"Oh, I have stuff to do before I leave. But it's not at home." Star laughed loudly and turned to latch onto Reed. He bristled at first, but he didn't bother to pry Star off even when she began kissing his neck.

"Nice," Taidem called out.

"More tongue," Marco coached.

"Gross." Ari turned back to the guy still sitting next to her. "I think I'm ready for that tab now."

He smirked and waved down the bartender. He dropped a tab in each of their drinks. They fizzed slightly as they dissolved.

"I want to erase that picture out of my mind forever." The drink tingled as it traveled down her throat with a sour taste. Placing the drink back on the bar, she gasped.

The rest of the night blurred past with drinking, and

dancing and talking to classmates. The pressure in her chest lessened with every tab. The worry of tomorrow faded, and the surrounding chaos lulled her into a sweet numbing blur.

Collapsing at the bar, Ari rubbed her temples to ease her spinning head. Marco and Taidem were propped against it, tangled in each other's arms. Marco leaned down to whisper something in Taidem's ear, and they both stood to leave.

Ari grabbed Taidem's hand. "Where are you going?"

"A virtual." Taidem pulled back, her face flushed with excitement. "Go dance. We'll be back later."

"No, no. He's not supposed to do virtuals." Their mother disapproved of Marco going in virtuals outside of school—not that he ever listened.

Most parents pushed the virtuals. It was a way for their children to act out their urges, whether sexual, physical or otherwise with no consequences. No unwanted pregnancies or police calls in the middle of the night when it stayed online.

Ari stood and Taidem swayed—or maybe that was her swaying.

"It'll be okay, Ari. It's a quick trip to the beach, and we'll be back before you know it." Taidem headed off across the floor, and Ari tried to follow.

Pushing her way through the crowd, she lost Taidem's blonde hair and somehow ended up on the dance floor. It was warm, too warm. People spun around the room, or maybe that was Ari, swaying, turning. She was going to be sick. She clawed her way through the bodies in search of fresh air.

The guy from at the bar, the one who bought her the tabs, grabbed her hand and pushed himself up against her, trying to dance. She shook her head. Shoving him back, she tripped, tangled up in his long arms and legs. She found herself on her hands and knees. Feet knocked into her, bodies kicking her out of the way.

A pair of strong hands pulled her up from behind. Remembering the guy who groped her, she struggled out of the stranger's grasp.

"Ari, Ari, it's me," Reed spoke in her ear.

His voice calmed the panic inside as she leaned into him. "Reed."

He pulled her into the darkened alcove off the dance floor.

"You wanna dance?" She slapped a hand over her mouth as words flowed out without any conscious thought.

He continued to hold her upright. "Where's your brother?"

"Making out on a beach with Taidem." She tossed a hand up dismissing them. "Or worse. Oh no, you don't think that they would do that here?"

Reed laughed. "Don't worry about him. I think I need to take you home though."

"Are you going into a virtual with Star?" Ari slurred. "She has big teeth you know, along with big other things." She fell into his chest, and he smelled good, like musky cologne, sweat and Reed.

He tucked Ari's hair behind her ear. "Star's dancing. She won't miss me."

Ari stared up into his face, distorted by the strobe lights. His hazel eyes turned to silver in the changing lights. "You have beautiful eyes, Reed."

"Um ... okay." His lips parted, so soft, so close.

She wanted to touch those lips and wondered, not for the first time, how it would feel to kiss them. She had a crush on him as a young girl, but it was long forgotten, or so she thought. Her vision blurred as the world spun around her. All thoughts of romance fled as she bent over and threw up on his shoes.

Something bounced her awake in the chilly night air. It

took a minute to realize she stared at Reed's backside, upside down. Not bad. He must have thrown Ari over his shoulder as he walked the familiar path home.

"Reed," she mumbled as she wondered how to get down.

"Glad to see you're awake," he said, but didn't make a move to put her down.

"Didn't you want to stay and dance?" Ari asked, not forgetting about Star.

"No. Someone threw up on the floor."

She snorted, wondering if he was mad or amused by it. "That sucks."

He gave a light laugh. She loved his laugh. Silence filled the night, the yellowed street lights lining their path home. His feet constantly plodded along the concrete.

He broke the silence. "Are you going to accept your assignment?"

If anyone outside of Ari's family knew the pain, the fear that consumed her since her father slipped into a coma, it was Reed. He had been friends with Marco since she could remember, and his own father had left town when he was young.

Ari considered the sobering question, but she wasn't sure of the answer.

The sun sliced through the blinds, the morning rays like sharp knives piercing Ari's head.

"Shut them, please." Ari begged her mother, who was picking up clothes and random pieces of equipment from off her floor. With little money to spare, Ari had become a pro at refurbishing old tech.

"Sorry, honey, but we need to talk."

Talking was the last thing she wanted to do with a dry mouth and her brain too fuddled to form complete sentences. "Water."

With an exaggerated sigh, her mother headed to the

kitchen. Their family clean bot entered the room with its noisy hum and occasional clunk. Ari would have to look at it again. The small machine had been torn apart and fixed countless times. Last year, Ari glued on two long eyeballs with gems in the middle and long eyelashes and dubbed it Pixy.

Her mother returned with a glass of apple juice. "Water alone isn't going to take care of that taste, dear." She sat on the edge of the bed and offered Ari the juice with a straw. It's what her mother often did when Ari was sick as a child. Ari sipped slowly, unsure of what would stay down.

"I'm not sure who I'm angrier at, you or Marco. He told me he would keep an eye on you last night. I didn't think that would include tabbing until you passed out. I thought you would know better. You're usually my sensible one."

That was true. Ari took over many of her mother's household responsibilities as she worked two jobs.

"Don't worry. Never again." After a few sips, Ari laid face down on her bed while her mother rubbed her back. Her head throbbed, and her body refused to move.

"Why do people get wasted?" Ari moaned.

"Lots of reasons. Not many of them worth it." Ari's mom rarely drank or used tabs but that probably had more to do with money.

"I have a double shift today or I wouldn't have woken you," her mother said.

"I know."

"Have you decided what you're going to do? I'm not going to force you to do something you don't want to. But if you don't go, you'll need to put your name in at the factory to find a position before winter." Her mother's hands, dry and cracked from work, smoothed out Ari's blanket. Maybe that's why people drank or did virtuals. It was better than real life.

Ari had another choice besides the life her mother

lived. With a higher education, Ari would have better paying jobs. The choice wasn't only about Ari not wanting to work in the factory, but a chance for her mother to leave the factory. Her mother had to work two jobs just to keep her husband's feeding tube full.

Six years ago, Ari's dad took a VR vacation down the Rhine River and never came back. Six years since she truly spoke to him. Six years of after-school jobs, of discount food, and watching her mother wither away every day. Ari watched her mother's hope turn into foolishness. Ari hoped he would drown in that damn river.

When Ari graduated from the VR Academy, she could afford to buy a place for both of them. She also wouldn't be completely alone there. Reed and Marco went to the same campus for training in computer security. The thought of Reed and what she did last night made her moan all over again.

"It's okay, honey." Her mother stood. "One more day won't hurt. I'll talk to Kent, my manager—"

"Yes." Ari would do this, for herself, for her mother, for a chance at a real future.

"Yes? Put in for the position?"

"No, I decided. I'm going to accept the scholarship." Ari turned her head away, not wanting to look at her mother's concerned face. Closing her eyes, she tried to block out the world for a few more hours.

CHAPTER 4

Her choice made, Ari reported to her principal with her final decision. With only a week to pack and say her goodbyes, the time flew by. When the morning of her departure finally came, she boarded the tram with Marco and, of course, Reed. Break ended for all them, and the boys were returning for their final year at school. She sat apart from the pair, not wanting to revisit her mortifying behavior from the party. Slumping down on the cold plastic seat, she watched the only home she'd ever known disappear.

Last night, her mother had insisted that Marco and Ari visit their father before heading off to the Academy. Normally, Ari refused since her father didn't acknowledge anyone. This time she went and soon became edgy and unsettled.

She hated watching his withered frame and sunken face. He didn't look like her father anymore and stopped being her father years before that. It didn't help that the facility reeked of old people, dying people.

Ari's mom carried on a one-sided conversation with her unresponsive husband, but despite her efforts, Ari wouldn't play along. She was done pretending this was okay when it wasn't. Instead, she fixated on the computer tied to his vitals and feeding tube. With coma patients, you could turn off the computer or whatever VR they were in, but their brains wouldn't wake up. Subconsciously their minds stayed in the virtual world even without the plug. They didn't want to wake up, not even to eat, drink or survive.

That one little box of wires and parts controlled their lives. She bit back the tears that burned her eyes. He didn't deserve them anymore.

Trying to block out the memory of the trip, Ari pulled up a book on her old tablet and read for the rest of the trip. A mechanical voice pulled her back to reality and informed them of their upcoming stop. Standing, she pulled her old leather bag onto her shoulder. It was her dad's or had been. The only reminder she had of him. Not sure why she even kept it anymore, she reached for the battered suitcase above her seat.

Reed appeared at her side and helped pull it down. "How are you feeling?"

Like an idiot, she wanted to say. Instead she kept her eyes down and mumbled, "Fine."

"Don't worry. School's not that bad."

Marco appeared between them. "Oh, my sis will do great. Once they strap her down for her VRs."

Ari glared at her brother and stepped off the tram.

"It's not like every class is in the VR." Marco kept close behind her. "Unfortunately."

"Whatever, Marco." Ari kept moving with the flow of the other students. People had spoken about making all of the Academy's classes purely VR, so the cost of schooling would be cheaper, but they found students suffered from too much VR use. VR comas were on the rise, malnutrition ran rampant, and muscular atrophy increasingly common. Ari grimaced at the thought of her future working with these wonderful machines.

Ari arrived at the gates and wasn't sure what bothered

her more: the armed guards waiting to let students into the Tech Academy, or the high electrified fence that wrapped around the school. Was it to keep people in, or out?

Students stood with their motorized luggage trailing behind as the line to enter the silver registration building crawled forward. The sun peered out through the clouds, warming them as they waited. The immaculate grounds sprawled in both directions with flawless engineered grass and bushes. Massive trees stood along the electric fence.

They finally entered the registration building, which entailed another line. This time though, they could watch the government news and alerts that ran on screens as the lines inched forward. Details on the current global conflicts played on the screens. The government referred to the various wars as the Continuing Struggle for Human Rights. Most people called it the Never-Ending War. One picture of a soldier stood out as he held an injured child in his arms. Large words appeared underneath him: "Our Democratic Union at Work." The line moved forward. Up ahead, guards processed the incoming and returning students.

"You're next, Ari." Marco pushed her toward the armed guard standing in front of the scanner.

She couldn't help but notice the weapons at his waist that stood out against his pale silver uniform. She placed her luggage on one scanner and walked through the other.

"Ariana Mendez?" The guard asked looking at his monitor.

"Yes."

"This way please." The barrel-chested guard motioned for Ari to step to the side. He pulled out a silver electronic wrist HUB.

"I already have one." Granted the sleek design would outrun her old HUB, which was battered and slow, but her HUB had all her favorite books, shows, and old contacts. Her life lived on her wrist.

"Every new student is required to have a school issued

HUB." He waited expectantly and motioned to the desk, which held a pad to rest her arm on.

She released her old HUB, slid it into her pocket, and extended her hand out. He placed the new device on her wrist and it automatically sealed shut. It would take pliers and a blowtorch to pry it off.

He must have guessed her thought. "Don't attempt to remove it. The school would be notified immediately."

"Great," she mumbled.

"Also, you have been requested to see Advisor Williams. You can request directions from your HUB."

Unease tightened her stomach. "What for?"

"Because he asked." The guard waved her along and turned his attention back to the line of students.

Ari turned to say bye to her brother, but he was already in deep conversation with a red-headed girl. Reed stood under the silver full-body scanner and was busy talking to a guard. She turned back around and walked through the doors, stepping into a world that could have been its own VR.

A variety of modern, polished buildings reached up to the heavens. Every building was different and unique. One mirrored its surroundings, almost disappearing as it traveled up to the sky. When her gaze finally returned earth bound, the grounds were no less stunning. Brightly colored shrubs and flowers were scattered around the greenery. On closer inspection, she realized they were manufactured. Genetic replicas that couldn't help but be flawless. The picture-perfect landscape sent an uncomfortable chill down her back.

Activating her new wristwear, she followed its directions. Students brushed by her, talking to one another or some flying by on boards. She couldn't help but stare at the variety of tech: projected on arms, hands, and glasses with display screens. Other people showed no sign of tech, not even contacts, as they talked with an invisible someone, probably using the new Push implant she'd read about—an implant that connected directly to your tech and was only steps away from a portable VR.

She was light-years behind these kids and that wasn't even talking about virtuals. Granted, even if she could afford it, Ari detested the idea of an implant. Why would kids even want an implant here when the school and government monitored all their data and controlled their access to the outside? With a huff, she continued down the path. Ari never felt like she lived in the dark ages at home, until now.

Once inside the large mirrored administration building, she took the elevator to the fourth floor and checked in with a receptionist.

"Please have a seat." The woman directed Ari to white chairs lined against the wall.

Ari sat stiffly, glancing around the office. Sleek angles and designs were muted with soft colors, but it still had a doctor's office feel.

"Ariana Mendez, Advisor Williams is ready to see you." A mechanical voice spoke from her HUB.

Ari stiffened. She'd forgotten she wore a new HUB, one that the school was hooked into. She hefted her bag on her shoulder and grabbed her suitcase, wishing it didn't look so shabby. Unlike the rest of the modern design of this room, the advisor's door was mahogany wood. Authentic wood doors were a rarity. They cost a lot more to add security to.

In the center of the gold knocker, a small camera was buried deep within. Since the advisor was ready see her, there was no reason to prolong the inevitable. She tapped the gold knocker and a mechanical voice replied, "You may enter."

She walked into a world of old and new mixed together. The furniture was obviously from an older era and a painting—an actual physical painting—of a golden field hung on one wall. Computerized screens covered the other wall, which sat across from his desk. This room had to be the most expensive place she had ever been in.

The man behind the desk had no trace of age, sitting tall with short black hair. The only thing that gave his age away was the surgically tight skin. Only rich people preserved themselves so well. He would probably be considered attractive, if his lips weren't pressed into a rigid line.

"Hello, Ms. Mendez. Please take a seat." Without looking up from his screen, Advisor Williams waved her to the over-sized leather chair in front of his desk.

She nodded while she slid into the chair.

"I have been reviewing your file for the past several minutes, and you have quite an interesting case."

Ari shifted in her seat.

"I can see you are a bright student. Top scores on your written tests. Even an aptitude for programming and advanced problem solving. Interesting that you were assigned Virtual Programming when you didn't complete the session though." His voice rose hesitantly as if he wasn't sure if he dared question the evaluation of the test himself.

Ari remained silent, the knot in her stomach twisting in worry.

Williams stared for a few moments longer before turning to Ari. "My responsibility is to make sure you are given the tools to succeed and to weed out any potential problems. Be that as it may, I hope we won't have any problems with your adaptation into this program. I know coming from your background may pose certain … challenges, but you'll need to immerse yourself in the program and strive for the excellence that permeates this Academy."

Ari had stayed silent throughout the conversation, but now she realized he expected an answer.

"I will complete the program, sir." She had no other choice but to complete. Failure wasn't an option.

"Good, good. That's the spirit. I have your class

schedule and some forms for you to read. Sign and return them to me by the end of the day. I can upload them directly to your tablet."

When she pulled out her old tablet from home, he tightened his lips. "That won't be adequate for your classwork."

"I can make do." Ari had rigged enough old gear. She was confident that she could manage.

Advisor Williams probably wouldn't consider her old tablet worth killing a rat with. "I'll send the tech department a requisition form right now, and you can head down there to pick up the new gear. In our student union, you'll find meals, and a basic shop for clothes and other hygiene items. Your monthly stipend should be adequate to cover your needs." He didn't bother hiding the judgmental disdain creasing his face. "You may go."

Ari stood and gathered her bags. She left the office as quickly as possible. Unfortunately, the cold chill he gave her took longer to leave.

Her HUB directed her along a path that weaved amongst the unique buildings. Every building was slightly different in shape, and used a mixture of glass, metal, and synthetic materials. Each dorm housed a different concentration: hardware, electronic security, network systems, and a few others Ari couldn't remember. This campus was the biggest in the west for electronics. She passed a shorter building with a constant flow of students streaming in and out. After accessing the map on her HUB, she discovered this beige building with arches on top was the student commons, holding the cafeteria, multipurpose stores, and a gym. The student tech supply center was in the rear.

She pushed back her hair and headed off. The flawless perfection of her surroundings pushed past the ordinary, becoming almost surreal, like she was on another planet. The bright flowers dotting the campus produced a rich, fragrant smell that trailed along the path.

HOOKED

At the tech center, she headed through the automatic doors. "The attendant will be with you shortly," a pleasant woman's voice spoke above her. The entry room appeared small, but behind the counter it extended farther back into a myriad of shelved rows, cubicles, and locked cabinets. An electronic sign-in screen hung from the ceiling. Her name appeared on the screen, indicating she was the next in line to be helped.

Behind the divide, a guy, entranced in a game, propped his feet up on the counter. He had canary yellow hair, which fell to his ears in a naturally messy style. It clashed horribly with the silver metallic uniform clinging to his slim build.

"Whatcha need?" He didn't bother to look up.

Ari stepped forward. "I need a … a computer, I guess. I'm in the virtual design program, and they said you could get me what I need."

The guy finally paused his screen and looked up at her through gaming contacts. Colors swirled around his eyes. He blinked several times, and his eyes cleared, except for a gold glint next to his iris.

"You're a newbie, right? First year?"

"Yeah."

"You didn't bring your own gear?" The ring in his eyebrow pinched slightly.

"Nothing from this century."

The guy exhaled slowly. "O-kay, so you like antiques."

"Like isn't the right word. 'All I can afford' is more fitting." Ari kept her gaze steady and chin high. She wasn't going to start the program by being ashamed of being poor.

"I'm Garrett." He stuck his hand out and smiled. "It's okay to be different. Most everything here is new and shiny. I'd rather see something original."

"Ari." She shook his hand and wondered if his meaning went beyond electronics.

He returned to his computer. "Just pulling up your

29

orders. Okay, Ari, let's get you hooked up with something that will give those geeks in the VR dorm a reason to drool." His smile was nice, with a bit of mischief in it.

An electric cart followed behind as he walked down the rows of equipment, picking up this and that. It kept a steady pace behind him, pausing when he did. He eyed one small piece that looked like memory, before putting it on his cart. It wasn't until the top of his cart was cluttered with random hardware, that he made his way back to the front.

"Has someone been good?" Garrett asked in a humorous voice.

Ari couldn't help but be excited as her eyes flew over the pile he'd gathered. She'd only seen stuff like this online. "And if I say no?"

"I'll ask you out." The smirk on his face made it hard to tell if he was serious. "I already have your number from the paperwork."

Startled by the turn in the conversation, her faced warmed and she adjusted the HUB on her wrist.

"Come on back and let's get to work." Garrett pushed a button and a short door around the side of the counter opened for her. She grabbed an extra chair and pulled it up next to him.

When Garrett said, 'let's work', what he really meant was Ari could watch and "ooh" and "aah" respectfully while he worked. She didn't mind and enjoyed watching him fly through the systems. He kept up a running commentary cluing her into the capabilities of her HUB and tablet.

"Your Advisor's requisition said to supply you with the equipment needed for your program. I love when they say that." Garrett turned to her with a large smile. "Then I can do what I want."

He turned back to the gear. "Okay, so here's your tablet that can port into any of the school's systems or desks. I'll order you a bigger screen to link to in your room and a backup drive too. Here's a ring or phone for your HUB. If you're tired of a ring, it can hook on your ear."

"An earring?"

He flipped the device open. She froze as he moved her hair back to place the device on her ear. He wasn't big on respecting personal space.

"I made them in my second year. They are finally starting to catch on around here. Much cooler than those web glasses. You look like a fool reading invisible messages."

"Thanks."

"No problem. Unfortunately, I'm not allowed to do implants here. Have you seen the new tat implants? They're amazing. The school claims I need a medical license for that."

She cringed at the idea of a permanent implant but kept her thoughts to herself as she didn't want to dampen his enthusiasm.

"One last thing." He reached over her to pick up her tablet and handed her a cord.

"This will help you record any notes you need while inside the VRs. By the end of the year you'll have whole classes inside. So, don't lose it."

She stared at the cord that would plug into the VR system going into her brain. Surprise and disgust must have been evident on her face.

"What's wrong?"

Ari took a deep breath. She couldn't freak out here, in front of the one person who'd been nice to her. "Sorry, I can't stand them."

"What? The tech I gave you is pretty sweet."

"No, virtuals."

He leaned back, confusion flashing on his face. "Really?"

She pursed her lips together and nodded.

"How are you going to pull off this program?"

"Not sure. I will though, because it's my only option.

No one gets two scholarships, so I'll have to make it work."

"Then you will." He stared off at the monitor in front of him. "Have you tried drinking?"

She watched him for a moment to see if he was serious and then shook her head. "Yes, but never again."

He held up his hands. "Just trying to help. VRs, they're second nature to me. I'm sure we can think of something."

Ari wasn't sure why that meant so much to her. Why would this boy with yellow hair and a ring in his eyebrow want to help her? It didn't really matter. She would take all the help she could get.

With a bag full of her new toys in one hand and her old suitcase in the other, she searched out her dorm. It stood on the edge of campus, glass windows covering it top to bottom. No, they weren't glass, but some type of clear reflective material. Colors, projected on the front, created the look of an abstract painting. By the time she made it to her room on the fifth floor, she would have sold a kidney for motorized luggage.

She opened the door to her new sleek dorm room. It was a decent size with two beds, dressers and desks, lining opposite walls. A white comforter fit tightly around her mattress. A laundry chute stuck out of the wall near her closet. Ari bristled at the idea of some machine run by a random person cleaning her clothes, her underwear. Brushing aside the unavoidable, she noticed a short fridge inset in the wall. That would be handy. Even a bright shiny bot hid under her bed. It might be used quite a bit, considering her roommate had left enough clutter to house a small family of mice. Food wrappers and old coffee cups littered the desk.

The room was painted in neutral blues and whites, probably meant to evoke some feeling of peace and openness. The colors felt sterile and cold to her. She couldn't wait to add some color and her own flavor to her side of the room. She tossed the old suitcase next to her bed, realizing how out of place it was here, just like her.

Someone entered the room behind her, interrupting her thoughts of home. "Oh, I wondered when I would get a roommate." A squatty girl with shoulder length purple and pink hair came bustling in with a small interface in one hand and some type of iced coffee drink in the other. She was pretty, or probably was, under the heavy eye make-up.

"I'm Ari."

"Tessa." She plugged in her computer and took a quick drink. "Don't worry. You didn't miss anything, just the regular losers chatting online."

"Good." Ari sat on her bed, not ready to unpack just yet.

"So, what's your story?" Tessa looked over Ari as if her life history was tattooed on her tanned skin.

"Ummm ..." Was she that obviously out of place?

"I already know you're one of the few scholarship students here. Do you already have published virtuals or what?"

"No." The level of gossip amazed Ari.

"Huh?" Tessa shrugged off her lack of response and brushed back a strand of pink hair. "Okay then, about me. My dad owns ... well, too much to name, my mom was trophy wife number three, and I'm the gamer they wish they could remake. Don't talk to me until I've had caffeine and don't interrupt a game."

Tessa didn't wait for a reply as she inserted ear buds, activating the gaming bands on her wrist, and logged into her game. She blinked repeatedly to activate her contacts. "Tessa here." After a short pause. "No, no. I'm logging in now. I knew that loser couldn't hold onto our lead without me. I'll take him."

Okay. Ari turned to her bags. She had no desire to unpack. Once she emptied her suitcase, this whole thing would be official. So, instead, she dug out her old tablet and proceeded to finish her book.

CHAPTER 5

T he next morning, Ari tugged at her purple shirt as she waited in the classroom. Tessa entered the room with a group of guys and took a seat across from Ari with no acknowledgment. She tried to catch her gaze to say hello, but soon stopped, not wanting to look desperate.

The class was on the second floor of her dorm. The bottom three levels of their building held classrooms, lecture halls and VR labs, while the top three levels were for housing. With the vending machines, the students didn't even have to go outside.

As several other students came trickling in, one stopped next to her desk. He had an olive completion and short dark hair standing on end, forming a widow's peak. His deep set brown eyes perched above a perfectly, almost too perfectly, shaped nose. Some might say he was attractive, except for the smug look which curled his lips.

"I didn't think the school had such nice stuff." He touched the edge of her new tablet.

Ari grimaced and didn't reply, hoping he would just go away.

Of course, just her luck, he took it as an invitation to

bend down and move even closer to Ari. His overpowering cologne wafted around her, and she leaned back against her chair.

"We're all trying to decide what you did to worm your way into this program." His fake smile displayed perfectly polished teeth.

"I tested my way into here," Ari said, then clenched her teeth. Testing into programs was the official way, but desired slots like VR always had exceptions for daddies with big paychecks.

He flicked Ari's long brown braid back over her shoulder and leaned down, his voice taking on a disturbing husky quality. "Maybe you did more than just a test, maybe 'who' is a better question?"

She swallowed her revulsion and realized her initial plan of ignoring him wasn't going to work. Before she could shove him back, Tessa appeared behind him.

"Really, Wake? That's the best you got? You've screwed the pooch in more games than I can count."

Wake turned towards Tessa, his shoulders tightening as if ready to attack. He wouldn't hit Tessa? Would he? "Daddy's unwanted little miscreant is going to give me a hard time?"

"Drop the act. Your sales couldn't pay for my coffee."

Wake stepped forward, but the professor spoke, "Please take your seat, everyone. We have a lot on our agenda today."

Ari mouthed "Thank you" to Tessa as her roommate took a seat.

She took a deep breath, rattled from the encounter, and turned towards the teacher, Professor Speltman. A tall middle-aged man, he appeared a bit wild. His beard was short and unkempt, and his brown hair swept long across his forehead. A defining nose took up major real estate on his face, but behind the facial hair and bushy brows were intelligent eyes. And once he started talking, Ari realized she had more trouble than some jerk named Wake.

Back in middle school, she was the top of her class, despite her fear of virtuals or, maybe, because of it. She had to work twice as hard studying books to achieve the feel of the world, while her classmates experienced a VR for an afternoon and came away with all the answers. The only reason the whole school day wasn't in VR was due to the health risks involved. Even after school, she spent her time reading or drawing, while most of her friends preferred the virtuals whenever they could afford them. Dances, and other school events, were always cooler in another country, on the top of the world, or wherever. Ari spent many nights with her nose in a book thinking it was the safest form of travel.

Even with Ari's top grades, she only caught about half of what Professor Speltman said regarding his programming class. She knew how to program, but not in VRs. It couldn't be that different, but from what he was saying, it obviously was. She turned on the auto-record on her interface and hoped she could make some sense of it later that night.

The lecture lasted over an hour, and when it was over Ari sat there stunned for a minute. The homework he gave would fill her entire evening, and she hadn't gone to second period yet. As someone walked by, they smacked her tablet to the floor. Ari's head snapped up in time to watch Wake and his friend walking towards the door.

"Rand, you should be more careful." Wake's voice dripped with insincerity. "I bet scholarship girl doesn't have money for another one. She'll have to take out a work loan."

Laughing, they left the room. Ari didn't have the energy to be angry anymore. She bent over to pick up the small flat tablet and prayed it still worked. It appeared unharmed, so she shoved it in her bag.

She stood up and found Tessa watching her. "No one ever said this program was gracious or obliging."

Smiling, Ari narrowed her eyes. "I never asked it to

be."

Second period proved to be easier. Professor
Tollingston taught History and Interactive Storyboarding,
two things she knew about. He had a gruff personality that
matched his gray hair and thick mustache, but the
homework was simple enough.

Her next class, Biological Psychology, was on the
second floor of their dorm. Taught by the only teacher
who was a doctor and a woman as well, Ari looked
forward to it.

"Welcome to the study of the human mind." A thin
woman stood before them with a serious expression. Her
hair was wound up in a tight brown bun, but a few curly
hairs fought themselves free. "I'm Dr. Cox. In this class,
we will delve into the study of human behavior, to help
you create realistic portrayals of humans in the virtual
world. In programming, you may be given scripts by the
writers, but you need to know human behavior inside and
out to realistically portray the emotion and behavior
needed in all types of situations."

Ari hoped she'd learn something helpful about herself.
If she could kick this fear, she might be able to graduate.
Dr. Cox gave her a good chunk of homework as well, but
Ari looked forward to it.

She stayed in the building for their lunch break, eating
from the vending machines. The HUB on her wrist gave
her permission to purchase food from anywhere on
campus. The machines were well stocked with a wide
variety of everything from meal bars to steaming fresh
pasta. She sat in the lounge on the first floor and reviewed
her notes. Even Speltman's lecture made sense the second
time through it.

Her HUB vibrated on her wrist, and Ari noticed she
had a message from Garrett.

Survive your first day? He really wasn't joking when he'd
said he had her number.

Her hand hovered over the screen, deciding what to

write. *I haven't been eaten alive by implant wearing monkeys if that's what you mean.*

Good to know you're safe from exotic animals but watch for those domestic guys though. They can bite.

Thanks for the heads up.

Thankful to have one friend at the school, she headed upstairs to her next class: VR Lab.

"Welcome," a younger woman, maybe in her twenties, greeted her. "If you'll give me your name, I'll find your assigned virtual."

Ari nodded as her gaze traveled over the room, full of larger chairs set up next to their individual VR machines.

"Your name?" The girl repeated, snapping Ari out of her state of awe.

"Ariana Mendez."

"I'm Mica, the teaching assistant." Mica was tall and slender with ink black hair, cut pixie short, barely reaching her ears. "I have you up front." She directed Ari to her chair, a comfortable recliner with the monitor and wires connecting to the computer next to it. A small portable desk hung from the side.

Ari tensed, as every cell in her body told her to run.

"Have a seat," Mica told her impatiently. Ignoring Ari's frozen stare, she continued, "Pull out your tablet. I'm sure Dr. Coleman will have you take a few notes first."

"Notes," Ari repeated. *I can do notes.* Sitting down, she exhaled not realizing she had been holding her breath. She opened her tablet and tried to ignore the machine to her left. She stared at her screen and opened up a game to keep her mind occupied.

Her mind kept drifting back to her nightmares. Corpses floating through virtuals, talking and dancing, unaware that their bodies were decaying while they lived a half-life inside a machine. The smell of death poisoning the air and amidst it all, her father.

She reminded herself, it was only a dream. *I am not my father.* Graduating in this concentration would provide for her family in a way her father had never been able.

After losing at cards for her fifth straight time, she realized the classroom was full. The professor appeared in front and cleared his throat. He was young, which surprised her. His dark skin was rich and black, and his hair cut short.

"Welcome to the virtual programming lab. I know many of you come in here with an expectation of getting to hang out in virtuals for free, but this isn't rec hour. There will be nightly homework, reports, and tests just like any other class. It's not easy. Ask around."

He jumped right into the syllabus which gratefully distracted Ari from the inevitable. They spent the first half of their two-hour class going over the long list of rules and expectations.

"Now, I have the address of all of your ports from the student tech store. I will be able to access each of your systems individually, or we can connect as a group for particular assignments." He came towards Ari, using her virtual to point out the hardware. "I shouldn't have to remind you to take care of your gear, and get it serviced regularly at our student center."

Then Dr. Coleman continued to go over more specifics for data storage. "Okay, I'm throwing you all in a common virtual that you guys probably used in middle school. It's from the early stages of our Continuing Struggle for Human Rights. I want you to pick out at least five discrepancies before pulling out. I'll be in and out of several of your programs to observe. Go ahead and plug in," Dr. Coleman said with a smile.

Ari's heartbeat picked up as she leaned back in her chair like the rest of the students. She moved her braid and cleared the way for the cable. Clicks of cables sounded throughout the room as people plugged in, while Ari still struggled with snapping it in place in the base of her skull. Her fingers shook badly, and the wires clattered to the floor.

Mica appeared beside her, taking the port from her hand. "I'll help." Her hands were cold but fast as she inserted the thick metal cord. "It's okay. A lot of kids get nervous on their first day."

Ari tried to console herself that at least she wasn't in the olden days when they had to port into several spots in the brain and blood stream. It had been almost barbaric. Ari lay back in the chair and clamped her eyes shut, forcing herself to go to the one place that scared her the most.

She opened her eyes to the war-torn chaos that surrounded her. Bullets screamed past while explosions flared in the distance. Cries of the injured bombarded her, while camo-covered men rushed the broken city with guns at their sides.

All students in her middle school were required to complete VR military training to select those capable for duty. And while Ari had read about this war, she'd never lived it. She'd never smelt the dust of the desert mixed with the smoke of destruction.

A bomb exploded in a small shop down the block. The ground shook, making her stumble. This wasn't some old 3D movie. These people could hurt her, as much as one could be hurt in a VR. She took off, running as fast as possible. She wasn't sure where she was going but standing out in the open was a sure way to get shot. Her logical mind told her that she wouldn't die. VR programs muted any painful experiences, so it was only a shadow. But even the shadow of a gunshot or bomb would be more than she wanted.

She sprinted around a corner and stopped short, almost running into two men, one severely injured.

"Help," the soldier begged. It was awkward to hear an English ancient from such a foreign looking man with dark and pointed features. Ari stood dumb for a second before she realized he wanted her to help with the injured man.

She hurried forward and helped lift.

"We need to take him to the hospital. We're almost

there." The soldier continued forward, sweat dripping down his temple.

As they rushed into a nearby building, bullets and debris rained over their heads. At the entrance to the hospital, Ari froze. There were lines upon lines of beds, with injured people crying out in pain. The smell of blood and dirt overwhelmed her.

"Come on," the uninjured man urged her forward.

Medical personnel dressed in bloody scrubs took the body from them.

With her arms now empty, her hands began to shake. People always joked about never leaving their VR vacation, but what if she remained stuck in this living hell? *None of this is real. It isn't real.* Cold dread seeped into Ari's bones, despite the heat. Glancing down, she noticed red splattered against her purple shoes. Blood.

She sprinted down the street but didn't make it to the end of the block before she disappeared. Gasping, she awoke back in the classroom. She lifted her stinging hands. Blood dripped from her palms. Her nails had cut into her hands. At the sight of blood, her stomach turned.

A hand touched her shoulder and Mica appeared above her. "Whoa, girl, what spooked you?"

Ari struggled to speak, her breath coming in short gasps. As soon as Mica removed the cord, Ari jumped out of the chair. Bent over, she stared at the thick wire hanging loosely from the chair. The cable could transport a person to anywhere in the world plus some, but it could also be an eternal prison.

Dr. Coleman appeared next to them. "Mica, what happened?"

"I'm not sure." Mica turned to Ari for an explanation.

"I was ..." What could she say? How could she explain that she would explode if she didn't get out of there? "I just ... the bomb, the smell," Ari stumbled over the words, trying to get out the problem.

"Surely, even in your area, you are familiar with this

VR."

"I'm sorry." Tears were hot on her face. She grabbed her bag and headed to the door.

"The reading assignment is due tomorrow." Dr. Coleman shouted, but Ari didn't stop walking.

If she stopped, she would break down, and she wasn't going to do that. She took the stairs down at a run. Her lungs burned for air, but she kept going. She pulled out some sunglasses to hide behind and pushed outside. She eyed the manufactured grass and fake trees with distaste. With everything fake, how could she tell what was real?

At first, she didn't know where she was heading. Once she passed the cafeteria, she thought of her brother. Marco would understand. He was there when she first freaked out in the virtual.

They had been in school. She was eleven and he was thirteen. Her father had recently slipped into another coma, and her teacher planned on taking the children to visit ancient castles for world history. When the vision opened, Ari's screams had sounded throughout the school. She wouldn't let anyone close enough to touch her until Marco came. He might be an annoying dink at times, but he knew her better than anyone.

His dorm stood at the far edge of campus, in a huge gun-metal building with heavy beams. It looked formidable, matching the security concentration perfectly. Walking through the doors she went for the stairs, not willing to wait for the elevator. Trudging up the four flights calmed her a bit.

She followed the narrow gray hall and knocked on Marco's door. It wasn't until the door opened that she remembered it was Reed's room too.

"Ari." Reed's eyes widened. "What are you doing here?"

Ari wiped the sweat from her brow and tried not to think that she looked even worse when Reed had seen her plastered at the club. "I'm looking for Marco."

"Sorry, he's not here. He's in class."

"Oh, yeah." She was supposed to be there too. "Why are you here then?"

"Study hour." Reed leaned against the door frame in a plain white tee, jeans and socks. Ari thought it unfair that guys could look so good with so little work. He probably didn't even have to run a comb through his short hair.

"So ..." he said as he tapped the door lightly. "Do you want me to leave him a message?"

"Message?" Somehow, 'Marco your little sister is crazy as a loon,' wouldn't be great for a message. That's why she hadn't messaged him to begin with. "No, don't worry about it." She glanced down the hall, unsure of what to do next, or where to go.

"I'll go." She pointed down the hall and turned to walk away.

"Hey." Reed caught her by the wrist. "What's wrong?"

She glanced down at her wrist, and he dropped her hand.

"Nothing." She shook her head. "It's just ... we had virtuals today."

"How long did you last?"

"Enough to see the hell that was the Never-Ending War." She blinked back the raw tears threatening to overflow. Her body didn't want to listen to her at all today.

"I'm sorry," he said, holding her gaze. "The programs the teachers use here are never pretty. They're trying to prepare us for the future, I guess."

Stunned into silence, Ari didn't want to imagine any reality or future that horrific.

"Do you want to come in? I have thirty minutes till my next class."

Her art design class was starting soon, but she didn't care. Ari was about to take him up on his offer, when she noticed someone approaching, a pretty blonde girl with a little too much make-up.

"Hey, Reed." The blonde waved. Ari hoped she was a

neighbor, but she kept heading towards them.

"Oh, I forgot. Ari, I have this thing with Talia," Reed said before the blonde made it to them.

A date or something like it, Ari realized, feeling stupid and small for thinking anything of Reed's offer to come in. Why was she even bothering Reed? "No big deal," Ari turned to leave. "I'll catch you later."

"Wait." He reached a hand out to her but then pulled back.

"It's fine, really." She assured him over her shoulder and kept walking. She shouldn't feel rejected. There was nothing between Reed and her.

Blaming her emotions on the VR, she hurried down the stairs and out the door in relief. Clouds drifted over the campus, casting shadows on the ground. Following the paved path, she curved around the building, through campus, and even past a small park she hadn't known existed.

The sun had set by the time she headed back to the dorm. She wanted to climb into bed and find some comfort in sleep. The first thing she noticed as she opened the door was her school bag that she had forgotten in the virtuals. Someone must have picked it up for her.

Thankful for her bag, she pulled out her tablet and flipped it on. A bright green message instantly popped up.

Thought you might need this. ~ Garrett.

Maybe she wasn't completely alone.

CHAPTER 6

Tessa pulled out her earbuds for the first time the next morning, and repeatedly blinked her eyes until her gaming contacts cleared. Tessa had her hair up in a messy bun, exposing the shaved underside of her hair and the port in the back of her neck. Grabbing her coffee, she turned to Ari. "What was the deal with you leaving the VR lab early yesterday?"

"I had to get out of there. You know?" Ari gathered her bag, ready to leave for morning classes. She really didn't feel like getting into it this morning.

"No, I don't." There was a brief, awkward pause that Tessa was in no hurry to fill.

"I have a problem with being in the program ... like I want to tear out my port." Ari didn't know why she told her roommate. Maybe she was looking for sympathy? Help? She got neither.

Tessa laughed. "That's a good one." She continued laughing as she grabbed her bag and headed out the door.

Ari swore under her breath as the door hissed shut. It was going to be a long day.

Her first two classes sped by in a flurry of notes. It helped that she came in just before the bell rang and sat on the opposite side of the room from Wake. She was up and gone before he could say a word.

Arriving at her third period class, she settled in the chair and pulled out her tablet to go through her schedule. The guy next to Ari uploaded a file directly to his desk and began manipulating his notes. The desks had ports to upload to and write on whenever they needed. Ari preferred holding her tablet in her hand, almost like a real book.

Her HUB vibrated with a message from Garrett.

Heard about Dr. Coleman's class yesterday. Wanted to see how you were doing?

She moaned and wondered just how many people knew about her meltdown.

How did you find out?

I know the TA, Mica.

I'm not as crazy as it probably sounds.

Don't worry. All the hot girls are a bit crazy.

Ari's mouth dropped, not sure how to take that. She didn't have time to reply before the class began.

The fast-paced lecture kept everyone's attention. In a slimming business suit, Dr. Cox paced in front of the students. Her strong voice carried without a microphone.

As the instructor outlined the syllabus, Ari realized this class might end up being one of her favorites. Hard, yes, but fascinating. The workings and reasoning behind human behavior was complex and engrossing all at the same time. The class dismissed all too soon for Ari.

For lunch, Ari headed down to the student commons building in the middle of campus. Not feeling like a big meal, she ordered a vanilla meal shake from the automated window. It tasted like ice cream but contained the vitamins and nutrients of a complete meal. Ari's mom hated the engineered food, but Ari could eat ice cream for the rest of her life. She grabbed a small apple, so she could tell her mom she did, and worked on the shake while reading about the circuitry of the human brain.

She read the same sentence several times, struggling to focus amid the noise of the cafeteria. It wasn't until someone pushed a white napkin across the table did Ari realize she was no longer alone.

"Hey, Reed." She studied the simple cartoon drawn on the napkin. A clown was sucking on a cigarette while making a balloon animal and getting ash on the large-eyed child waiting in line. A smile grew on her face which turned into a laugh. "I haven't gotten one of these cartoons for quite a while."

"You haven't needed one for a while."

She didn't want to tell him she had kept every drawing he'd given her back at home. Reed used to sneak cartoons into Ari's bags, or books, and even one into her breakfast box when she was younger, right after she lost her dad. They always cheered her up, no matter how bizarre. Maybe it was because they were so bizarre.

Looking up and meeting Reed's gaze, the laughter slowly died. It wasn't very often she found herself alone with Reed. And the last couple of times hadn't been promising.

"Thanks." Her thumb brushed over the cartoon. "I never thought I'd miss the old neighborhood." She realized he was just taking care of her, like he had done when her dad abandoned her. He treated her like a younger sister, but unfortunately, Ari's thoughts weren't very sisterly.

"Just remember these rich kids are jealous. Their parents had to sell their vacation home to pay for this."

"Not my roommate. She still has her vacation home and a couple others to spare." It was hard for Ari not to be jealous of Tessa.

"Yeah, some are luckier than others, but that's why we're here. Right? To have more opportunity than our parents did."

She reached for the spoon in her shake and swallowed a cold bite. The freezing lump hit her stomach and cleared her head. It was easy to forget about the worry of tomorrow with Reed nearby. "It's totally over-rated."

"What is?" He glanced up, meeting her eyes, and those eyes of a million colors shone back with curiosity. In the middle of a noisy cafeteria, a small bit of quiet spanned the distance between them.

She lowered her gaze, which made it easier to think. "The money. These people all spend it on a fake life, with plastic faces, and perfect bodies. Give me ice cream, fake or not, and I can die happy."

CHAPTER 7

After missing Art Design the day before without any major consequences, Ari decided to skip her VR class. Better to take a demerit than freak out again, and it gave her one more day to figure out what to do. She completed homework during her VR class and then headed to her last class of the day.

"We missed your theatrics in class today." Wake brushed by as she entered the classroom.

She glared at him while taking her seat. Why wouldn't that creep just leave her alone?

Professor Mienka taught art design and dressed the part. She was a tall woman with a heavy accent. Long curly hair fell to the middle of her back, and she had a natural beauty that Ari guessed many men fought over. And the woman insisted everyone call her by her first name, Irina.

By the end of the day, Ari welcomed the homework; at least, the kind didn't require trips to the VR. She studied until the words blurred together on her small interface screen and then passed out for the night.

The next day, she tried to become invisible as she found a seat in the back for her first class. She kept to herself and tried to focus on the lecture and not her upcoming class with Dr. Coleman. She couldn't skip again and avoiding it wouldn't help anything.

Her HUB vibrated with a message from Garrett.

Want to meet for lunch today?

Ari wondered if he was asking her on a date. She didn't have much experience with dating. Most guys wanted to take girls on VR dates to foreign destinations. Ari had to admit Rome or Greece probably impressed girls more than a coffee shop.

Sure. Where?

I'll meet you outside your dorm.

Thoughts of Garrett helped distract her as she finished class. As promised, Garrett stood outside her building, bag in one hand and drink carrier in the other. Instead of the lab uniform, he wore slimming jeans and a green shirt. His yellow hair had a cute, messy look, and his smile was infectious.

"You, me and some killer meatballs."

She returned the smile. "Lead the way."

He curved off into the fake manicured grass behind her dorm. A small lake bordered the north of campus. They strolled to a grouping of large boulders overlooking the water.

"Need some help?" he asked, nodding to the large boulder.

"No, I got it." She climbed up easily and then grabbed the food, so he could climb up beside her.

"Just to warn you, these meatballs go beyond mere mortal food at our campus. Once tasted, your diet will never be the same again."

Ari laughed. "Okay. I've been warned."

With one bite, a flood of flavors flooded her mouth. Messy and delicious, the meatball tasted like a complete meal, like her mom's lasagna with bread rolled into one ball. She devoured the meatballs and cleaned up afterwards. "You're right. That was amazing."

Garrett had already polished off his meatballs and was

sucking down a drink. She looked over at his bright yellow hair and several hoops running up one ear. The black eyeliner and goofy grin belied his age.

He handed her a drink. She grabbed it, but he didn't let go.

"Do you have a plan for the virtuals?" His grin gone and his large eyes containing no hint of laughter.

Her stomach sank, and she wondered how he knew. "No. Just hope they don't kick me out until after Christmas," Ari gave a forced laugh. It was either laugh or cry.

He relinquished his hold on the cup. "Okay, then."

She sipped her soda, a unique rich flavor, with a hint of cream and salt. The soda reminded her of her father, something he'd always splurge on. She rubbed a spot on her chest and cursed herself for missing her father. *He left us.* She stared out at the lake for a while longer wondering if she had the courage to even show up for the next class.

"You ready for your class?" Garrett asked.

"No," Ari replied, "But do I have a choice?"

"We could get drunk, steal a boat, and roam the river like pirates." Happy Garrett was back, with his bright eyes and smile.

"Ask me in two hours, and I might take you up on it."

Garrett hopped off the rock first then turned to help her down. For some reason her muscles didn't want to work as her brain requested. She stumbled a bit, and Garrett reached out to catch her.

"You okay there?"

His voice sounded farther away than usual. She looked at him, wondering what he was talking about. He could almost be a fairy with his pointed nose and light pink lips. Why was she thinking about fairies?

"Ari," he called her name.

He asked her a question, but she struggled to focus on the words coming out of his mouth.

"You'll be fine. It will relax you."

"What?" Something wasn't right. He took her hand and led her back to the virtuals building.

The sun warmed her skin, a fuzzy heat she drank up. She tried to stop and bake in the sun, but Garrett kept pulling her hand.

"Class," he said loudly. "School. Remember, not getting kicked out till after Christmas?"

Then she did. She hoped she wasn't late to class. The virtuals. She should be freaking out, but again her body didn't want to obey.

"What did you do to me?" she asked Garrett. "Did you put a tab in my drink?" She would have tasted it.

"Sort of. A relaxing tab I got after a skiing accident. A little help to get you through your virtuals."

Ari grabbed his shirt, angry. "You drugged me?"

Her third day away from home, and she'd been drugged. She could be a poster child for those warning posters in school, showing you what not to do. Her mother would probably reprimand her for trusting boys with colored hair and rings in their ears. If he was a fairy, he was a bad one indeed.

"It wasn't a lot. I didn't think it would affect you so much. You must not tab often. Get through your class and then you can yell at me. Okay?"

"O ... kay." Ari's speech slowed as her brain took in everything he said. "Class first, then yell at you." She wiped his chin where he'd missed the sauce from his sandwich and then licked her finger.

Ari couldn't help but laugh, happy everything else was gone.

"Come on. You better hurry to class or you'll be late." Garrett led her to class like a gentleman, except for the whole drugging thing, of course.

Everyone was already seated when Garrett handed Ari her bag and pushed her through the door.

The teacher stood in front of the class with an unhappy look on his face. "Welcome, Ms. Mendez. Glad you made it to class today. I hope you can stay."

Unsure if he asked a question or made a statement, she played it safe by heading straight to her chair. Her purple painted shoes took one step after another. She slumped into the chair with a bump, letting a surprised squeak escape.

"Sorry," she mumbled. Sitting was good.

Dr. Coleman resumed his lecture. Ari only caught phrases about sending homework to their class hard drive and what to focus on in today's virtuals. Without warning, Mica appeared at her side to help her hook into her virtual.

"Mica, will you give me a happy virtual today?" Ari asked.

"Dr. Coleman assigns the virtuals, not me. Let's get you hooked in." Mica directed Ari's head to the chair and inserted her data port.

The next time Ari opened her eyes, a gray bird—a pigeon maybe—stared at her, cocking its head from side-to-side as if curious.

"Caw," Ari squawked at the bird.

The bird twitched and then flew off.

It took her a few moments to realize where she was. The damp air and smell of old fish and seaweed brought an unexpected smile to her face. She loved the ocean.

Her feet ran along on a wooden walkway. Dodging tourists, she weaved her way around small brightly painted restaurants and gift shops. She turned a corner and hit the railing. Gripping the cold bars, she watched the raw power of the ocean as it crashed onto the shore.

A loud breath escaped her lips. The beauty overwhelmed her, the immense nature of the water. Waves shattered with a force of a wild animal. Pushing and pulling, back and forth. She briefly glimpsed Professor Coleman, but the waves demanded her attention.

Dark over-sized rocks blocked the path down to the

beach, creating a wall of sorts. She'd never been in the ocean before, and she wasn't about to lose her chance. Lifting herself over the ledge, she climbed down. It probably wasn't her smartest decision. It took longer than she wanted to maneuver herself amongst the dark craggy rocks. The wind off the sea chilled her to the bone and tugged at her hair. Determined to stand in the water, she had to touch the end of the world. A loose rock fell under the weight of her foot. She slipped and lost her footing. She caught herself on a sharp rock, cutting her hand.

She paused to regain her balance. A quick glance down showed her she still had what looked like ten feet to go. The blood on her hand made her head spin. *This is not real. I'm almost there.* Glancing down again, she wondered if her eyes were playing tricks on her. The ground appeared closer. What was ten feet looked like one or two. She ignored the anomaly and jumped off. Her feet landed softly on the sand beneath. *Could Garrett's drugs affect my perception inside the virtual?*

She dismissed any worries and headed to the sea. She kicked off her shoes in the sand and waded into the icy water until it reached her calves. Her toes squished deep in the sand as goosebumps covered her arms. Starring out into the great abyss, Ari hadn't felt so alive, so at peace, since her father left. The crash of a nearby wave sprayed her, leaving drops of salt water clinging to her skin. She lifted her arm to taste the ocean.

A small voice crept in the back of her thoughts, distracting her. *This isn't real. You're in a machine with cable coming out of your neck.*

Lifting a hand to her face, she was surprised at the tears she found. Unsure whether to laugh or cry at the irony that she couldn't quite enjoy the virtual even with a drug in her system, she decided it was okay to do both.

Squinting against the bright lights, she found herself back in the class room without remembering that she left the VR. For the first time, Ari experienced what others called 'coming down' after a VR. Her body sagged in the chair, void of any energy or desire to come back to reality. The sandwich sat heavy in her stomach.

Hands soon found her and unhooked the cable from her neck. Ari turned around to thank Mica but instead found the large hands of Dr. Coleman putting the cable back in its spot at the terminal. Anger etched the sharp lines in his face. Glancing around, she found the rest of the students still hooked into their chairs.

Ari lowered her gaze and focused on her hands. She rubbed her fingers together and marveled the numb feeling, like rubbing silly-putty. *Focus, dammit.* Dr. Coleman grabbed a nearby chair and sat across from her.

"Ms. Mendez." Dr. Coleman waited until she lifted her gaze. His jaw clenched, his cold eyes held an undeniable anger.

His silence unnerved Ari. "Sorry, I didn't understand the assignment." Which was an understatement.

"You show up two days ago only to leave in hysterics, and today you come in high. Is this really the way you want to start out your career?"

She shook her head, not trusting her voice.

"You got nothing, huh?" He stood walking over to his desk. "I'll mark down a demerit in your file and talk to your advisor."

"No, it's just ..." She froze, unsure of where to start.

He stopped and turned around. "It's what?"

"I have a ... problem with virtuals."

"I don't think 'problem' begins to cover it."

"I don't like them."

"Then leave."

"What?"

"You heard me. Leave. Grab your bags and head out that door, because there are plenty of kids wanting to get accepted here and they actually *like* virtuals. *Love* them, to be honest."

Leave, I could just leave. Standing there, every cell in her body ached to go back home, to the comfort of her room, her mom, her life. But that was why she was here, to make a better life for her family, for herself. Lifting her chin, she resolved to do better, be better, to remember why she came here.

"Your tests show you have a lot of potential, but so do a lot of people. You have two days to get over it. The first test is on Friday, and you will need at least a C to continue in the program, especially since you have failed your last two assignments. I don't care about excuses."

"Okay." Ari grabbed her bag to leave. She wasn't sure how she was going to do it, but she'd worry about that when she was sober. All she wanted was to bury herself somewhere.

"If you show up high to class again, you're gone."

"I understand."

"And, Ariana," Dr. Coleman added. "Did you mean to jump down off the rocks? Even if the pain is muted, it is there to keep you safe."

"The jump wasn't that far. It didn't hurt." A brief look of confusion crossed Dr. Coleman's face, but Ari dismissed it, getting out of there as fast as she could.

CHAPTER 8

A ri walked around the school grounds aimlessly. Her thoughts meandered, trying to see how she felt about Garrett's actions. He drugged her and, on every account, that was wrong. On the other hand, she experienced a VR for the first time without the stress and panic that drove her to flee. Being tabbed every day at school was not an option though. Mr. Coleman's threats made that clear. He didn't have the patience for hand-holding or incompetence—his words at their first class.

Finally, thirst steered her towards a drink machine, and she grabbed a coffee to help sober her up. It probably had as much sugar as coffee, but it would help. She found a nearby bench, and as soon as she sat down her HUB vibrated. It was a message from Garrett.

How did it go?
Still deciding whether or not to kill you for drugging me.
WRU?

It took Ari, a moment to reply, unsure if she wanted to meet him. Finally, she opened her satellite location to Garrett.

See u there soon.

While on her HUB, she sent a message to her brother,

but she knew better than to wait for a quick reply. As the high wore off, her thoughts finally calmed down, so she pulled up some assigned reading for class. She didn't make it past chapter one before someone plopped down on the bench next to her. Garrett wore his silver work uniform. An odd smell radiated off him, a mix between smoke and sugar.

"That bad, huh?" He leaned over and nudged her with his shoulder.

She clicked off the device and looked up.

Garrett wore a wary expression, his shoulders tight as if preparing for an incoming punch. Ari decided that the glimmer of innocent mischief in his eyes was just that, innocent and meaning to be helpful.

"If you ever try anything like that again, I'll hurt you. Bad." Ari glowered at him. "That being said, it was my best trip through the virtuals."

Ari proceeded to tell Garrett about the virtual and Dr. Coleman's threat.

"Somehow I have to figure out how to do this sober in three days or I'm a goner." She leaned her head back against the bench. The cloudy sky darkened.

Garrett leaned back as well, his arms barely touching her. "I can't believe you've never been to the ocean."

"Really?" Ari straightened up. "That's what you got out of that story? I have bigger issues than my lack of traveling."

"I'm serious." His gaze remained sky bound. "I wish I could have seen that."

"If I'm around long enough, maybe you can, but let's see if I survive to next week." She checked her HUB again; no message from Marco.

He pushed himself up. "That's easy, I'll help you."

"No drugs. He'll fail me."

"You're right. Today was only supposed to show you that you can do it." Garrett leaned in close to Ari and pushed back a strand of hair that had fallen into her face.

It felt intimate, even though he barely touched her.

Glancing up, Ari spotted Reed nearby, talking with a black phone in his ear. Once he noticed her, he faltered for a moment, his brow furrowing. She waved slightly.

"Hey, Reed." Garrett leaned back next to Ari.

Reed regained his composure, gave a forced smile, and headed off, continuing his conversation with someone in his ear.

"Careful," Ari said as Garrett accidentally knocked over the remains of her coffee. She wiped at it with a napkin. "What is this master plan of yours that doesn't involve drugs?"

"We'll go to the lab tonight to practice."

"You have access to the lab at night?"

His eyes sparkled with mischief. "Yes, one of the perks of working there."

"Is anyone else there?"

"Depends who I let in." Back came Garrett's mischievous smile. "Being a third-year manager has its advantages. Meet me out front at midnight."

"What about my HUB? Wouldn't the school realize I'm not sleeping or even in bed?" The electronic device strapped to her wrist kept constant tabs on Ari. She found the health alerts quite annoying and had to disable them, like she didn't already know her heart rate and stress levels were through the roof.

"You have to break into your HUB and put it into a loop." He reached for her wrist and pointed to a small crease in the edge of the screen. "You can pry the screen open from there and I'll send you the schematics for the rest. You switch one wire. Use tweezers or pliers and change it back when you're back in your room. It's pretty simple. Everyone does it. Don't worry."

Don't worry. Really? Anyone who knew Ari, knew that those two words were impossible for her, but she had to try. First week at school, and she was moving on from tabbing to sneaking out. The school security guards might get the chance to kick her out before Coleman did.

After saying goodbye, she headed back to her dorm, hoping to get through some homework. In the dorm room, Tessa wore her head phones, engrossed in her game, like the example of a perfect VR student. She probably had a waiting list for her game's release.

Ari dropped her bag and fell on her bed. Tessa logged out of her computer and grabbed a soda from their fridge.

"Hey, roomy." Tessa leaned back in her chair and kicked up her black boots that probably held more tech than Ari's HUB. "I didn't see you in the virtuals today when I awoke. Did you freak out again and I missed it?"

Ari gave a dry chuckle. Laughing was always better than crying. "No."

Tessa didn't bother holding back her belch. "Oh, well that's good. Right?"

"Yeah, I guess. What are you working on?" Ari motioned to Tessa's computer.

"A new planet in the Pultzer Galaxy was causing a few glitches."

"A few glitches ... that sounds like me."

Tessa laughed. "Don't worry about it. This program is full of geeks hoping to be at the forefront of virtual programming. You're an alien to them. The only decent girls they come into contact with are in virtuals, and most of those are just overly sexualized versions the guys dreamed up. There are only five girls in this program. Remember?"

Tessa took a drink. "And it's all about pecking order here. The first week is spent finding out who has sold what and to whom, and you are a virgin."

"Virgin?" Ari knew they weren't talking about her sexual experience, though if they were, Tessa would be right. She didn't even date a lot at her last school.

"A virgin to programming and going inside your first creation. Granted, the pervs here use that term in other ways."

"Ewwww." Ari shook her head in disgust.

Tessa laughed at her again, lifting her head back and putting a hand on her belly. Most people, especially rich people, would have taken care of that little extra fat with a few simple procedures. But Tessa was definitely not status quo. Ari liked that about her.

Tessa pushed back a few strands of hair escaping the knot on top of her head. "Sorry, I know the mental image is a little much. I hate using the open lab for that reason."

"They don't do that there, do they?"

"The techs monitor all the virtuals, but kids always try."

"Nice," she replied sarcastically. Ari grabbed her leather bag and pulled out her tablet to read.

Tessa stared at the electronic notebook. "Is that the Azio 7.1? Where did you get that?"

"From the tech store."

"I didn't think they had anything past a 6.5 here for students. I might have to grab one. I don't like teachers accessing my custom one, especially with my gaming contacts on it. How did you get one?"

"A friend," Ari replied not sure how to quantify her relationship with Garrett. Friend felt safe.

Ari didn't know why she asked her next question. Maybe it was the easy grin on Tessa's face, or maybe pure desperation. "Tessa, would you ever be willing to tutor me?"

Tessa narrowed her eyes, lined with heavy black eyeliner and mascara. "Do I look like a tutor?" She shook out her colored hair, edgy techy clothes, and a dark green shirt that read: "My other body has wings and claws."

Ari motioned to her own dark hair, that unlike most people, she constantly wore down to hide her port, her homemade clothes, and shoes that had glued back together more than once, making her stand out amid her classmates. "Do I look like a virtual programmer?"

CHAPTER 9

Ari set an alarm for her meeting with Garrett and then pulled up some reading on her tablet. She stayed awake until Tessa dropped off and then got to work on her HUB. After reading the instructions, it took her about thirty minutes to get it set. Granted, wiping her nervous sweaty hands every couple of minutes didn't help.

By the time she finished rewiring her HUB, her alarm went off. Her stomach churned with nervous energy. She pulled on a dark hooded jacket. Once she stepped outside her dorm, the crisp night sky set Ari on edge. The idea of sneaking into school property sent fear, and a bit of excitement, coursing through her veins like caffeine. The last time she'd snuck out her brother had urged her to do it.

When she'd began her eighth year of training, the other kids at school had often harassed her for her fear of VR. Ari had already missed out on birthday parties and games, but some bullies never let up. Marco fought them for a while, but he thought Ari needed to get her own revenge.

Trying to help, Marco had hacked social parties and

retrieved pictures of kids in compromising situations. Having printed the pictures in poster size, Ari and Marco posted them all over the school campus. The administrators probably knew who had done it, but Ari never heard about it. Apparently, they thought some people needed to be held responsible for their actions. Hopefully, tonight would be as successful.

Ari continued out into the night. The dim security lights gave an eerie feeling to the silent campus. She walked in the shadows alongside the path to the student lab, the silver buildings turning into menacing mountains, looming over her like robotic monsters with so much power silently sleeping.

A slight tune traveled down the darkened path. She wrapped her arms around herself, fighting against the chill. Garrett's dark figure leaned against a tree, whistling his melody.

"Hi," she said, grateful to see him.

Dressed in dark colors, he casually pushed himself off the tree. Even his hair was black as night.

"You changed your hair." No wonder Ari hadn't seen him near the tree.

"Yeah, I thought it fit in with the whole sneaking around thing. This will be fun."

"If you think hanging around a phobic girl who may burst into hysterics any minute sounds like fun." As much as Ari wanted to agree with him and to enjoy the night, in the back of her mind remained a nagging reminder of what lay ahead.

He gently picked up a piece of her hair and twirled it around his fingers. Her stomach fluttered at his closeness. She wondered if he was trying to distract her on purpose.

The simple gray tech building stood behind the student union, where Ari first met Garrett. He used an electronic card to unlock the door, and the gray glass door slid open in a silent rush of air.

"Won't someone realize we came? You know cameras,

data records or something?" Ari searched the empty room while crossing the threshold.

"Cameras are never looked at unless there is an unlawful entrance." Garrett waved the key. He spoke at a normal tone, but the empty building amplified his voice, reverberating in the dark metal cavern. "I will hack into the virtual records to alter the time of use. It's easier than deleting and that way your teacher can see that you have been practicing."

"Can they see everything we do inside?"

"No, it would take way too much data to record every student's usage. When it's open, they have monitors, sort of like Dr. Coleman sets up in class. Tonight, it's just us." Garrett inserted his card and entered an electronic code.

With a swoosh, the door opened. Bright light flooded the room. Blinking repeatedly, Ari glimpsed rows and rows of padded reclined chairs with computer terminals, hooked up next to them. The VRs held an infinite world of possibilities and places to go, if only she could let herself relax.

"You ready?" He startled her out of her thoughts, standing close enough for her to smell the coffee on his breath. He teasingly traced a path down her arm, which brought her back to the present.

Pull yourself together. Standing here, alone with a cute boy, a third-year at that, who was trying to help her, overwhelmed her a bit. She stepped back and tried to force a smile.

"Come sit down." Garrett took her hand and led her to a nearby chair. His casual touch surprised Ari. She assumed it probably didn't mean as much to him as it did to her.

He booted up the system. Staring at her from above, he connected the data port in the back of her neck. She shuddered at the feel of cold steel connecting to her brain.

"You're okay." His free hand swept her hair off her shoulders. "Think of this as a first date. I want to take you out."

She should have been flattered. Her gut twisted in so many knots that she didn't know what to think. He quietly took a seat next to her, plugged himself in, and reached for her hand.

"I am in control of this virtual. I am the main user and you are set up as a participating spectator. You can always get out on your own, but I can force you out at any time. You'll be safe."

Ari swallowed once and nodded.

He put pressure on her hand. "The real question is: do you trust me?"

She hadn't known Garrett long, but at that moment she was drowning in school and he was the only life preserver. She gripped his hand in return.

Squeezing her eyes shut amid the darkness, she focused on Garrett's hand to keep her grounded.

"Open up, Ari. Come on," Garret's playful voice drifted around her, carried on a cool breeze.

A warm light greeted her. Blinking several times, it took a minute for her vision to adjust. The smell of salt water carried past her on a cool breeze. She glanced down. Garrett's grip remained tight, tethering her to reality.

"Look, Ari." He tugged her forward like a little kid anxious for a surprise.

Lifting her gaze, an endless expanse of water filled her view. The ocean, but nothing like the ocean she saw before with its cold gray waves. Instead, an exquisite aquamarine sea rose and fell, lapping towards flawless white sand. Palms trees stood to her side, with a netted hammock hanging in between them. Down the beach, a small white house stood with open windows. She turned to find more palm trees and green plants dotting the landscape.

Its perfect beauty pricked against her neck, where her port should be. "Where are we?"

He pulled her into the ocean. Garrett had on gray trunks that fell low on his hips, and his chest was bare with lean muscles built into his thin frame. "A small island. I can't remember the name anymore."

The warm water lapped at her ankles, her feet melting into the cool sand. "Wait, I'm not dressed for the—" Before she could finish, she glanced down, and realized she wore a short white sundress with a teal bikini underneath.

She shivered at the idea of the VR accessing her subconscious to dress her appropriately. Most VRs had a program that allowed the player to choose or change their attire. Pushing down the frantic voice in the back of her mind, she continued to let Garrett guide her out to sea.

"Did you make this virtual?"

"No, just an upperclassman I know. I'm only the techie who gets to play with all the fun toys."

The warm waves crept up her legs. Despite the beauty, her nerves unsettled her. She pulled her hand free and crossed her arms.

He stepped closer. "What's wrong?"

"Nothing, everything, this place ... it's so real, so perfect. Don't you ever worry that one day you won't be able to tell reality from fiction? That one day you'll wake up but not be really sure if you're awake?"

"This virtual isn't that good." He glanced at Ari. "You must have covered it in your classes, the errors in programming? You have to see them?"

Ari remembered visiting the carnival with her brother, and how the clown glitched, static covering its face. "I haven't stayed in one long enough to get a good look."

"Well, look." He pointed to the fish. "See the fish and how they swim, so symmetrical and perfectly timed. Step into their path."

As she stepped forward, the fish blinked out of existence for a brief moment, with a short burst of static, then appeared again and continued along their path past her leg.

He stepped closer to her, blocking the path to several others. "See?"

She watched for several moments the fish blinking in and out of existence. It was so bizarre when considering they looked so genuine. Reaching down, she stirred the water, watching the fish scatter and the program restart in the same spot.

"With the obvious errors in this cheap VR, I don't think you could ever get lost in it." He rubbed a hand through his hair which stood on end. "Granted, it's a bit of a buzzkill when I focus on those things. Most of us want to get lost here and be oblivious."

A nervous chuckle escaped her lips as she turned in a slow circle, searching deeper into the program. The trees swayed, but the corresponding shadows in the sand didn't move. The clouds had a similar precision, timed with a warm breeze. Even the sand where they once stood on the beach was smoothed over as if with an air brush. A student must have written this, and not as a sightseeing program.

With every error, a bit of the stress and anxiety peeled off. She still itched to get out of her virtual skin and take a real breath, but it helped to look at things differently. She had never lasted more than a few minutes in the VR and nobody really cared to help her work through it. One of the disadvantages of attending a poor school had been that her problem was brushed under the rug. With every error, she realized she couldn't get lost in this fabricated reality. And wasn't this what her teacher wanted her to do, find the errors?

She turned to asked Garrett another question. But before she could say anything, he splashed her, soaking the front of her dress. She sucked in a breath, and then lowered her brows, giving him a narrow glare. "You started a war, buddy." She slapped the water and nailed him right in the face.

It was on. For a few moments, Ari forgot about the fear and panic and just enjoyed being with Garrett. They ran and played in the low waves. At one point, Garrett picked her up, threatening to dump her all the way under.

"No, no, no," she begged as he headed into deeper waters. Of course, laughing while telling him to stop didn't help her case. Finally, he threw himself in the water with her in his arms.

Thoroughly exhausted and soaking wet, they returned to the shore. Ari took off the wet dress to ring it out, but then realized how exposed she was in her bikini.

Relaxing into the sand, she wrapped her arms around her knees. Unease gathered in her stomach, but she was unsure if it was due to the VR or being alone with Garrett while wearing so little. Garrett plopped down next to her, shaking out his hair. They faced forward, watching the low waves, but close enough for their shoulders to touch.

"You haven't left yet?" He nudged her with his shoulder, a sly grin on his face. He hadn't shaved in a couple days, and despite her generally liking boys clean-shaven, she had to admit it looked good on him.

"Nope." She rubbed a hand over her arm. Her emotions revved up a notch, playing pinball inside her head. "It's amazing. Too bad it's not real."

"It's real in our minds. When we come out won't we remember this conversation or our water fight?"

"I suppose ..." She straightened, his words not settling quite right.

"A VR is a set built for whatever our imagination wants." His hand reached over to brush sand off her arm.

A shiver crawled up her skin, despite the sun. "I wish I could dry off my dress."

"Now why would you want to do that when you look so great?"

Ari shoved his shoulder making him tip over in the sand. Her face suddenly grew hot, like the warm sand beneath her feet.

"Hey, I was only asking why you would want to. Only a warper could do that, anyway." He dusted off the sand.

"A warper? I didn't think those were real." Ari had heard the old wives' tales about people who could manipulate or create VRs with a wave of their hands, but no one really believed in them. If one believed the conspiracy theories online, warpers were responsible for everything from government hacks to alien landings.

"I knew a buddy online that claimed to be a warper. He supposedly made millions but disappeared. I haven't heard from him since."

"Then how do you know he was telling the truth?"

"I guess I don't. He just didn't seem like the type to brag or lie about stuff. He was something else." He shrugged. "I'm glad you're sticking around."

Ari took another breath. "I'm surprised I'm actually able to stick around in here."

"Most phobias just take constant exposure to overcome."

She looked at him sideways, narrowing her eyes. "When did you become an expert?"

He smiled. "The school has a fabulous computerized counselor."

She cringed in embarrassment. She was the crazy girl. But part of it made sense. She tried a virtual at the beginning of every school year, and when she freaked out, the teacher let her opt out for the year. She learned to loathe the first day of school.

He reached for her hand. "I think I've been a nice distraction too."

Taking his hand sent her heart racing. Her other hand restlessly adjusted her swimsuit. While she definitely was improving, she was far from comfortable here. The fabricated world could hold anything or nothing. After being held at bay for so long, her panic pushed to the forefront of her mind.

Sensing her panic, Garrett turned her head with a

gentle hand. "Hey, Ari, look at me. I'm real. You're real. That's all that matters." He cupped her face with his hands. "Look at me." His dark eyes were calm and his breathing even.

She tried to mimic it.

"I'm real. You're real," he slowly leaned forward. "This is real."

His salty lips pressed against hers, and she lost all focus. *This wasn't real. None of it.* In a second, her world blackened.

Ari stared at the ceiling, struggling to catch her breath. Garrett's hand hung open and empty by his side as his eyes fluttered open.

Her hands reached behind and slowly unplugged herself. Now awake, Garrett unplugged himself, and then came over to help her. She knew how to do it, but without years of experience like everyone else, it took her longer.

Even the dim lights couldn't hide the disappointment in Garrett's heavy eyes.

"Thanks Garett," she said. "I'm sorry, I just ..."

"Don't worry about it." He spoke in a brisk manner. "It'll take a while. I get it."

She stood, and they both headed outside. The cool wind brushed against her skin, and for the briefest moment, she wished she was back on that beach. Instead, she tugged her cardigan around her body to block the chill. They walked back, an awkward silence settling between them. He stopped at the door to her building. She kept the distance between them, not ready to relive that moment in the VR. Not that he wasn't cute or nice for helping her. It just messed with her mind, having reality and the virtuals mix so closely. Her feeling swirled in her mind, unsure of how she felt about him. He was a great friend, but as a boyfriend? Maybe that was her answer right there.

CHAPTER 10

Tessa shoved Ari's shoulder repeatedly. "Hey, are you going to class? You slept through both of our alarms."

"What?" Ari bolted upright, though her mind took a bit longer to catch up.

"You slept through breakfast and have about ten minutes until class."

"Damn." Ari stumbled to her desk, shoved her tablet in her bag, and slung it over her shoulder.

"Your clothes?" Tessa watched her in disbelief.

Looking down, Ari realized she still wore her pajamas, gray sweatpants and a purple tee. "Ugh!" Ari headed to her dresser.

"Don't mention it. Here's a coffee, you're going to need it more than me." Tessa placed the drink on her desk and headed out the door.

Ari made a mental note that she owed Tessa big time and rushed to finish getting ready.

Ari slipped into class a few minutes late. Wake and his friends snickered in the back as Professor Speltman reprimanded her. Warmth flooded her face as she mumbled her apologies and took her seat.

The caffeine had not hit Ari's system effectively enough for her to comprehend Professor Speltman's lecture on the common templates for coding. Although she'd better figure it out by that afternoon, since she had to create a template herself. By the time she found her seat in programming, she had wiped the sleep from her eyes and the caffeine had kicked in. With thoughts of the previous night, a nervous energy kept her sitting up straight in her chair as Professor Tollingston lectured on the seven basic plots in storytelling. He claimed that there were only seven stories ever told in history, and those were retold with different variations.

Despite her interest in the topic, Ari's mind wandered back to her night with Garrett. Part of her found hope in remaining in the VR for as long as she did. Yet leaving mid-kiss had made things a bit awkward in the lab with Garrett. Though, as they texted through the day, he had guaranteed her that he didn't take offense at her fast departure.

While trying to keep up with her notes, thoughts of Garrett and his almost-kiss twirled around her mind. He was cute, nice, and ready to help when no one else seemed to care, but something was off. Maybe it was his objectionable methods of helping by slipping a tab in her drink or sneaking into school property in the middle of the night? That kiss wasn't anything like she imagined her first kiss. Did that even count as a kiss if it was electronic?

She shoved the memories of the night away and focused on the lecture. Professor Tollingston was giving examples of stories told throughout history.

The red-headed kid, Rand, raised his hand. "Why does it matter if history falls into the regular stock stories?"

Gutsy to ask, Ari thought, or just stupid.

"There is a high demand for periodic pieces amongst educational institutions, and the study of military strategy and wars is extremely important to our country. Yet people want to be constantly entertained, so you must follow the plots given to you. You students are storytellers, every single one of you, and virtuals are a story taken to the ultimate platform."

As her professor assigned homework, Ari realized why she might have been chosen for the scholarship. She loved stories, relishing the characters and intricate plots. The only problem was she preferred them on her tablet where she had more control over the experience.

The bell rang, and Ari headed to lunch. Her shoes hit the warm pavement, and she welcomed the sun as she continued on her way to grab a bite to eat.

She was surprised to find Reed approaching and wondered what he was doing near the Virtuals building. It was on the other side of the campus for him.

"Hey, Ari." He looked good with his perfectly mussed hair and green eyes. She nervously touched her hair, currently wrapped in a messy bun, and wished she'd fixed it after class.

"Whatcha doing on this side of the world?"

"Not much. I had to run a couple of errands." He looked around for a moment.

She wondered if he was meeting someone, maybe the blonde she remembered from his dorm.

"Can I talk to you for a second?" He moved to the grassy area next to the Virtual building, and Ari followed, a bit curious as why he would need to talk to her.

"Is this about Marco? I haven't seen him for a week, and I thought he might be avoiding hanging out with his first-year sister."

"No, it's not about Marco."

"Then why hasn't he called or returned my texts?"

"He's busy lately, studying, and he's been in the virtual lab a lot this semester." A chill ran up Ari's spine at the mention of virtuals. She still needed to get used to the fact that they were a part of her daily life.

"You better tell him to text me soon." Ari's stomach grumbled, signaling time to go. "I'm heading to lunch."

"No, wait." He stopped her.

She glanced at his hand on her arm. She's known Reed for a long time, and his touch shouldn't affect her so much. Looking back up, she noticed color flooding his face. She'd never seen him flustered before.

"What is it?"

"It's Garrett."

She pulled back slightly. *How could he know?*

He must have seen the surprise on her face. "I saw the both of you the other day and I was a little worried."

"What about Garrett?"

"I know Garrett. We work together."

"Where?"

"We do a side business together to make some extra money." Reed dropped his hand and his eyes. "It's just that I know what kind of guy he is, and I don't think you should be hanging out, especially with you being a first-year and all. He has a reputation with girls."

"Really?" She bit back her frustration at being left in the dark. Why didn't anyone tell her? She waited until Reed met her eyes before she continued. "Garrett has been the only one in this whole school to help me out and even care what's happening to me. I can't even get my own brother to text me back, never mind give a damn about how I'm doing."

"I give a damn."

"Until the next pretty blonde comes along." Ari didn't mean to say it. The words slipped out. She had no reason to be jealous, and she didn't think she really was. It just felt like ammunition.

A momentary flash of surprise crossed his eyes. "What are you talking about?"

"The girl in your room."

"That was work," Reed protested.

"The work you do with Garrett?"

"Yes." He ran a hand through his hair. "I never knew you needed help."

"Don't worry about it, Reed. You don't have to tell me anything." Tired and hungry, she wasn't in the mood to fight anymore. "I'm going. Thanks for your concern. Tell my brother I say 'Hi'." Ari walked off, leaving Reed behind.

She made it only a couple steps into the cafeteria before Garrett found her. She smiled, relieved. He lightly brushed her arm as he approached, and, just like that, the anger dissipated. Reed worried like an older brother, or like an older brother who actually was around, nothing to be taken seriously. She wouldn't have been able to make as far as she had without Garrett, and she still had a way to go.

"Ready for tonight?" he whispered in her ear.

"Depends." Ari's phobia of VR hadn't died after one night.

"Depends? A date with me isn't something to look forward to?" Garrett smiled with mock sincerity.

"You do make virtuals bearable."

"I have to run a couple errands, but I'll try to be more than bearable tonight." He squeezed her hand and headed off.

Ari's face warmed, and she hoped her tanned skin hid any blush.

She grabbed food and headed back to her room. Over lunch she scanned a message from her mom, checking up on her. Ari took it as a reminder that as bad as school was, things could be worse, like working in a warehouse for the rest of her life.

Ari kept her return message brief, not wanting to say much when the threat of coming home still hung in the air.

A message flashed from her advisor, Dr. Williams.

Your VR teacher, Dr. Coleman, has reported your recent behavior, and I decided it would be best to place you on academic probation. We have high standards and expect all students to follow the school's code of conduct. I will be periodically sitting in on your classes to see if any further action is needed.

Ari let her breath escape in one big rush, and she

leaned back in her chair. Probation. What did that entail?
She had until Friday. She felt sick.

Tessa entered in a bustle of energy, tossing an empty
coffee cup in the trash.

"Thanks again for this morning." Ari closed her screen
and spun in her chair.

"No worries. You going to Coleman's class today?"

"Not sure." Ari bit her lip, not sure if going today
would help or hurt. Freaking out might make her situation
worse. Maybe she should get her fear under control before
returning, and she had until Friday to do it. Would
Coleman buy the excuse that she was sick? "I'm not
feeling great. I'll probably skip Coleman's class today."

Tessa kicked off her shoes. "Not to pry, but I don't
get your problem with virtuals. You do great in all of your
other classes."

Ari shrugged. "Not sure. I just prefer to read pages
than live them." She didn't feel like going into the problem
with her dad. That would take a therapist to truly
understand.

"Then why did you come here?"

"Beats the alternative." The memory of her advisor's
message tightened her gut as she considered that
alternative.

Thick clouds promised rain and blocked out any chance of
moonlight. The campus's emergency lights lit the path a
pale orange as she left her dorm to meet Garrett. The
perfected landscape took on an eerie frozen appearance in
the shadows.

Despite the quiet, she couldn't shake the feeling that
they weren't alone. With all the technology and cameras on
campus, how could they be getting away with this? Yet,
they were.

"Ari." Garrett's shadowed figure stepped onto the
path and continued walking by her side.

"Where to tonight?"

"If I told you, then you wouldn't be surprised."

"I'll fake it. I swear." Ari smiled. Her mind traveled the globe of possibilities. If she was going to risk her mind and body to these contraptions, it might as well be worth it.

"Sorry, still not telling you." Garrett opened the door and led her through the empty building.

The quiet darkness curdled the fear lurking in her stomach, and she focused on her breath. In and out, nice and even. She took the same seat as the previous night and gripped the arm rest.

Leaning back, Garrett helped her plug into the device, and then leaned over. "You ready?"

"No, but since when does that matter?" She smiled and nodded for him to continue.

She tried to remember the glint in his eyes when she turned to face the ceiling and shut her eyes tightly. This time he didn't have to pry her eyes open. Water roared in the distance as the air turned hot and heavy with humidity. Her eyes flew open to find a waterfall. It fell over a rocky cliff face into a small pool of water. In this tropical forest, greenery grew everywhere while flowers of every color dotted the landscape, so wild and beautiful in its own unique way. Turning in a circle, she found green jungle surrounding them.

Her breath picked up, nerves fighting their way out. This place seemed so real, so visceral. "Where are we?"

"Another island." He pointed to the mountain in the distance. "This one even has a volcano."

"Really?"

"Yeah, but we'll save that for another time. Come on." Garrett took her hand and pulled her towards the waterfall.

"One minute." She held up a finger. Like in the previous VR, she searched for the errors, digging past the surface. She bit the inside of her cheek. There had to be something. A new pair of hiking shoes hugged her feet. She scratched a shoe along the rocky path she was on, but nothing moved. Not the rocks, not even the dirt moved. *This isn't real.* Above, the sun shone bright in a clear sky, but as she looked at it, it didn't burn her eyes, it just stayed a fuzzy yellow color with no true warmth. There was more still off about the world, she could feel it. Before she could investigate the deep vegetation, Garrett pulled on her hand.

"Are we gonna stand here all day, or are you ready for an adventure?"

At the word, 'adventure', she cringed internally. I can do this, she reminded herself. "Okay. What is this adventure?"

Garrett's mouth lifted into a mischievous smile. "Race you." He disappeared on the narrow trail through the trees. Was he purposely being flippant or maybe he was trying to distract her? If so it was working. Almost.

She swallowed her fear and took off up the hill after him. By the time she made it to the top, she was out of breath and her legs burned. "I know this isn't real, but my legs hurt."

"Just because this is happening in your mind doesn't make the experience any less real." Garrett reached out and took her hand.

While his action appeared extremely casual, Ari couldn't help but wonder what it meant. He tugged her to the edge, to a breathtaking view of water below. Vegetation surrounded the pool with a variety of colored flowers. Their tropical smells drifted up to greet her. He stepped closer to the edge, pulling her with him.

"What are you doing?"

"Jumping, of course. You'll love it."

"I don't think so. What if I died here? I know I won't really die, but it still has to hurt. Right?" Unable to control her nervous ramblings, Ari pulled against his hold.

Garrett must have seen the panic in her eyes, because

he pulled her into a hug. "Don't worry so much, Ari. Remember I said it's all about trust?"

They were at the edge of the cliff. She didn't know if she trusted Garrett. Granted, she was there with him, and sneaking out in the middle of the night required some trust. While the mental war waged on, Garrett held her tighter, and before she could say a word, he stepped off the cliff with Ari screaming all the way down.

Ari tried to hit Garrett several times after she recovered from the jump, but he ducked under the water out of range. Struggling to fight while staying afloat, she swam to the side and sat on the rocky deck in her wet clothes.

"Don't be mad. I really thought you'd like it." Garrett floated in the water in front of her.

Ari could almost admit that it had been pretty fun, but she didn't like him making choices for her in the virtuals. She needed to learn how to do things for herself.

"I promise no more cliff jumping without your permission."

"Oh, so cliff jumping is a regular thing for you."

"Bungie jumping also. You should try the Eiffel Tower."

"No thanks. I'd love to see Paris, but not in a blur as my life passes in front of my eyes." Ari's anger receded as her heartbeat finally slowed. The panic hadn't left her, but it took up less residence hiding in the recesses of her mind. She didn't know if it was Garrett's surprises or his casual flirty behavior and she didn't care. If she could play in here, she could work. She had to.

"Ready?" Garrett swam towards her and climbed out.

"No, but I don't have a choice, my test is tomorrow." Ari grabbed a small rock on the ground and threw it in the water. "I need to try this on my own."

"Go during lunch then. It's pretty empty." Garrett's wet hair dripped into his mischievous eyes.

DeAnna Browne

"Garrett," Ari swallowed unsure of what their relationship was growing into. "Thanks for everything. I couldn't have done this without you. I owe you."

"I can think of one way you can repay me." Garrett eyed her in a manner that made it obvious what kind of payment he was hoping for.

She stood, nervous about what had happened the last time he tried to take things too far. "I can think of one too." Ari shoved him back and watched as he tumbled into the water.

CHAPTER 11

L iving on a constant caffeine drip, Ari slept for only a couple hours and woke up early the next day. She read the school policy and learned that every student was allowed two absences a quarter, and she was cashing in that day. Coleman's deadline was up. Messaging Tessa, Ari asked her still sleeping roommate to take notes for her morning classes and headed off to the VR lab.

Despite her lack of sleep, anxiety and fear kept her awake and followed her every step. She had to do this, before she talked herself out of it. The open lab in her dorm was next to her VR class with Dr. Coleman. The glass door slid open with a whoosh as she approached. Ari's normal teaching assistant, Mica, wasn't in the room, but another tall lanky guy sat behind the counter, his head in his hands.

"Wanting to check in?" His brows lowered as if wanting to ask, instead, why she was here so early.

"Yes." She gave her full name so that it would match her HUB and waved her wrist over the black pad on the desk. Her name and picture popped up onto the screen.

The guy looked over her info and then typed

81

something. "I'm Toby. You must be getting some last-minute cramming in for Dr. Coleman's test. Number eight is open. What do you want to run?"

As determined as Ari was to come to the lab, she'd never thought about what VR to choose. She wanted to conquer the last one she'd run from. "Can I do the one from the first day of his class?"

"Sure. Give me a second to find it." He focused on his screen. "Most teachers use the one from the Never-Ending War to scare all the newbies away."

Well, it worked, but not this time.

"Okay, you're all set."

Ari made her way through the small cubicles filled with leather reclined chairs and VR stations. A few of them were filled with unconscious students. The smell of cleaning solution filled the air, and it reminded her of a hospital, and her father. She was determined not to lose her nerve so easily, so she continued down to number eight. She set down her bag and pulled her hair up into a high ponytail. It took a moment to get settled.

"You can do this," she reminded herself and dove into the program.

The familiar dust and noise bombarded her instantly. Voices screamed, calling for help. Bombs exploded in the distance. Her first reaction was to flee. She scurried back to the shelter of a nearby building and struggled to draw in a clean breath.

This isn't real. The dust and smoke suffocating you isn't real.

Squeezing her eyes shut, she drew in a breath through her nose. When she reopened her eyes, the noise and chaos continued to attack and disorient her. She clasped her hands over her ears to block out the craziness. With the world in front of her muted, it helped her pounding heart to slow. This VR put a lot focus on the sounds of war, but as she scanned the horizon, there was something missing.

While bullets and bombs sounded overhead, there

wasn't any evidence of any of their destruction. No explosions of dirt or debris in the landscape or people being struck down. Several injured people littered the dirt path along the building, but their wounds were bandaged already.

Down the block, one injured woman cried out. "Help me. Dear God, help me."

Watching the woman, Ari lowered her hands and approached.

The woman's image scattered ever so briefly, and then reformed. "Help me. Dear God, help me."

This woman's script must run in a loop, repeating for whoever walked past. Several other errors stuck out so obviously that Ari wondered why she'd never seen them before. Granted, she'd never stayed in a VR long enough to find them. Out in a nearby field, the same soldier kept running a similar path every minute or so. The explosions, still loud and annoying, sounded like a pattern that could be predicted.

This was a flawed program. Dr. Coleman wanted them to see these flaws, so they can do better. Be better. With a world so complex, every little detail mattered. For the first time since coming to this school, a kernel of hope burned in her chest. She just might have a chance here.

After scanning the horizon one more time, she pulled out of the VR, not out of fear, but because she had another class soon. The sickening noise of unplugging herself from the machine, still churned her stomach.

Grabbing a drink from her bag, she realized that her class had already started. Despite the nausea building in her stomach, she had to go back in. She completed a couple of easier VRs, not lasting over fifteen minutes. But it was enough. Exhausted, even though she didn't move a muscle for most of it, Ari picked up her bag and headed out of the cubicle.

Walking down the hall, she read the screen in the wall flashing student reminders. Then the screen glitched.

Numbers and letters sprawled all over the screen. Ari blinked again, and it was gone. She rubbed her temple, not sure what she saw in the first place. *Maybe I need to get my eyes checked again.* She'd had corrective surgery once already for her vision.

Turning the corner towards the exit, she paused. Reed stood in front of her talking with the lanky TA that had checked her in. Reed finished his sentence and glanced her way. "Ari."

"Hi. What are you doing here?" She worried that he would give her another warning or lecture to avoid Garrett. He had never given her a tough time about boys she dated at their old school. Granted there weren't many when most dates took place in the virtual realm.

"Just helping Toby with a last-minute assignment."

Toby took the small drive on the counter and inserted it into his personal device. "I owe you one."

"I think it's more than one." Reed turned to Ari. "Walk you to your next class?"

Taken back, it took Ari a moment to answer as she tried to figure his true reason for being there. He could have transferred data electronically to Toby. Couldn't he?

"Are you going to class?" He tilted his head slightly in question.

Pull it together. Ari shook off the awkward surprise and exhaustion enough to answer. "Actually, I'm headed to my room." She figured she should sleep for an hour or so before Coleman's class if she was going to make any sense.

"We can ride together."

They walked down the hall. The inches between them felt heavy, like miles filled with uncomfortable silence. In the elevator, they were alone, which was rare. He pushed her floor and then turned to her.

"I wanted to say sorry about yesterday." He glanced down. "It's not my business who you date."

She had been thinking about it a lot since their run in. "If Garrett is so bad, why do you work with him?"

"He's not bad. He's just more ..." He appeared to struggle to find the right word. "Let's just say he has a reputation."

The elevator opened, and Ari wasn't sure how to take his comment. Was Garrett a male slut or did Reed think she was naïve? She didn't have time to worry about it and stepped out of the elevator.

With a hand, he stopped the doors from closing behind her. "So, are we okay?"

She turned back to Reed, his hazel eyes the same eyes she often lost herself in since she was twelve. He was trying to watch out for her. Even if he thought of her as a little sister, he cared. She couldn't blame him for his behavior before. "We're good, Reed."

A smile lit up his face as he stepped back into the elevator. "Have a good class."

As she headed to her room, an elated feeling grew in her chest. It felt good to settle things with Reed. Walking one staggered step at a time, her bed called to her like never before. Inside her room, she dumped her gear and kicked off her shoes, ready to sleep in her clothes. Before she could collapse on the bed, a message vibrated on her HUB.

It was from her bank. They confirmed her withdrawal of $200. She hadn't taken any money out of her account. On a tight budget, she planned her money from her part-time jobs to last her all year. But there it was on the bank record, removed this morning at 9:52am. It was clearly an error, but she'd have to deal with it later. She fell onto to her bed and closed her eyes.

A few hours later, Ari's hands gripped the arm rest, and she couldn't stop chewing her bottom lip. She thought she was ready but wondered if she'd ever *feel* ready. Dr. Coleman didn't speak to her but gave her a look of expectation that told Ari he was serious about her performance. She ignored the looks from the other students, especially Wake glaring at her.

Mica approached with a sympathetic smile and a new ring in her left ear. "You okay?"

"I got it." Ari was really getting tired of that question.

Ari inserted the cold metal cable into the back of her head. No matter how many times she had to be in virtuals, she would never like that feeling. Closing her eyes, she headed towards the void.

Before she could gather herself in the VR, a cacophony of sound assaulted Ari. She spun sideways as a gush of air and neon lights raced by her.

"Watch it," someone shouted as they pushed past her.

Standing on a busy sidewalk, buildings surrounded her and rose higher than she could see. Lights blotted out the night sky. Horns blared as cars sped by, ignoring the mass of people flooding the walkways. Distant music carried through the night, but Ari couldn't say from where. Foreign words flashed on the side of the building. The Chinese symbols told her she was far away from home.

The chaos fed her fear. She clenched her hands against her thighs and focused on what needed to be done. She hadn't traveled enough to be sure, but this appeared to be a major city in Asia. Never having been there before might make it harder. She ignored her doubt and searched for the problems.

Dr. Coleman's voice cut through the noise, reminding them of their assignment. "Your test will be to find the limitations and errors in the program. You may have to push, but there are over twenty. You will have thirty minutes."

Thirty minutes. That would be the longest Ari had ever been in the VR. Hopefully, she wouldn't need it. A man on a bike raced by, forcing her back. She pressed up against the wall of a building. Closing her eyes, she focused on her breath. *I can do this. It's only code, little numbers floating through my brain.*

When she opened her eyes, the scene in front of her flashed in gray and black as if a 2D movie had been scratched. Blinking, the scene returned to the busy street in some city in Asia. Time to work.

Ignoring the twist of nerves in her gut, Ari completed the task in front of her. She pushed in stores, talked to people, searching for any error. It wasn't as easy as it looked. Searching down the crowded street, she noticed the same Asian man on a bicycle forcing people out of his way. That in itself was an error, but Dr. Coleman would want more than a repeating bicycle. She realized if she really wanted out of this VR, she needed to think outside the box. This was fake, right?

When the bicycle approached, she grabbed a nearby woman with a bag full of groceries and shoved her into the man's path. Ari braced for the worst, spilled fruit and a bleeding woman. Instead, the scene in front of her flashed black for a moment and then returned to normal as if the bicycle had never hit the woman.

The woman still held her bag of groceries and turned and shouted at Ari. Thankfully, Ari didn't understand the streams of what was probably Chinese swear words, and she turned to continue down the sidewalk. As she navigated the noisy street, she easily spotted many of the characters in the time loops. The freeze or glitch when each one started over appeared almost too easy to find. It took her more time to memorize them. Mentally she ticked them off: man on bicycle, woman selling flowers, man calling for the same cab, another young man selling tickets, and the list continued.

Coleman would want more thorough specifics on the coding problems. Anyone could pick out repeater loops. She pushed into a nearby store and found herself in a tech shop. A young salesman greeted her at the door in a language Ari didn't understand. She ignored the man. He was only numbers, she reminded herself. She touched a couple of computers, tech, and other personal links as she headed to the back. Once Ari passed the sales desk, the associates began shouting at her. She knew the problem before she even went into the back. They put the supposed back rooms around a corner. Dark and downplayed, they didn't want anyone going there. Another associate hollered something and grabbed for her.

Ari made it around the corner and found the door. She reached for the knob and pulled it open. Then in a flash, her world was turned upside down. Colors morphed into a drunken swirl. She closed her eyes, her stomach rolling with unease. When she opened them, she found herself standing back on the sidewalk. The program had spit her back outside. *I guess, that's one way to get rid of unruly customers.*

Dizziness still plagued Ari, and she wished for a bit of peace and quiet. She thought she had enough to pass the test and for a moment was tempted to leave. A group of girls headed down the sidewalk towards her. With fluffy crowns and open drinks, it appeared they were part of a bachelorette party or something.

Ari decided to get one more error for the test before leaving. Determined to stay still, she hoped to watch the girl's glitch at running into her. Maybe they would go around her and then Ari would be out of luck. The girls didn't even notice her as they laughed and carried on. When they reached Ari, one stumbled into her, *actually* stumbled into her, shoving her out of the way. Surprised, Ari fell awkwardly off the sidewalk. Someone shouted, and she reflexively turned to face an oncoming car.

She didn't have time to move, and the car slammed into her. Ari flew through the air, pain bursting in her body.

Ari woke in the classroom with a gasp. Her hands trembled as she reached for her stomach. Just a second ago, there had been so much pain and darkness. Her breath came out in harsh gasps as her adrenaline raced. "I'm back."

"You okay?" Mica appeared at her side.

"Yeah." Ari tried to rein in her emotions. It wasn't real, but her racing heart wouldn't listen.

Ari removed the plug and rubbed around her port. Dr. Coleman sat at his desk in the corner of the room, not even bothering to glance her way. The majority of the class remained unconscious, plugged into the VR. Without speaking Ari logged onto her tablet and completed the test by writing down her observations and errors in the system. She prayed it was enough and headed to grab a drink before her last class.

Her last class blurred by as she waited numbly for her future to be decided. With no appetite, she headed to her room, checking her HUB every couple minute to see if Dr. Coleman had posted grades. Her whole life had been spent in fear of VRs, and now she wanted to stay in a program for them. Funny how life worked sometimes. She had finally began seeing a future here, not only for herself but for her family. She could make enough money for her mother to quit both of her jobs.

The afternoon passed in its usual fashion. Tessa kept busy on her game, bickering about the rate of currency exchange. Ari plugged her earphones in her tablet, turned up her music, and opened a book.

About a hundred pages later, the sun started its descent, casting shadows through the small windows in their room. Tessa stood up to stretch and grab a soda.

"Want one?" Tessa asked when she noticed Ari's gaze.

"No thanks."

"How did the test go today? I didn't hear anything about a first-year screaming through the halls." Tessa smiled easily, but Ari wasn't quite ready to laugh at herself yet.

"I think it went well, but we'll see."

Her HUB went off with a new message. She opened it. It was from Garrett.

Congratulations on your test. Ready to celebrate? Party

tomorrow night in virtuals at midnight.

This took Ari back a bit. Tessa must have noticed her surprise.

"What is it?"

"I guess I passed." Ari flipped through the school site on her tablet. There it was, a high B. That was better than even she expected. How did Garrett know this? Grades weren't public. She'd figure that out later.

"I passed," she told herself as well as Tessa. "I got a B+ on the test."

"Good. I would have hated to have a new roommate. You never know who you'll end up with."

Ari rolled her eyes at her roommate's flippant remark, but it didn't bother her. "Tessa, get ready. We're going to party this weekend."

CHAPTER 12

After hacking their school issued HUBs, the two girls walked through the campus guided by the orange glow of the school's emergency lights. Ari tugged on her fitted blue sweater as they approached the building. Uncomfortable, she wished she wore something else, probably just nerves from her first party.

"If this is supposed to be a date with your boy toy, why did I have to come along again?"

"First, he's not my boy toy. Garrett is ... I'm not sure what he is, but I know what he's not. And second, this is a party, not a date. I thought you'd have fun." Truth was, Ari didn't want to go alone. Ari didn't know why she felt uneasy, but having Tessa there, somebody besides Garrett, helped. "I'll owe you okay? I'll get morning coffee for a month."

"Don't skimp on the Danish." The corner of Tessa's mouth lifted at the idea. "And stop pulling on that sweater or I'll dump a drink on it."

Ari stuck her hands in her pockets and tried to stay calm. This would be the first time she entered a VR for no other purpose than to have fun. She spent all of her pre-teen years wishing she could do this.

They approached the lab. A couple of students turned in front of them and entered through the dark metal doors. Just inside, a scruffy guy collected Tessa's money.

"I was supposed to meet Garrett here," Ari told the guy.

"Oh, you must be his current girl."

Ari grimaced at the word current, as if Garrett had girls on a rotating roaster, replacing them for whatever fit his pleasure.

"I got it from here, Paul," Garrett interjected as he appeared behind Paul. Garrett grabbed Ari's hand and pulled her into the dark corridor.

"Congratulations, Ari."

"Thank you. By the way, how did you know I passed?"

A mischievous smile crossed his lips. "Mica is a friend, remember?"

Ari inwardly cringed thinking about what Mica had probably told him. It also made sense how Garrett always knew when she needed help. It didn't sit well that he knew so much more about her than she did about him. "Oh, so you have spies."

"Spies, friends, contacts, however you would like to put it." Garrett led her through the usual doors, but this time only dim light cast shadows around the room. Green lights pulsed from numerous VR stations. Someone familiar passed down a row. Her brother maybe? With the darkness she couldn't tell.

"And how can you pull this off with so many students?" Ari whispered as the room quieted with each student plugging in.

Garrett guided her through rows of unconscious students whose eyes flickered unnaturally in their semi-conscious state.

"There are only about twenty or so people. Any bigger would attract attention. But don't worry. We have a couple people we pay to look the other way. Do people really expect students to not party or have fun? At least this way no one gets hurt."

"Sure," she half-heartedly replied as Garrett repeated the same government line she had heard since a child. "Why the dim light?" When it was just two of them the lab was well lit.

"That's for the ambiance." He waved his hand like a true showman. "Here you go, Ari. I hope you like it." Garrett led her in a chair and then leaned close. "I'll be joining you shortly."

Ari plugged herself in, closed her eyes and then opened them to a dark city street. Cars and cabs rushed by, sending a polluted breeze her way. Tall, old buildings surrounded her. The one in front of her had an old gray brick face with fire escapes that led up to the roof. She turned in a full circle taking in the looming aged monstrosity of the big city.

A flashy young couple walked down the street and entered the building before her. The guy wore dark pants and a striped shirt, while the girl matched in a small black dress and four-inch heels. *This has to be it.* Looking down, she noticed her dress—a frumpy old black Sunday school type dress with black flats.

"Really," Ari cried to the starry night. She wasn't going to a party looking like a poor nun. Ari closed her eyes, trying to force herself to change. Her thoughts traveled to dresses that flashed across the celebrity blitzes on the screens.

When she looked down again, she wore a small gold dress that fit perfectly and strappy heels to match. A smile crossed her lips in satisfaction. It might not be perfect, but it was definitely an improvement and much easier than she thought. When she reached the end of the block, she noticed Tessa leaning against the building smoking.

"You clean up nice, girlie." Tessa pushed off the building. She wore ... well, it took a minute before Ari could figure out exactly what Tessa wore. Black leather wrapped around Tessa's body covering the bare necessities. A long black skirt trailed behind her.

"You look amazing. How did you do that?"

"Plan out your outfit when you close your eyes. It's easier to get dressed on your way in." Tessa blew a cloud of smoke in her face. "Come on. You have a boy toy to see."

They crossed the street and approached the aged building. At the door, a large man checked their names off a list. "The full bar is on the first floor. Second floor is for dancing. The next two floors are virtuals, and the heated rooftop is also opened tonight." He opened the door for them.

"Virtuals?" Ari had heard of a virtual in a virtual but why here? She turned to Tessa who ignored her question and headed inside.

"This club has several top destinations. Have a good night." He ushered her in without further comment.

Ari walked inside to find a large, gold trimmed bar that went decades past the crumbling exterior of the building. Velvet couches littered the room as people lounged around with drinks in their hands. Candles on the tables flickered, producing a seductive atmosphere that unsettled Ari.

There had to be more than the twenty or so people Garrett invited. The others had to be from the program, but being unfamiliar with the upperclassman, how did Ari know who was real and who was part of the program? She followed Tessa as she struggled to keep the panic at bay. Maybe a drink or a tab would help? But that wasn't even real.

At the base of a large staircase, Tessa turned to Ari. "I'm going to check out what games they have on the VRs. You want to come or are you waiting for him?"

Not in a hurry to go hop in another VR, Ari replied, "I'll wait for him here."

"Catch you later." Tessa headed upstairs, her skirt billowing behind her like a dark bird.

A shiver ran over Ari at the thought of what Tessa was

about to do. But Tessa was a big girl. Ari headed towards the bar and found a seat.

As she climbed on the stool, a familiar voice spoke nearby. "Yes, two beers and an ounce."

"Marco," Ari called down the bar.

"Hey, little sis." Marco headed towards her. "What are you doing here?"

"I was going to ask you the same thing."

"I'm an upperclassman, and this is a party." A familiar smile lit his face as he strolled towards her.

While she was so happy to see him, she had to wonder where he had been and what he really was doing here. "How can you afford the party charge?" Ari whispered. The cost of the party was a lot of money for them. Her mother brought that home in a day, with double shifts. Ari only got in free due to Garrett. Granted, the drinks and drugs were free here, since they weren't technically real. It still didn't feel right.

"I work on the side." Marco brushed off the question. "But look at you, dressed up and everything. How did you score an invite?"

"Garrett."

"Garrett?" It took Marco a minute to register this. "You're the freshman he's dating?"

"We're friends." She shrugged.

"Sure." He lowered his brow and stared at her. "I'm not sure I approve of that."

"A little hypocritical, isn't it?" Ari motioned to the two drinks and the small mirror with powder and a straw that was placed in front of him.

"Virtuals don't count."

"I could say the same." She bristled against his desire to control her. He'd never been the type, and she didn't want him to be. She decided to turn the tables. "You're not in the virtuals a lot, are you?"

Marco rustled her hair. "Don't worry, little sis." He picked up his two drinks. "Don't do anything I wouldn't do." And then he was off.

Those instructions left things pretty wide open. She sighed and watched him head across the room.

Before Ari could worry too long about her brother, a hand slid around her shoulders.

Garrett sat at the chair next to her in a dark suit. "What are you drinking?"

"Not sure yet. What's the point of drinking in the virtuals?"

"It's as real as you believe it is. Why do you think we come here?" Garrett asked but didn't wait for an answer.

"Most of these rich kids have actually been to this club. The more closely tied to reality it is, the more believable it is. Then, if you want something more exotic you can go hit up a virtual."

"I thought a virtual in a virtual wasn't safe." Ari had read reports that the more levels you go down in a VR, the harder it was to find yourself back to reality. After her father, she'd read a lot about it.

"Amazing isn't it?" Garrett eyes flashed with excitement. The bartender came by and Garrett ordered a couple of drinks for them.

"So, what's it going to be tonight? Drinking, dancing, or head to another beach?"

Ari wasn't ready to think about another VR. "How about the roof?"

Before Garrett could answer, the bartender pushed the two drinks in front of them.

"The roof it is." Garrett lifted his glass in agreement. "I've got to take care of a little business, but I'll meet you up there."

Ari nodded and watched as Garrett headed off into the crowded bar. He greeted several people as he passed. He headed to a dark table with a few girls too perfect to be real, and, of course, her brother sitting in the middle. Ari wanted to know what was really going on with Marco and what he knew about Garrett. Annoyed by this possible friendship, she grabbed her drink, and headed to the elevators.

Ari squeezed into the crowded elevator. The mix of alcohol and a variety of cologne and perfume colliding in the small space overwhelmed her senses. As the doors started to close, a familiar face slid in. Reed. He wore a dark blue vest with a fun tie and shirt rolled up to the elbows.

"Hey, Ari." He smiled that adorable smile of his as he squeezed in next to her.

"Hi," Ari replied.

The elevator stopped on the second floor to let people in and out. In the shuffle, someone pushed Ari next to Reed. Her drink almost spilled, and he held onto her arm to steady her.

His gaze trailed up and rested on her face. "You look nice."

"Thanks." Ari stepped back, heat rushing to her face.

A guy, visibly drunk, entered the elevator and slapped Reed in the arm. "Great party."

Did Reed throw this party? Ari couldn't worry about that right now. She focused on breathing in this confined coffin and watched the numbers rising on the display.

While Reed replied with niceties, Ari considered how getting drunk in a virtual worked. If you didn't really believe the alcohol was real, then would you get drunk? Ari took a drink of her cranberry vodka, telling herself it wasn't real. Once she focused on the illusion though, it continued to other things. Was she really rising with the elevator? What happened if she only believed in parts of a VR? Would she fall through the elevator?

By the time the elevator reached the top, Ari couldn't breathe. Her fears snowballed, imagining her mind running in a program that might never end.

Reed was at her side. "What is it?"

Ari tried to push him off, searching for ... something. She struggled to stay in the present. Flashes of glitches, black and white static lines, spotted her vision.

"Breathe," he said, close by. Close enough that she could smell him, an odd scent, a cologne that she didn't recognize.

"Ari, look at me." Reed's voice was commanding.

Her eyes flicked up to meet his worried gaze.

"You're okay. You're with me in a virtual. One that I have control of ending whenever I need to. You're safe with me."

"You're holding my hands." Ari's breath came in short gasps. She couldn't think of anything else to say but couldn't find the energy to care. He must have taken her drink at some point.

"What?" Reed gave a nervous chuckle and dropped her hands.

"It's these damn virtuals. They mess with my head sometimes."

"That is what they're supposed to do." He led her to a chair and sat down next to her.

His eyes became intense, as if he was asking for everything she never wanted to tell him.

She turned to look at their surroundings. It didn't look like a roof at all but an extension of the club. Plants and vines hung as a backdrop with comfortable couches, reclined chairs, antique-looking coffee tables, and even a small bar.

Beyond the roof, large buildings and a twinkling of lights scattered the night sky almost like stars—a modernized galaxy in its own accord.

Reed leaned forward. "You sure you're okay?"

"I will be." She pulled on the hem of her dress. "Still getting the hang of these things."

"Ari, I'm sorry about before, but you're amazing."
"What?"

"Do you know how many kids from our neighborhood have been placed in the VR program? None for over ten years. I checked. You've overcome your fears, and one day you will be creating worlds that will make this VR pale in comparison." He reached forward and brushed the top of her hand and then lifted his gaze. "That's why I warned you about Garrett. A lot of people will want to know you as you're headed towards something amazing. He doesn't have the best reputation with girls, and I worry about you."

A warm stillness spread throughout Ari's body. "You worry about me?

"When I was ten, your mom told Marco and me to watch over you on a school trip. She told us the same thing before we came back here." He glanced down. "She didn't have to though. I would have anyway. It's a hard habit to break."

Ari let a breath go, not sure whether to be annoyed or grateful to have an extra big brother around. "Anyway, if Garrett's such bad news then why do you work with him?"

"We need each other to pull this off." Reed spotted someone behind Ari.

"How do you pull this off?" Ari asked.

Before Ari could turn around, Garrett placed his hands on her shoulders. "Reed can't give away all of our secrets or there goes our mystery."

"Why the mystery?"

"Everyone needs a little mystery." Garrett squeezed Ari's shoulder hard, and she gave a little jump.

Reed couldn't cover the look of disgust that crossed his face. She wasn't going to feel guilty though. She had seen him with countless girls himself; he was in no position to judge.

"Right. I'll head off. Ari, you sure you're okay?" Reed asked one more time.

"Promise." Something inside of her sunk as she watched Reed walk off. She realized she missed him, but he wasn't hers to miss.

Garrett pulled her up from her seat. "Do you need anything else to drink?"

"Do I?" Ari returned the question. "It's all fake anyway. Can't I tell my brain to release the chemicals that make me act like the rest of the stupid drunk girls?"

"Some people might call you a buzzkill, ya know?" Garrett pulled her into a hug, his mouth brushing against her neck. His lips sent a tingle throughout her body.

Ari scanned the balcony to see who else was up there. There were a few couples lying down on the couches making out, while others were drinking and talking. Garrett would probably expect something like that, being up there. Her stomach tightened, wishing she would have stayed at the bar.

Stepping back, he led her to a plush reclined chair. "Have a seat, and I'll grab a couple drinks." Ari watched him cross the rooftop to the other side of the bar. She took a seat and wondered how many other girls had he brought here? She was letting Reed and Marco get in her head, and they had occupied too many of her thoughts already. It was time for her to live her own life.

Garrett returned and handed Ari a green concoction. She took a small sip and the taste of apples flooded her mouth.

"Sweet apples."

He lifted his drink, a dark amber color. "Here's to you and your educational success."

Ari took another drink and inhaled afterward as the sweet liquor warmed its way down her throat. She set down the glass, remembering her last incident drinking—virtual or not.

"Anything wrong?" Garrett asked.

"No, my mind's all over the place, taking in the fact that this is my new life."

"It is only beginning," Garrett said as he leaned forward, kissing her softly on the lips. It was so gentle and warm, she melted against him. His mouth tasted of alcohol, warm and rich. Soon his drink was put down, and they reclined against the couch with Garrett on top of Ari, pushing her into the back of the couch. It wasn't long before Garrett's hands were all over her body.

Ari tried to close her eyes and enjoy being with Garrett. But soon Reed's annoying voice crept into her head. She couldn't help but wonder how many girls, in how many places, he had done this with before. And despite what everyone said, this felt all too real.

Garrett's hands were warm as he touched the bare skin on her leg. As his fingers traced it higher, Ari froze.

"I'm not that drunk," Ari said, trying to keep the panic out of her voice.

"No, you're not. Just like that wasn't real liquor, this isn't real either." He went to kiss her neck, pushing the limits of her dress.

"Garrett there are people up here." Ari eyed the other couples who didn't seem to notice anything beyond their partner.

"They aren't real." He waved them off with a free hand. "Just part of the simulation. Most people headed to the virtuals."

He kissed Ari again with more determination. Her thoughts flew a mile a minute. Was this wrong? She never had gone beyond kissing before. She hadn't known Garrett for long, but he had saved her butt. She owed him.

She wasn't going to do this because of obligation though. She tried to push her way free of Garrett, but he wasn't giving up easily. Since he could do this with any computer animation here, she failed to see the appeal. He kept murmuring things about her body that made her feel like she needed to shower. His grip tightened on her body, his tongue a dead slug trying to invade her mouth.

She couldn't take it anymore and wasn't sure if she could fight her way out of his hold. Her heart raced with a panic which had nothing to do with the VR and everything to do with Garrett. Without a second thought, she left.

CHAPTER 13

A ri sat at her computer, retyping the same code into her programming interface for the sixth time. She was supposed to be working on the physical world for her first virtual. At least she'd decided on her setting. That had taken an hour in itself.

It didn't help that her interface ring, which was securely stowed in her bag, was flashing with unread messages. Garrett.

It had been a week since she'd talked to him. A week since she'd left the virtual in the middle of making out with him. She had woken in a panic and pulled the plug. The guy who had manned the door, had watched in a dazed stupor as she'd sprinted out of the building, not looking back.

It had been a long week.

With her grades barely above passing, she had been working hard at her assignments. She typed in the code in for a sky for the seventh time. She finally closed her tablet, which was plugged into her hard drive, in exasperation and reached for her ring. She checked her HUB and scanned the messages.

Twenty-five were from Garrett. The first few started

with apologies. By the end she could see the anger
dripping into them. His last one read: *If you won't call me,
I can't fix it.*

Ari knew he deserved an answer, so she decided she
wouldn't finish her homework that night without talking to
him. She didn't think "I'm a scared prude" or "It didn't
feel right" was really an answer he'd understand. After
everything he'd done for her, she didn't want it to end like
this.

She wrote: *I need some time to focus on my grades. Thank you
for all your help and hopefully we can talk soon.* Her thumb
lingered over the send button. The "we can talk soon"
didn't even feel right. She hit the save button instead and
thought another hour wouldn't hurt.

Another message flashed. This one from her bank.
The bank received her complaint about the missing
cryptos and claimed she had legally withdrawn the money.
Frustration boiled under her skin. Her academic
assignment covered all of her food and board, but she
would need some funds for Christmas. She should have
several hundred cryptos in there from her part-time jobs.

Tessa came in, arms full of bags and coffee. That girl
should get a straight IV of that stuff.

"Hey, roomy." Tessa dropped her bags on her bed.
"How's the homework coming?"

"It's coming," Ari admitted. She closed her messages;
she would deal with them later. "I think I need a break,
actually. These damn walls seem to be closing in on me."

"You could head up to the virtual lab upstairs and
send your mind to get some fresh air." Tessa gave a
sarcastic smile, knowing Ari's love for virtuals.

"I think I'll go for some vitamin D from the real
source." It was a Saturday, and she had been working all
morning. A walk by the lake sounded great.

"Whatever. I don't have to worry about skin cancer
though."

"If that was my only concern," Ari mumbled as she

headed out the door.

She walked the path near the lake behind the dorms. A cool breeze brushed off the lake, and she tightened her jacket. Up ahead, a bit off the path, two guys argued.

As she neared, she realized it was her brother and Garrett. Her stomach tightened, and she hurried towards them. Marco's face tightened in anger.

"You can't cut me out of something that was my idea to begin with." Marco shoved Garrett back.

"I can and I am." Garrett had a coldness in his expression that was foreign to Ari. His hair, still dark, matched his icy exterior.

Ari placed a hand on her brother's shoulder. "Marco."

He shook her off. "Here's my sister you screwed over too."

Garrett narrowed his gaze. "Leave Ari out of this. She has nothing to do with this."

"You're the one that brought her into this," Marco said.

Ari's mind spun trying to figure what this was about. Was Garrett working with Marco too? "Marco, stop." Ari approached him and laid a hand on his arm. He was thinner. When did he lose weight? When he roughly waved her off, Ari turned to Garrett for some answers.

"Garrett?" she asked.

He finally turned his gaze to her, softening it a bit, but his cheeks remained flushed.

"Your brother is a loser, Ari. He is hooked up all—" Garrett didn't get to finish the sentence because Marco tackled him to the ground.

Straddling Garrett, Marco punched him, repeatedly. Ari yelled at Marco and tried to pull him off. Amid the chaos, a fist flew in her direction, slamming into the side of her head. Darkness encompassed her.

Sitting on the grass with an ice pack nursing her jaw, Ari

shot a passerby a dirty look. By the time she woke, Garrett had already taken off. Marco at least went to get her ice.

"Don't you have a life to live or something? Oh wait, you probably don't." Marco hollered at an embarrassing level to one of the spectators.

The small group didn't bother to look embarrassed.

"That's all I need, more people talking about me." Ari winced as she talked, her jaw aching.

"Don't worry about those losers." Marco brushed at his pants.

"Like I'm one to talk," Ari said. Most of them, except Tessa, avoided her, online and in person. "Yesterday, Dr. Coleman's version of a compliment was to tell the class that I was pretty good for someone who has logged fewer hours than his dog."

"Don't worry about it. His dog is pretty damn good from what I hear."

Ari chuckled, and pain shot up the side of her face. "Who hit me? It hurts like hell."

"Sorry, that was me. I didn't see you," Marco said. But he didn't look sorry enough for Ari.

"Figures." The running joke in their old school was "How do you know what block kids come from? How hard they could hit." Rich kids who only fought in the VR, fought like crap in the real world.

"Marco?" Ari asked, waiting for him to look her in the eye, "Are you going to tell me what's going on? I haven't been able to really talk to you since school started."

He didn't reply, and she turned her gaze to the lake, waiting for an answer. The wind brushed the top of the water, sending slight ripples across the pristine surface.

"Reed, Garrett, and I started the underground VRs at school last year," Marco gazed out over the lake. "Garrett has access to the lab from his job, Reed watches out for us while we're in the virtuals, and I hack the system to cover our tracks." Marco played with a piece of grass, avoiding her gaze. "I've been busy lately, and we've had a couple of close calls."

"So, the fight wasn't about me?" Ari couldn't help but feel a little relieved.

"Garrett's pissed about business, but it's partly about you. Garrett deserved having me beat him down either way. Everyone heard you jumped ship on him at the last party—which I was glad to hear." Marco leaned into Ari, bumping her shoulder playfully. "But this argument has been going on for some time, so don't stress about it, sis."

"Easy for you to say. What if the school finds out about this? I thought virtual-in-virtual programs were banned here since they're so dangerous."

"We don't do much V-in-V, but we still make good money. The advanced students sell the programs at half the cost." Marco looked proud of his business venture.

"Oh." Ari didn't know what to say. She'd spent most of her life quietly chastising her brother, like her mother had, but he did what he wanted anyway. She couldn't muster enough energy to reprimand him anymore. He'd told her enough times that she wasn't his mother, and he was right.

"Do you do them?" Ari already knew the answer but had to ask.

"Sometimes." He kept his eyes on the grass in front of her.

Ari bit her lip for a moment. "Aren't you afraid that you'll get stuck and end up like Dad?" For the past five years Ari had been angry at her father, whereas Marco had never said much about it. Yet sometimes, especially after visiting their dad, Ari could see the pain in Marco's eyes.

Marco spared her the briefest of glances before turning back to the lake.

"Ari, virtuals aren't so bad. Life ends up being a boring movie." His usual sarcasm laced his words, but his eyes remained cold and serious.

She was about to question him when his HUB pinged. He looked at it briefly, reading the message. "It's

Reed." Marco huffed as he stood up. "I'm going to have to clear this mess up."

Ari stood, grabbing her bag. "Please, be careful." Marco was pressing his luck by fighting on campus and running virtual parties. Maybe going to the same school as her brother wasn't such a good idea.

"I'm not the one with a shiner." He smiled.

"You owe me, ya know." Ari would have to get this taken care of before people asked questions. Hopefully, the first-aid kit in the dorm was well stocked.

"Yeah, I do." Marco said, the smile completely leaving his face.

Ari hated watching him leave. He might not be the best brother, but he was family. She wiped at a tear, flinched at the pain in her face, and went upstairs to try to contact her mother.

CHAPTER 14

For the next few weeks, Ari threw herself into her studies. Now that she could somewhat handle a VR, she had to work to pull up her grade. Watching herself improve and thrive in the program, felt nice. The only downside was the nagging feeling in the back of her mind that she'd handled things poorly with Garrett. She'd never claimed to be experienced with guys—at sixteen she'd never had a boyfriend—and walking that fine line between friend and boyfriend was harder than she thought.

On the plus side, she'd actually had dinner with Marco last week. Tessa and Ari hung out more often, too. Once Ari had learned to ignore Tessa's brisk manner and brutal honesty, she'd warmed up to her roommate. Both figured that in an industry filled with men, girls had to stick together. Tessa even let Ari play her game once—for free. Granted Ari didn't last long until an angry dwarf killed her, but the game was impressive. Slowly, she was finding her niche.

After dinner one night, Tessa and Ari rode the elevator back to their room. "Have you heard from your IT boy?"

Ari shook her head. "Not lately." Not after he'd fought with her brother.

"Is that a good thing or a bad thing?"

"Probably a good thing," Ari answered honestly. "I was never sure how I felt about him anyway."

"He did give you some great gear though."

"Yeah. He had his moments." Tired of talking about Garrett, Ari tried to change the subject as they entered their dorm. "I have to finish this code before I go to sleep tonight."

"Do you need help?" Tessa asked.

"Thanks for the offer, but I think I can manage."

Tessa kicked off her shoes. "I only have an upgrade on my game to work on, but I'd rather work on my procrastinating skills instead."

"Good luck with that." Ari headed to her desk. She started her computer up and tried to open her coding interface IDE, or Integrated Development Environment. It took longer than usual. She tapped on the file, and the response time seemed delayed. While she waited, she realized there was a program open in the background that she hadn't recognized. Suddenly, the program closed by itself.

An uneasy confusion grew in the pit of her stomach as she rebooted her computer and tried to access the IDE again. Her breathing quickened as she calculated how many hours she had already spent on her homework. She kept tapping the screen, swearing under her breath.

"What's wrong?" Tessa pushed back from her desk and looked over Ari's shoulder.

"Not sure," Ari replied. "Something is wrong with my system. Seriously delayed response times. One program opened that I've never even seen before."

"Calm down. I'll look at it."

Ari stepped out of her chair as Tessa sat at her desk. She paced watching Tessa work on her computer.

"You have a ghost."

"What?"

"Someone is screwing with your system."

"Who?" Ari asked.

Tessa furiously typed on Ari's computer. "Dunno. A lot of people here could hack into your system."

"Could it be Wake?" That jerk had been shooting her dirty looks and making snide comments every chance he could.

"Maybe, but it doesn't feel like him. I'd be surprised if Wake is this good."

"Great. I just finished Tollingston's paper that's due tomorrow." Ari couldn't help that her mind went to Garrett next. She didn't think he'd stoop that low, but how well did she ever know him?

Tessa spun around in the seat. "I'd see if your brother or his roommate can fix it. If I pry too hard, whoever it is could trash your system."

Ari couldn't afford a missed assignment, not since her performance at the beginning of the year. She briefly closed her eyes, willing herself not to go into panic mode yet. "Could an IT person do this?"

"You thinking of Garrett? Sure. He probably even set up the system passwords."

Anger boiled inside of Ari. Sure, she hadn't ended things well with Garrett, but did she deserve this?

"Maybe your brother can help? Set up a new firewall to protect you?"

"Yeah or beat the crap out of Garrett until he fixes it," Ari said through her clenched jaw.

"That works too."

Ari disconnected her tablet from her screen, threw her bag over her shoulder, and stormed out of the room.

"Good luck," Tessa shouted as the door hissed shut.

She headed towards Garret's room at first, formulating every diatribe she wanted to spew at him, but as she approached the turn off to her brother's dorm, she changed her mind. As much as she wanted to rip Garrett apart, she didn't have time to deal with their past. Her assignment came first.

So, instead she found herself in front of her brother's door. Pinching the bridge of her nose for a moment, she tried to push back the killer headache looming behind her eyes. Lights flashed onto the back of her closed eyelids. She had been staring at her computer for too long.

When she finally knocked, Reed answered barefoot in a pair of pajama pants. His thin yet muscular physique stole her words for a moment. She hadn't seen him shirtless since they were kids swimming in the community pool. He had certainly grown up.

Avoiding his gaze, she looked past him for her brother. "Is Marco here?"

"No, he's doing homework in the lab." Reed opened the door for her to enter. "What's wrong?"

Ari stepped inside and pulled out her tablet. "I hate to bother you, but I have a ghost on my computer."

"What? A key logger?" Reed took her tablet drive from her hands and hooked it into his system. "Do you know who placed it?"

"Not sure. Maybe Garrett."

Reed's shoulders tightened, and lines creased his face. "If so, I'll talk with Garrett."

Ari wondered just how much Reed had heard about what happened at the party. Gratefully, she'd taken care of the bruising already with the first-aid kit. Yet, her face warmed with embarrassment. "If you can't fix it, I may just kill him."

"It might take an hour or so to fix, but feel free to kill him." He glanced up and his face softened. "Pull up a chair, and we'll see what we can find."

Ari grabbed an extra chair and sat next to Reed at the desk. "Thanks so much. I can't afford another bad grade. I was hoping Marco would be here. I hate to bother you." Ari couldn't seem to stop her nervous rambling.

"It's not a problem." Reed placed a hand on top of

hers.

Ari froze and stared at his hand. The touch sent a warmth through her body, settling in her stomach. It went beyond comfort to something else entirely. She fought the romantic notions that threatened to carry her away.

Their gazes met, speaking more than either could have said, and he took his hand away. "Ari, really, it's not a problem. I'm glad you came. I can have it fixed in the hour."

"Me too," she said softly.

Reed sat up stiff in his chair and his fingers flew over the keyboard. "What is this?"

"What?"

"This can't be."

Frustrated at his lack of communication, Ari leaned forward to look at the screen. "What can't be?"

"Your key logger. The person recording your every stroke you make ..."

"What?"

"Nothing." He quickly closed the computer and stood up.

"That wasn't nothing."

He grabbed her hand and pulled her out into the hall.

"What is going on, Reed? Is this all Garrett?"

He shut the door behind them. They stood inches apart as she searched his face for an answer.

"It's not Garrett?" She waited for the answer.

He glanced down the hall. "It's the school."

"The school?"

"Yes. I knew they watched our online access, but they normally don't watch individual students."

"Why would the school be watching me? Maybe because of my grades?" Her thoughts traveled to Advisor Williams who had been coming to her classes and keeping a close eye on her, and all of a sudden it didn't sound so farfetched. What worried her was Reed coming out in the hall to talk, and how he whispered only inches away from her.

Worry creased his brow. "Not sure. I can't remove it without alerting them though. You need to be careful of what you do online or even say. I'm not sure how far they went."

A cold chill traveled up her spine, and she tried to rub her arms for warmth. "This can't be real. Why would they bother?"

He shrugged. "I'll ask around, but until we have more answers, please be careful."

She nodded and glanced down the hall, realizing she'd never feel comfortable at school again.

CHAPTER 15

Ari spent the next two weeks focused on her school work, memorizing code, learning about art design and so much more. On her weekly chats with her mother, she almost admitted that she enjoyed the program, except she couldn't. Not with the school watching her every step. She tried to ignore it, but the idea of someone spying on her set her on edge. It forced her to be more determined to finish the program. Two more years felt like forever.

As midterms approached, Tessa and Ari spent hours studying, surfacing only to eat and shower. With two days left until her tests, Ari thought her brain might explode.

"Do you want anything to drink?" Ari stood, trying to stretch out the massive kink in her back.

Tessa let out a sound that was half moan, half yes, then clicked off her computer. "I need a break. I think I'm going to break out the chocolate stash in my closet. We deserve it."

"I won't argue." Ari stood and grabbed a couple of drinks from their fridge. She handed one to Tessa and plopped down on her own bed.

Tessa tossed a package to her, brownies. Ari's mouth

watered as she set the timer. Less than a minute for steamy fresh brownies. Her mouth watered in the wait.

Tessa took a long drink. "Are you going to The Grid this weekend?"

"No." Most of the campus had been planning parties after midterm tests. The city was a popular tourist spot, often catering to the students. Ari didn't have the money to go and was still trying to figure out what happened to the cryptos she lost. The bank said they were looking into it.

"Want to come with me?"

"Sorry, no money."

"My parents own a condo there. It wouldn't cost a thing," Tessa offered.

Ari stalled, knowing that there would be other expenditures besides housing on the trip. Before she could reply, someone knocked on the door. Ari and Tessa looked at each other.

"I provided the chocolate." Tessa pointed out.

Ari stood and pressed the code to open the door.

Marco leaned against the door frame with wet hair and his goofy grin pasted on. "Miss me?"

Ari rolled her eyes but couldn't help her smile. "Come on in."

"What are you gals up to?"

"Not much."

Marco turned his attention to Tessa. "This must be the famous roommate, Tessa. Nice to finally meet you. How's it been living with my sister?" He pasted on a huge grin as he sat on the edge of her desk.

Ari knew Tessa wasn't his type, but that fact was irrelevant to Marco, who acted like it was his duty to flirt with all of Ari's friends.

"I'm trying to convince Ari to go to The Grid with me for the weekend," Tessa said.

"The Grid, huh? Not bad. You might have fun there." He paused for a moment then turned to Ari, "Is that the problem, fun?"

Ari glared back at him. "I have fun."

"Yeah, but do you like it?"

Ari grabbed a nearby throw pillow and threw it at him. He caught it easily.

"You could come." Tessa offered. "My parents own a condo there."

Ari turned to look at her roommate in surprise. This wasn't like Tessa. It had taken more than a week for her to offer to eat with Ari.

"Anyone else coming? Or can I invite a few friends?"

"No, Marco. You're not throwing a huge party at someone else's condo." Ari wasn't going to let him take advantage of her roommate.

"Not a huge party. Just a few friends. Reed, and a couple guys from our dorm. We'll be out most of the time anyway. Just need a place to crash."

Ari began to protest again, but Tessa spoke over her. "Sure. Why not? I haven't pissed off my dad yet this semester." Tessa's eyes glimmered with the excitement.

This wasn't going to end well.

"Great." Marco clapped his hands together and pushed up off Ari's bed. "I have to go. Ari, walk me out."

"You just got here."

"I have loads of studying. Exams, you know. See you this weekend, Tessa." Marco nodded in her direction and headed out the door.

Ari followed. Before they reached the elevator, Marco turned to her. "Ari, I need to borrow some money."

I shouldn't be surprised. She let out a long breath. This wasn't the first time he'd borrowed money. "No."

"Only eighty cryptos."

"Why?"

"I owe someone, okay? Please, I know you have it."

"How can you be so horrible with money?" Ari had already lost two hundred cryptos and wasn't going to part with more.

They both had worked part-time jobs on and off since they were twelve. And while Ari was usually fine through the year, Marco couldn't even make it to Christmas. He said it made for better homemade Christmas presents, but Ari had a dark feeling about where the money went.

"Please, Ari. I really need it."

Ari paused, realizing his jovial face had fallen into something serious, almost anxious.

The elevator dinged, and two boys exited.

Marco held the elevator open with one hand. "Please?"

Her resolve crumbled. "Here's twenty bucks and get a job."

Marco leaned in for a quick kiss on her cheek. "I have one, remember"

She doubted after Marco's fight with Garrett that things were going well with their underground VR ventures. "Try a legal one."

Marco smiled, the desperation gone from his countenance. "Now where's the fun in that?" he asked as the doors closed on him. Ari couldn't help but worry about him, and she found it frustrating. He was the older brother, and she wished he would start acting like it.

Building up to midterms, her nerves were harder to deal with than her tests. She fell asleep in front of her computer too many times to count, and flashes of code mixed with her dreams. Fortunately, her studying paid off. She turned in her assignments on time and flew through most of tests with no problems. When Ari walked into Dr. Coleman's VR class, Advisor Williams sat near the back of the classroom, next to Dr. Coleman's desk. She swallowed and nodded at his steely gaze. Suddenly, Wake's annoying glares seemed trivial. She wondered if Williams was the one behind the hack on her computer. Pressure built inside her, her chest tightening. She couldn't afford any mistakes, especially not here.

She spent over thirty minutes in the VR, double checking every step, carefully and methodically. When she finally left the classroom, the weight on her chest lifted. She'd aced the test, or pretty close. Coleman and Williams would have nothing to complain about. She finished her last class and then spent the night with Tessa gorging on pizza and packing for their trip.

The next morning, while driving into the city, Ari began to see why everyone from school went there. It was only a couple hours from campus, and this place had everything. Unique restaurants, hotels, and clubs were squeezed into every extra inch of the city. Ari could step into a different world with every door and VR port. Pools, fountains, and even a hot air balloon promised a fun-filled weekend for whoever could afford it. Even without money, Ari was determined to enjoy it.

She tried to push Dr. Coleman, her tests, and school out of her head as Tessa pulled into a small cream colored five-story building. They left their car to park itself. An attendant came to help with the bags. With a scan of her hand and a simple code, they rode the elevator to the top floor.

"Welcome, Tessa," a mechanical voice boomed as Tessa pushed through the front door.

"Wow." Ari couldn't help her open mouth as she scanned the place where she'd be for the next couple days. Her feet sank into the thick carpet and the light scent of vanilla greeted her as she took her first steps into a side of humanity she'd rarely glimpsed. Rich colors painted the walls, browns and deep reds, with chartreuse accents adorning the doorknobs and drawer pulls. The doorway opened to a room where dark leather couches surrounded a flat wall, completely made out of some sort of screen. It currently displayed a picture of a field of flowers, with a villa of some sort in the distance. Yet, it was fully loaded with sleek keypads discreetly stationed on every wall.

"First order of business, disable our trusty AI, Max." Tessa threw her bags on the floor and headed down the hall to a control panel. "We don't need a record of the weekend."

"You weren't kidding. Your dad is loaded. Is this whole wall computerized?"

"My current stepmom redid this after their honeymoon," Tessa shrugged. She threw her large brown bag on the couch. "Tacky in my opinion."

Ari slid into the soft couch and enjoyed the scenic view. "The couch in our dorm room will never be the same." She didn't want to add her thoughts about her own home which could easily fit into the entry room.

Tessa twisted her mouth in disgust, her cheeks squishing up into balls. "That's the one I caught my dad on with his last wife."

Ari immediately jumped up. "Really? Thanks for ruining that for me."

"Yeah, trust me. It's a memory I wish I could get rid of. I'm hoping we find a smoker who can burn a hole in it."

Ari brushed her pants, though she was sure the couch would have been cleaned. She hoped.

"Hey, can your brother help me with the security system?" Tessa asked.

"Why? Are we not allowed here?"

Tessa played with the interface in the wall. "Relax. I have the code and everything. But my dad is jealous and a bit neurotic, so I'm sure they have some digital record of us coming in and out that I can't even find. He's on his fourth wife and never seems to be able to trust one of them."

"I'm sure Marco can do it when he shows up tonight, or if Reed comes, he could do it too."

"Oh, right, Reed," Tessa smiled. "You may want to sleep in the room with the Jacuzzi in it."

"What? I don't need a bed. Well, in fact I do, but not

119

in the way you are thinking."

Tessa laughed at her. "Whatever. Let's get dressed. You can raid my stepmom's closet. You're about her size."

"I'm fine in what I have." The idea of wearing other people's clothes didn't sit well, especially after the mental image with the couch.

"Come on. You'll see." Tessa lips curled into a smug smile.

Ari knew rich people lived in a different world but knowing and seeing were two different things. Tessa's stepmother had over sixty pairs of shoes in a vacation rental. Ari counted them. The wardrobe was about the same. Shirts, dresses, and pants hung tightly together in every color, shape, and style that she could imagine.

Ari walked through the closet, touching the different textures. Even though it was an excess, part of her loved all the different colors and fabrics. All of her life, she had worn hand-me-downs or homemade clothing. There was no need for her colored dyes or pens in this closet. A large grin grew on her face at all the choices before her. "How can she even wear all of these?"

"She doesn't. You should see her home closet, but she comes from old money." Tessa grabbed a black jacket off the hanger. "One of the reasons she is wife number four."

A small black dress called to Ari. When she moved the dress, a rainbow of colors appeared. It was unlike anything she had seen before. Computerized lights were somehow constructed into the soft material. Amazing, didn't begin to describe it. "Won't she know if we borrow her clothes?"

"Probably not. She'd be happy if she thought I could fit into one of those dresses. She's been pushing me to go to a cosmetic doctor before school."

"Ouch." Most wealthy people paid doctors to change their size, color, or pretty much anything, but Ari was surprised a stepmother would be so bold as to offer it. It was one of the things Ari liked about Tessa: she was who she was with no apologies.

Tessa shrugged on the jacket. "But I can't ever go to a doc, for spite, you know."

"You don't need to anyway. Who wants to be a plastic?"

"Hurry up. We want to get first dibs on team members." Tessa grabbed a pair of tall purple boots and headed out.

"What team members?" Ari asked a now-empty closet and realized this weekend was going to be like nothing she imagined.

The girls exited the condo, and instead of getting in Tessa's car, Tessa lifted an arm to flag down a cab. "Parking is a nightmare, so I thought it would be better to catch a ride." She wore a bright neon green tank top under the black jacket, which held a variety of micro drives sewn into it.

Ari decided on electronic dress that changed color with every step. She pared it with a bright blue jacket and black dress shoes that crawled up her ankles in a myriad of straps. The three-inch heels had her towering over Tessa, who was already a couple inches shorter.

As they waited outside the building, someone crept out of the shadows next to them. She was younger than Tessa and Ari. Her small frame hunched over. Before the stranger could speak, an attendant appeared.

The young man wore a stiff uniform of blue jacket and pants. "You can't beg here." He waved the young girl off and then turned to Tessa. "A car will be arriving shortly."

Ari watched the girl wander off into the darkness and wondered why she wasn't in school. Suddenly the extravagance of their outfits sickened her and made her feel guilty. Their outfits could help that girl. Soon the quiet black car pulled up in front of them, and Tessa opened the door.

"Come on, Ari," her friend motioned her into the car.

Safely tucked in the confines of the car, Ari questioned Tessa about the girl.

"People like that used to infest the city, usually druggies or prostitutes. VR eliminated most of that. She's probably a runaway and just needs to go home."

Ari wondered if Tessa ever saw a rundown VR center full of desperate people looking to escape and willing to do anything to do so. Granted, druggies and prostitutes were less frequent since the upstart of VRs—the government helped with that—but Ari wasn't sure VR centers were much better.

Once they arrived at the club, Tessa paid with a swipe of her electronic bracelet.

Guilt gnawed on the corners of Ari's mind. She hated feeling like a freeloader. "Can I help?" she asked even though this weekend would wipe out the rest of her savings.

"I put it on my family account. Don't worry. Good old Dad is paying for this weekend." Tessa climbed out of the cab.

For a moment, the assaulting smells and noise of the busy street gave Ari déjà vu of her time in the VR. It took a minute for her to orient herself amongst the chaos. Large buildings crammed together on the street. Hotels, clubs, and restaurants all vied for attention, with each sign bigger and brighter than the last.

They approached a dark club tucked into the corner. Instead of flashing pictures and neon lights, the black four-story building only had patterned green lights running along its name: Hooked. On closer inspection, there were numbers—binary code actually—running through the words. Old school for sure, but cool.

With a wave of Tessa's electronic bracelet, they entered. A sheet of binary code hung in the air, and the girls walked through a cascade of code and dense fog. There was no dance floor or tables for conversation. This was for gamers. Colors of code raced in lines along the ceiling, casting eerie lights on the throngs of people inside. On one wall, an enormous bar ran the entire length and a 3D screen floated behind it. It displayed statistics of the ongoing games and upcoming tournaments. Electronic music blared overhead, not giving her a chance to talk to Tessa, so Ari followed her to the bar.

Tessa approached a couple of guys and talked to them with a familiarity that told Ari she was probably a regular here.

Looking around, Ari controlled the fear in the pit of her stomach. This was how she'd always imagined it would be like getting trapped in a virtual, like getting caught in a huge computer, yet the rational side of her brain knew she was wrong. That very moment her father was probably enjoying a cruise in his mind for the hundredth time.

"She is our fourth," Tessa told the guys by way of introduction.

Ari pulled her attention to the others and gave a weak smile.

"Is this girl any good? We don't need eye candy." The boy with dark blue hair and tats on both arms looked her over. His nose was sharpened to an unnatural point.

She leaned forward slightly. "I'm Ari."

"You better be as good as Tessa says. I'm planning on winning this thing."

"Hey, I already told you I'm good enough for two, so don't worry about it," Tessa turned to Ari. "The stress case here is Aron."

"And I'm Logan." The guy with curly brown hair gave a friendly smile. "Don't worry about Aron. Tessa will tear it up in there. I've never seen someone take on so many wizards at a time. Epic." He raised his hand to high five Tessa.

While the two guys continued to discuss strategy, Ari leaned to her friend. "What in the world did you sign me up for?"

"It's the latest version of Shadow Lands. Don't worry.

We'll be fine. This was my summer vacation last year."

"I think I'm going to pass on this one. I don't have extra money right now." The excuse was true even if it wasn't the main one.

"Don't worry about the money. Trust me, you won't regret it," Tessa said.

Ari wasn't sure how she felt about being Tessa's charity case. At least by the sounds of the game, Ari wouldn't confuse the VR with reality. But VR gaming was low on the list of things she wanted to do.

A shoulder brushed against hers. She turned to find Garrett, his hair a blue-black. On his side was some girl. Ari recognized her as a second year in the IT program.

"Don't waste your time on this one," Garrett told Tessa.

Tessa looked as if she found something disgusting on the bottom of her shoe.

Ari ignored the insult. "Hi, Garrett."

"Oh, is that the problem we had?" He tapped his finger on his temple in a mock sense of enlightenment. "Maybe you swing the other way?"

Ari grabbed a drink on the bar and threw it at him, not at all confused about her feelings now. "You really are a jerk. You know that?"

Garrett's girl sent some choice words in Ari's direction before they stormed off.

"Am I supposed to take offense to you saying you wouldn't want to be with me?" Tessa's sarcasm lightened the mood.

"I'd pick you over Garrett any day," Ari said.

"Let's go to the Shadow Lands, and maybe you can really kick someone's ass."

Anger burned through Ari's veins, and it pushed her to be more daring than normal. "Let's do this."

When they signed in for the game, Tessa had Ari use her stepmother's ID. "Don't worry my dad will pay for it. Plus, it will drive him crazy to see she's doing virtuals here.

You could make out with a few guys, then if he pays to have the history checked, he'll really go nuts."

"I'm not going to make out with a 'few' guys. Hit them, maybe."

Tessa laughed. "I hope so. I set up your user profile as Oya the Undergoddess. Try not to die 'cause it'll take twenty minutes to get you back in."

"I'll try." A thin dark-haired woman assisted Ari into the leather recliner and hooked her into the VR port. Ari closed her eyes and let herself fall into the other world.

CHAPTER 16

W hen Ari first awoke inside the game, blue filled her vision. Make that a blue man standing right in front of her. The guy with blue hair from before, Aron, now was completely colored a rich blue from head to toe. Dark tribal tattoos covered his bare chest which bulged with defined muscles. The tattoos moved with the man, swirling and drifting as if animated. The only hair on his body that she could see was a short beard. He wore black leather pants that fit a lot better than they would on the human version of her teammate. He held a scimitar in one hand and a ball of swirling purple light in his other. He glanced at Ari and then continued walking around, scanning the surroundings.

A huge knight, Logan, stood off to the side. He had to be at least seven feet tall and clad in a gold and red armor that hid most of his features. A massive sword hung at his side.

Turning from the guys, she took in the landscape. A thin layer of green grass blanketed the world in front of them. Gray boulders created rock formations dotted with patches of grass, and an arch loomed in the distance. Foreign white trees were scattered amid the rocks, creating a lone path leading into the unknown.

A hand grabbed Ari from behind and she whirled around, knocking the person several feet back. *Whoa.* Ari's strength astounded her.

Tessa stood, no floated, several feet in the air with the help of slowly flapping dark wings. She wore a blood-colored outfit with leggings and a tight shirt that could be a second skin. Her hair stood out like fire rising from the ash, wild and free. She had transformed into some kind of beautiful dark creature. Her dark eyes and plump lips were the same, but her cheek bones were sharper, stronger.

As Tessa approached again with a definite scowl on her face, Ari noticed the other differences. She now had red eyes, swirling in a mesmerizing pattern. Her features were also darker, her teeth, sharpened to points, and a growl came from her. "I'm glad you know how to use your powers, but please don't use them on your teammates."

"Yeah, sorry about that." Ari looked down at her own personal changes. Her skin kept its tanned color, but her hair, which fell around her shoulders in curls, was now silver. Her body appeared taller as well, and her fingers were longer, ending with long sharp nails polished in silver. She touched her clothes, a smooth light blue color. The top was clingy but flexible. She wore a skirt on the bottom with slits up to her waist and tights underneath.

A shiver of fear coursed through her body. Ari had played her share of fantasy games but never in VR. The errors of the program were harder to find here, but they were here, she told herself. *This is a game, and only a game.*

Tessa had sped through some pre-game instructions that Ari pretty much had all forgotten. "Who am I again?" Ari asked.

Tessa gave a blow of exasperation. "You're Oya the Goddess of the sky. You can control wind, tornados, lighting, and whatnot."

"Not bad." She played with her fingers, and the power between them sparked as if alive. The electricity that pricked her palms didn't hurt but was like nothing she had ever experienced. Not reality at all. But definitely interesting.

"Get your head in the game, Oya. The others are already probably up and ready to fight."

"Who is everyone else?" Ari asked as she took in her surroundings. The blue man had scaled a tall rock formation and was surveying their position.

"The blue man is Torq," Tessa said, then motioned to tall knight. "He is Ra-soon."

"It is time," Ra-soon said.

The others walked ahead while Tessa leaned in close to explain the rest of the game. The teams had to find the Jewels of Achman. There were only enough jewels for one of the three teams to win and participate in the revelry back at the castle with the winning teams from other rounds.

Leaning in closer, Tessa added, "And I told these guys you were good, so don't let me down."

"Why would you say that?" Ari had never even seen this game before, let alone played it.

With a shrug of her shoulders, Tessa picked up her pace. "Just try not to get yourself killed too much." Then she lifted off into the sky, her dark wings carrying her high.

The next few hours flew by in a rush. She had never been so scared or so exhilarated as she fought, ran, and tore through imaginary monsters. Her body had strength and endurance beyond a human, and the smile remained on her face even when a gremlin that reeked like rotten eggs punched her. The hits didn't hurt as much as in the real world. Ari assumed that was part of the appeal. She only died once and hated waiting impatiently back in the club to be allowed back into the game.

It didn't take Ari long to realize that she was the weakest link in the team. Tessa made up for it though, and they quickly collected five out of the six required stones. As they approached the den of Auni, they ran into trouble.

A different team had already arrived and was battling a fifteen-foot troll and the gremlin creatures they had run into before. Gremlins weren't too painful, but they drained your life and were difficult to kill.

Tessa and the team discussed their strategy before they attacked. They'd need to not only avoid the warlock and the gremlins, but also outfight the other team. The blue man, Torq, spoke first. "Okay, I will kill the troll. He looks large and stupid. Then I'll distract the gremlins. You two," he said pointing to Tessa and Ra-soon, the knight, "Take out the other team. And Oya, can you manage to secure the jewel?" He said this with such attitude that Ari was tempted to hit him. Something that she would normally never consider, but as Oya it was more appealing.

"I can do it," Ari replied pushing her hair out of the eyes and wishing for a ponytail for the hundredth time.

"You're her back up," Torq said to Tessa.

"I said I'll do it," Ari snapped.

"Yeah, and Tessa said you knew how to play. Pardon if I don't take your word for it." His eyes flashed in disbelief.

Before Ari could reply, Tessa pinned Torq to the ground. "Take care of the damn troll and we'll get it. Remember who is a level four champion here, huh?"

Torq rolled his eyes as Tessa released him, and he did a back roll to get up. Ari couldn't take too much offense. They probably had no idea she'd never played before. And as annoying as he was, Ari loved to watch Torq. When fighting, his intricate tribal tattoos spun wildly around his body.

"Let's do this," Ra-soon said, and they all went charging over the rocky cliff face into the battle.

While Tessa carried down the guys, Ari crawled down the side of the cliff so as to not to draw attention to herself. At the base, four gremlins charged her. Despite the fact they were slow, they were also strong. She took care of three with a gust of wind, but the last one held on to a nearby rock. Ari took her small blade out and finished him off with a swift jab in the general direction of where his heart should be. He dissolved into a black miasma that clung to the ground.

Ari approached the battle from the side. Tessa repeatedly dove towards another winged fighter, attacking and pulling back before the counter-strike. She had a finesse and grace to her that the other purple-winged fighter could not match. Tessa toyed with them, while they struggled to stay afloat.

Torq had almost defeated the huge troll, while Ra-soon fought off gremlins and the other team on the ground. The needed jewel laid in a cave directly behind the battle. As Ari neared the fighting, she cast a spell. The wind obediently picked up dust to cloud her from the warriors' vision. With the needed cover, she sprinted for the cave.

Once inside the interior appeared dark, almost blood red, with a small light shining deep within. The jewel. She was almost there. As she crossed the entrance, someone slammed into her side, taking her to the ground. He grabbed her hands, restraining her powers. They struggled, but he obviously had the upper hand.

"Why, hello there." A guy, dressed in slim green armor, sat on Ari's chest. A metal mask surrounded his head, with large insect like eyes poking out. "You really think we're going to let a newbie get the last Jewel of Achman? Sorry, sweetie."

His voice sounded familiar, even with the computerized lilt to it. Changing your voice was another option in the game, one Ari never bothered with. She didn't have time to figure out who he was as he gripped her hands together over her head and used his other hand to slowly squeeze her neck.

There were a number of ways to kill someone. Most went for the quick kill, hoping to make them start their quest over with a time delay. Or if a person was injured, with their life levels near zero, they remained in the game, helpless until their life levels regenerated.

But this guy seemed to enjoy restraining her, slowly draining her life and in no hurry to finish her off. She fought his grasp, sending electrical currents through her hands. He didn't move. She struggled to turn her head and out of the corner of her eyes she could see the fighting outside. It was evenly matched with both sides sustaining losses.

"I guess I don't have all day to win." He cut off any reply by increasing the pressure in her throat.

A small gasp escaped her mouth. Black dots danced in front of her eyes and something else, too. Code. A variety of multi-colored letters, numbers, and symbols danced through her vision. Was this the same type of code she learned in school? It looked similar. Enough so that upon further inspection, she could read it and see what exactly this character was. She found his strengths, saw the code that gave him his armor and other protections.

The characters mesmerized Ari for a moment, like reading or speaking a foreign language for the first time and realizing she was fluent. The black spots floating in her vision brought her back to reality. Without a thought, she shifted the code.

She easily picked out the code for the green man in front of her. She shifted the color of the armor out of the code and watched it float up into the air. Letters and digits spun around, and the guy in front of her glitched for a moment only to return colorless. This new aspect of the game was like a whole different game within a game. Piece by piece, she stripped away the green armor. Any perceived strength and power fled with another mental flick. Stripping off all the code that made the character, she found Garrett, in his usual jeans and shirt, sitting on top of her.

His hair stood on end, yet with his normal eyes and pale skin he looked alien in this environment. With his powers stripped, it only took a second for Ari to change the positions, ending with her on top, straddling his chest. Garrett's eyes widened in disbelief.

"What happened to the game?"

"You mean why am I on top and you're on bottom?" Ari had a sick pleasure in pinning him to the floor. Briefly, she wondered if his powers were stripped what would happen to his pain response.

"What happened? Who screwed my game?" Stripped naked of his power, he lost his usual bravado.

"What the hell is your problem?" Ari yelled, tired of his attitude.

"Why did you stop answering my texts?" he replied with as much force, his face flushed and angry.

Her response froze in her throat. What was she going to say? He was going faster than she was comfortable with? Might as well tell him she was the biggest prude on campus. He tried to sit up, but she pinned him down again. The pained expression on his face warned her that he had a normal response to pain in his stripped condition.

"I ..." She struggled to find the words. "What does it matter? I was just another first-year anyway, Garrett."

"Yeah, just another first-year I spent hours with. You must think I have all the time in the world." He spit out the words, muscles tightened and strained under her grasp.

Before Ari could question him further, Torq entered the cave.

"Oh, I see. While I'm getting thrashed by a troll, you're getting freaky with *him*." Torq's blue patterns on his skin spun, his adrenaline racing. "Nice costume, bud," he added dismissively.

Torq picked up the jewel. The golden color shimmered against his blue skin. It signaled the end of the game. Before Ari could say another word, the world rapidly dissolved in front of her.

CHAPTER 17

A t a heavy wooden table, Ari nursed a draft of ale. Next to her, Tessa flirted with a tall dark elf. Still reeling from her encounter with Garrett, Ari silently watched this exotic and almost alien world called the Winners' Circle. Small purple nymphs danced on the open floor, colored ribbons highlighting their magical acrobatics. King and Queen type figures sat on their gold thrones at the front of the room. They appeared more magical than human as they applauded the nymphs' entertainment. Torq perched on a bar stool, whispering something to a tall fairy of some sort. Her pristine hand landed on his arm, and his tattoos spun wildly.

Tessa's elf left, and her eyes followed him briefly before turning her attention back to Ari. Tessa's obvious infatuation surprised Ari. Like a friend getting tipsy for a first time, it opened up a whole new facet to their persona. Who knew, maybe Tessa was drunk? "Do you want to dance or drink the night away, Oya?"

Ari sipped the cold drink in her hand, its earthy flavor flooding her mouth. "Not sure."

"What is it?"

"What's what?"

Tessa adjusted her wings tight into her back as she turned to Ari. "What are you thinking about instead of drinking and enjoying this crazy world? There are a lot of people who wish they could be here. It's my fifth time. Hence, why I pick my second despite Torq's constant complaining."

"Is it possible to change code mid-game?" Ari couldn't shake off the encounter with Garrett. What were the chances that the game made a mistake at the same time she noticed the code in the game?

Tessa took another drink and winked at a large troll across the room. "It depends if you believe in warpers, aliens and all that other stuff. It's great to dream of super powers though."

"Sure." If that was true, then Ari really didn't know what to think of the game.

She ignored Ari and locked eyes with the elf from before, who was now returning. She leaned towards Ari. "Remember who may be watching before you hook up with an elf or warlock in the most unspeakable manner, as I am about to do."

Ari shivered. Corporations often watched or sold information from virtuals, but she hated being reminded of it.

The elf stood next to Tessa and reached for her hand. "My lady." He bent over and kissed her hand. "Our chariot is waiting."

"Where to?"

"To the ends of the world. Where else?"

Tessa turned back, her features strangely beautiful. "Try to have some fun, will you? Enjoy the fairy folk. Watch out for the green ones though."

Then Tessa walked out, her black wings shimmering in the candlelight that filled the hall.

Have fun, Ari thought. Not easy with a whirlwind of thoughts bombarding her.

A gorgeous faerie with tall icy features approached

her. Before he could open his mouth, she held up her hand and shook her head. Closing her eyes, she willed herself out of the virtual.

Ari awoke in the dark room, the smell of bodies and an odd mixture of perfumes overwhelming her. Hurrying out of the VR room, she continued through the lobby. Glancing at the old code littered around the room in decoration, she wondered if maybe the code in the game was a glitch or product of her imagination. She'd glimpsed those errors before, but she'd figured everyone saw them.

But to change the code? She needed to ask Tessa more about it. Maybe this was in Ari's head, or maybe this was why she was selected for this school. Either way, Tessa would be in the game for a couple more hours. She scanned the crowd briefly looking for her brother, but with no luck, she headed out into the dark night.

Ari wasn't about to spend cash on a cab though, so she walked the five blocks or so back to the condo. The sun had fallen long ago, and the neon lights of the businesses colored the night sky. Masses of people blurred past, laughing and talking as they forged in and out of the clubs and hotels. The buzz of their excitement carried her for a couple blocks.

The crowd thinned, and her feet ached. The black heels were as uncomfortable as they were impractical. She assumed Tessa's stepmother never had to walk more than a block in these. When she stopped to pull off the shoes, she noticed a man behind her. He caught her watching, he quickly turned his attention to an advertisement in a nearby store. He wore a blue baseball cap that hid his face, except for a goatee on his chin. She shook off the uncomfortable feeling creeping along her spine and continued down the street barefoot.

After another block, someone called her name. Turning around, Reed shouted from the back of a cab. He waved her towards him. Since, the cab was already crammed full, Ari shook her head, declining his offer. She didn't feel like hanging out with a group of people she barely knew.

"Hey, Ari, wait up."

Ari turned to find Reed jogging down the sidewalk after her. He looked handsome in dark jeans and a button-down shirt. He chased away any other thoughts and worries. The butterflies in her stomach were solely because of him. Why did he always have to look so good?

Reed slowed and walked next to Ari. "Thanks for waiting. I thought I would have to sprint all the way down the street."

Ari smiled and focused on the spot ahead of her.

"What are you doing here? Walking alone at night around here isn't safe."

"I was sick of gaming." Remembering the events with Garrett soured her mood, and worry replaced the butterflies.

He nudged her with his shoulder. "I wanted to see how you've been doing with your computer. Has it been giving you any more problems?"

Her stomach tightened as they crossed the street, heading towards the condo. "Having it report my every move isn't enough?"

Once on the other side, he grabbed her hand and pulled her to a stop, facing him. She regretted her snippy tone. Reed didn't deserve it.

His gaze bore straight through her defenses to the fear she'd been struggling to keep at bay. Averting her eyes, she realized they were in the more residential area with more condos and hotels than clubs.

"Ari." He waited for her to meet his eyes.

Once her emotions were firmly in check, she lifted her gaze. It made her want to crumble all over again. Not because of her fears this time, but because of the way he not only looked at her, but saw through her.

His brow furrowed in concern. "What's going on? Did something happen?"

She shook her head, not ready to voice what happened yet. "It's just stress. Don't worry. I'll be fine."

One eyebrow lifted. "Really?"

She hated to lie to him. "Don't worry." Lies of omission don't count, she told herself.

"If you say so." His gaze traveled down the street to the tall hotel built with a light smooth sandstone-type material that glimmered in the night sky. He then glanced down to her bare feet. "I can't help a bad game, but if you can stand wearing shoes for a bit longer, I may be able to come up with something to improve your night."

She was game, especially if it took her mind off things for a bit. She slipped on the torturous shoes. They made her a couple inches taller and closer to Reed's face. Reed smiled, the lopsided one that she had always loved. Heat spread through her face as they closed the distance between them. She wondered for a moment how he saw her. As a little sister he had to take care of, or something else?

"Come on, let's go." Reed broke the silence and led her to a sleek high-end hotel. The door man, dressed in a crimson suit, gave the pair a questioning look, but Reed strode in with confidence. A large fountain stood in the middle of the lobby with a statue of some man, barely dressed. They passed a noisy bar, and Reed turned to the elevators instead. Inside, one wall scrolled through pictures of the hotel and the different amenities it offered. An older couple boarded the elevator with them, but soon got off on the third floor which appeared to be lined with 3D games and virtuals. The doors finally shut, and they continued upward.

"Do you have a key to where you're staying?" he asked.

"Yeah, right here." Ari pulled out the electronic guest key card that Tessa had given her earlier.

Reed pulled out his interface from his back pocket and went to work.

"What are you doing?" Ari asked, her curiosity getting the better of her.

"Getting us a master key. Thought we could check this place out."

Ari gave a short laugh until she realized he was serious. "Really? You can do that?"

"One of the perks of going to school for security is I know how to build it and break it."

"Yeah, but are you supposed to? Won't they notice you in the system?"

"Nah. I'm not doing anything that would set off an alarm. They might notice a room key, but hopefully not this." He swiped the card with an attachment on his HUB.

"How did you get a card reader?" Ari asked, a bit astonished.

Reed looked up and smiled, his lips remaining sealed.

They continued until they reached the top, fifty floors up. They exited the elevator and passed many rooms until they arrived at a door marked 'Roof Access'. Reed used the card to open the door, and they emerged into the dark night once again.

This wasn't like the virtual she was in with Garrett where the roof was decorated like another floor. This roof was empty except for large mechanical units. It didn't have drinks and a pool but, looking up, Ari found a whole other world. Fifty floors provided a better view. Stars littered the sky with a beauty only nature could give.

"Wow." Ari turned taking in the night sky.

"Come on." Reed pulled her to the edge of the roof facing the busy street. He sat on the edge, his legs carelessly swinging down.

She paused for a moment, peering over the side. They were up really high. She had enough phobias and was glad a fear of heights wasn't one of them. She climbed onto the wide edge, next to Reed. From up there, the buildings flashed in a variety of colors, like glow sticks on end. People the size of ants swarmed below them.

"A miniature world with neon lights," Ari said.

"There's supposed to be fireworks soon."

She scanned the horizon, amazed by the never-ending trail of lights. "Cool." She hadn't seen fireworks since her days at the summer carnival with her family, back when she had a father. She shoved those thoughts aside, not letting herself miss him.

Reed suddenly shook her shoulders. A scream erupted from her mouth as she clung to the edge, and Reed laughed as if it was the funniest thing he'd ever seen.

Once she'd regained her balance, she realized his arm had stayed on her shoulder. She hit him lightly. "You are almost as bad as Marco." When she turned her head, she realized how close he really was.

His playful smile softened as he glanced at her mouth. She thought about closing the distance, but that was the difference between the virtuals and real life. In actual reality, kisses meant more, so did failing off the edge, even though they sort of felt like the same thing.

It took a moment for her to realize he wasn't moving away either. She had changed a lot since she left for school, doing things she never thought she would. Why not this? Before her brain could tell her all the reasons why not, she leaned in to lightly kiss his lips. He held still for a moment, and she worried that she'd made a mistake. But before she could pull back, he reached a hand up to cup her face. At first, his touch was hesitant, soft. Soon the space between them diminished and his soft lips held a hunger that she matched kiss for kiss. Bliss, true utter bliss blossomed in her chest as she lost herself in his touch.

When Ari moved her hand up to touch his face, an unsteady moment caused her to tighten her grip on the edge. Out of breath, she pulled back, a little flushed as she met his eyes.

One side of his lips lifted, his eyes never leaving her face. "Maybe kissing this high up isn't the wisest choice."

"And I thought you were worried about kissing your

best friend's sister," Ari replied, not able to keep the smile off her face.

"I am."

"We don't have to tell him," Ari suggested. She had always wanted to kiss Reed, but never thought through any sort of relationship afterward. It was always a little girl crush. But now that they started, she couldn't picture it any other way.

"I think it might be worse to keep it from him. He's already told me you're off limits."

"Really?" Ari fumed at the idea of Marco telling her who she can date.

"It was after he told me my mom looked hot one day, and I told him he wasn't allowed to think of my mom that way. He was offended and told me if my mom was off limits so were you. Guess I'd better warn my mom," Reed joked.

Ari avoided his gaze as she asked him the question that she didn't want answered. "You don't have to tell him if it doesn't happen again."

He pulled back slightly. "But what if I want it to happen again?"

Heat rushed to her face. "Then Marco can have your mom."

Reed laughed, his gaze turning to the night sky. "You probably don't realize just how long I've wanted to kiss you."

"Me too." Ari studied their intertwined fingers, his familiar, artistic hands that she admired, that held hers. She didn't trust herself to say more, to put what she felt in words. He was a childhood dream, a friend, and now ... she couldn't even qualify it, but it was definitely good. Fireworks exploded in the distance, and they both ignored them, leaning in for another kiss.

CHAPTER 18

The Tuesday after their long weekend break was bleak, gray and wet. Even those that hadn't left campus spent the majority of their weekend gaming. Unlike the gloomy expressions on the other students' faces, Ari was still riding the high of her time with Reed.

The lack of sleep did catch up with her though. A zombie herself, Ari struggled to keep up with Professor Speltman's lecture on logical and conditional loops. She recorded the lecture in case she needed it again. His monotone voice could be a cure for insomnia, but Ari tried to follow along.

Speltman paced slowly across the room. "Poorly constructed loops are an easy out in virtuals and will not be tolerated in my classes. I don't want to see the same cloud sequence floating by unless you want to fail. I expect at least a minimum of five different conditional loops streaming, whether it be clouds, birds, or a neighbor out for a walk." He stopped to face the classroom. "Minute variety is what brings depth to your worlds."

Ari raised her hand.

He nodded at her. "Yes?"

"How do you avoid an error when the loops transition or start over?" She often saw a slight glitch when a loop started over, like the fish in the ocean with Garrett.

The teacher's brow lowered. "There shouldn't be an error. Reread your coding manual. As elementary as it is, I'd be surprised if a child could screw that up."

A voice traveled softly from the back. "Sounds about right for that girl."

Ari nodded and lowered her eyes. Her face burned, and she wanted to kick who ever said there were no stupid questions. But if it was such a remedial error, why did she see it so often? She wasn't about to bring up what happened to her and Garrett in the VR.

Ari spent her lunch hour drinking coffee in her room while searching through online rumors on warpers. She sifted through a myriad of claims and rumors. One guy claimed to be a warper and was experimented on by the government. Another site claimed they were warpers and could recreate anyone's sexual fantasy to perfection. *Gross.* They boasted about their ability but never explained how they manipulated the code or what exactly they did. Could they create programs quicker if they wrote them while in the VR?

She was mulling over the implications of warpers as she headed to Dr. Coleman's class. While finding her seat, her stomach churned. She no longer had full blown panic attacks in his class, but that didn't mean she didn't feel ill every time she went in.

Dr. Coleman walked in between the chairs, in black slacks and a dark, crisp shirt. "Today we're going to see if you're worth your salt in programming. Dr. Speltman had you submit the skeleton you completed for your midterm assignment. You will walk through it, criticizing the flaws and assessing potential for the next level of design, the user interface. Please run your program for twenty minutes and then after a brief discussion, we will move on with our normal agenda."

Ari exhaled a bit loudly, which drew Dr. Coleman's attention. "Is there a problem, Ariana?"

She shook her head.

"I should hope not. After the weekend you should have no problem with the VR, should you?"

How would he know about the weekend?

His look was piercing though, and there was no doubt that he knew. "We're going to see if you really have what it takes to do this."

"Yes, sir," Ari answered and, under his heavy gaze, reached for the cable to plug in. She ignored an uneasiness in her stomach that had nothing to do with the VR.

The world Ari had created was sparse, but she'd done that on purpose. Lush green countryside traveled for miles in every direction. A small hill rose to the east, next to a wooden house surrounded by several well placed over-sized trees. She'd even created a stream to run behind it. Ari wanted to create a piece from history, when things weren't as crowded, but with the benefits of indoor plumbing. Her VR world wasn't amazing, but it wasn't bad.

She strolled near a small plant, a bush really. And without thinking about it she concentrated on the bush, trying to see the code, like she'd done with Garrett. But all she saw was a bush, boring and plain. At least at first.

Continuing to focus, the characters in the code appeared, showing what she used to create such a small simple bush. She laughed out loud in spite of herself. She wondered if that was why she was here. Could that aptitude test she had taken at home somehow predict this?

Ari wondered how easy it would be to change the bush. Not that she would do it, but she itched to try.

"You must be really pleased with your bush there." Ari turned around to find Dr. Coleman. He always oversaw the VR trips and interacted with students, but today Ari wasn't prepared for him.

"No, sir. I was thinking about how fake it looked."

"Good, because you are right. It's abysmal. What else?" he asked.

Before Ari could continue though, Dr. Coleman put his hand on his temple in a concentrated expression.

A mechanical voice broke into the VR. "Please exit the virtual immediately."

Dr. Coleman turned to Ari and talked over the voice. "We're going into lockdown. Leave immediately."

Panic rushed through Ari's body. *Lockdown*. They'd gone over this in the beginning of the semester, and they'd even had lockdown drills at her school, but for some reason this didn't seem like a drill today. *What was happening out there?*

Dr. Coleman must have noticed her hesitation. He put a hand on her shoulder, grabbing her attention. "You need to leave. Can you do that? Or does Mica need to pull you out?"

Ari shook her head. "No, I got it."

Then Ari forced herself to leave, leaving her imperfect world for a scarier, more real one.

Mica appeared, took out Ari's port without even asking and moved on to the next student. Ari glanced around the classroom, unsure of what to do. The other students were slowly waking up from the VR, asking questions.

"Everyone can be seated." Dr. Coleman stood at the front. "The room is secure, at the moment."

Ari clutched her bag onto her lap in case they needed to leave.

"What happened?" Tessa asked from the back of the room.

"There was a gunman apprehended at the entrance of our facility. They are worried he may have an accomplice, so they are searching the rest of the campus. Our systems may also have been breached so only internal network communication is allowed." Dr. Coleman pulled out a stool to sit on. "All the VR facilities are shut down in case we need to be evacuated, but they should have the place cleared in a couple of hours."

A moan went through the students.

"Don't complain to me. This is your fault," Dr. Coleman said to the class.

"What?" a dark hair boy asked in the back.

"Every time after break, the school has to double security. People watch the students partying on break and are reminded of what we are creating here. It makes the wackos come out of the woodwork. Crackpots from religious groups think virtuals are evil. They think VRs teach kids to have sex, do drugs, and kill others."

Ari swallowed, thinking that they might be partly right.

Dr. Coleman stood up and resumed his pacing, his argument turning into a lecture. "Ironically though, they seem to have no problem slaughtering us despite their moral objections." He stared off in the distance for a bit, and then a cough from the back of the class revived his attention. "Nevertheless, here we are. Please start your essay on your virtual and continue with reading the next chapter."

He began to walk off as the students pulled out their small computers. Then, as a second thought he added, "There will be a quiz tomorrow on the reading in case you decide to skip it." With a smug smile, he disappeared to his desk in the corner.

The campus was on lockdown: the VR College, IT, IT security, and network management. It seemed the whole world, or Ari's world, was frozen for the time being. She spent the first hour of lockdown completing her homework. Reed texted her once to make sure she was okay. She'd sent a message to her brother but hadn't heard back. Reed had told her not to worry about Marco, but something didn't sit right. Why wouldn't Marco text back? Maybe he was making out with some girl and locked in her room.

As time ticked by students became restless, stretching out their legs, or having quiet conversations. She ignored Wake and his buddies' comments and snickers from the back of the room. Tessa sent her a video of a comedian who specialized in jokes involving AIs. When Ari let a laugh escape. Dr. Coleman cleared his throat and glared at her.

She didn't have time to apologize before gunfire sounded outside the class. A girl shrieked in the next room. Ari jumped at the noise hoping, praying, it wasn't as close at it sounded. Several students cowered in their seats.

"Please!" Coleman said in a firm voice. "A gun cannot make it through these doors. And being hysterical will not help this situation."

The air in the room hung heavy and thick. Ari struggled to breathe as she unconsciously scratched her fingernails along the inside of her palms.

"You guys have gone through enough simulations to know how to control your emotions. If I passed out weapons, I would expect you to be the soldiers you have been trained to be."

Ari had never gone through those simulations that trained students in emergencies and even on the battlefield. It was one way the government could pick the perfect soldiers. Ari had always been exempt from all VRs with a note from the school psychologist. But by the look of the other students, Ari wondered if Coleman himself understood the difference between simulation and reality. These students were computer geeks, not soldiers, no matter what VR they did.

Dr. Coleman paced restlessly in front of the classroom, angry with his class for their less than exemplary behavior. He finally returned to his desk in the back. The class resumed its mumbled conversation, and Ari turned back to her screen.

She flinched as a hand fell onto her shoulder. It was

the moron, Wake. "You're not scared, are you? Maybe they want to destroy your brain from creating anything. Don't worry, I'll tell them it's not worth wasting a bullet on you, on the other hand—"

Ari slapped his hand away. "Get lost," She'd said it louder than she'd meant to and earned yet another glare from Dr. Coleman.

A brief noise sounded overhead, and a voice came on the speaker. "The threat was terminated. Please continue regularly scheduled classes and, as always, report any suspicious behavior."

Terminated.

Ari wondered what that meant exactly as she left the classroom. In the hall, students pushed against the glass windows. She moved further down the hall and looked out a different window. Authorities had gathered on the grounds. A stretcher was pushed out of the front of their building with a black body bag on top, and she realized the gunshots they heard weren't aimed at the students but at the intruder.

CHAPTER 19

Once dismissed, Ari headed to her next class, art design. There was only ten minutes left in class after the lockdown, but she didn't want to miss any assignments. The teacher had the door closed and locked with no note. Ms. Weber might have been just as rattled by the lockdown as everyone else and didn't bother catching her next class.

On the main floor, several students stood at the glass doors, watching the darkening sky, and complaining about the intruder. Ari stood slightly apart from them and watched large drops of rain pelt the path. She loved the rain, but today it felt dark, melancholy almost. The dead body being wheeled out of school might have something to do with it. Tessa came running down the path, her arms full of white bags, distracting Ari from her thoughts.

Once inside, Tessa brushed water off her jacket. "Man, it's cold outside. I wish it would snow already." She passed a bag to Ari and ran her fingers through her newly colored dark purple hair. She even had purple eye liner on to match.

"Wanna eat?" Tessa asked, looking up, drops falling from her hair.

"I'm starving."

"I got a lot of food just in case of another lockdown. Our fridge might overflow, but at least we'll have food."

"Bless you," Ari's stomach growled in agreement. They rushed up to their room and sat in the middle of their floor with their array of food in self-warming packages, steaming with a variety of flavors. They even kept their door ajar, sharing with some of the neighbors.

Stuffed to capacity, Ari leaned against her bed and watched the rain hit the window. The dark sky made it feel later than it really was. Coming from a desert climate, she excitedly awaited first snow, even if she didn't have clothes for it. She'd have hit the student center soon to stock up.

Tessa sat on her bed with her tablet. "Have you started Tollingston's paper yet?"

"No, I can't believe he gave us a paper on our first night back." Ari turned from the window and grabbed her bag.

"Probably was jealous that we actually enjoyed our break."

"Enjoying your break was an understatement I believe." Without notice, a richly dressed man had appeared in their doorway.

Ari jumped. The man, dressed in an expensive navy suit, had smooth tight features that had a too-perfect feel about them. What he spent on his appearance could probably sustain a family of four for a lifetime. A school security guard stood several feet behind him.

Tessa didn't act alarmed, but her lip curled in annoyance. "Number Four is always telling me that I need to be more social."

"Not so social that we have to face complaints from the condo board. Sheri's pass is under investigation."

"Are you sure Number Four wasn't having some of her own fun?" Tessa asked in an innocent voice.

The barb hit its mark. The man, presumably Tessa's father, stiffened and his jaw flexed.

"Her name is not Number Four, but Sheri. You will show respect to your stepmother." His voice raised in volume.

"My roommate has a name too. This is Ari."

"Hi," Ari said, trying to turn invisible in the confrontation. Neither Tessa nor her father seemed to be worried about having an audience though.

"Ari, the girl from the block?"

Ari kept her chin up, refusing to react or be embarrassed by where she came from.

"Nice, Dad," Tessa said.

"What? I think Ari should be proud. Not many scholarships are assigned such high-paying occupations. I wish my own daughter could rise to something besides online gaming. It really shows when people make something of themselves out of nothing. Not like Tessa here who has had every opportunity in the world. Did Tessa ever tell you how I started my first business?"

"Dad, really? I think that was a new record. Three minutes before we're talking about you again."

"I just remembered," Ari interjected. "I was supposed to meet my brother for something." She grabbed her bag and took off. Ari would brave any storm to avoid that conversation.

Outside, the rain poured down as she ran towards Reed's dorm. She should've called first but didn't think he'd hear her over the rain, and she didn't want to stop running to text him. She also could have stopped in the cafeteria or student center, but if she stopped she would've lost her nerve. They'd messaged each other but hadn't talked in person since coming back to campus on Sunday.

Part of Ari worried if it was a weekend fling, or maybe a dream that she wished would come true. She wanted to know if what they had was real.

By the time she arrived at the door, she was drenched. She had only one more hour until visiting hours were over and then a key was required to enter. On the way up the elevator, a couple of guys eyed her questioningly. She ignored their stares and tried not to think about what she must look like. By the time she knocked on the door, she was shivering.

Reed answered the door, his lips pulling up in a grin.

Words stumbled out of Ari's mouth. "I had to get out of my room, and I wasn't sure if you were around or if you wanted—"

He ignored her words and quieted her rambling by pressing his lips against hers, warm and welcoming. He pulled her close, holding her tight despite her sopping clothes. It was the whistles and cheering from two guys down the hall that made them finally separate.

Reed glared at the two guys. "Come in." He closed the door. "You must be freezing. Do you want something to wear?"

"I'm fine," Ari lied, distracted by Reed's side of the room. He always had pictures up, some from home, many of them of the desert trees with their broad twisted branches. She loved to look at them. An unfinished drawing on his desk caught her eye. It was a portrait of a girl, with a long wave of hair covering half her face. It was her.

"I haven't finished this one yet, but it's of you." Color flooded his cheeks as he reached for the black and white drawing. "It still needs a lot of work."

"It's amazing." The detail in her eyes held more emotion than any photo she'd ever seen of herself. Looking up at all the pictures, the familiarity brought a bit of homesickness. She pointed to one bush with thorns twisted into the air. "This should be in a program. You would have been amazing in design. They are so surreal. Like a world, beautiful, twisted, scary."

Reed was a scholarship kid, like most kids from the block, and art was one of those things that might be a great hobby but didn't pay the rent. As an only child with a single mother, he had to be more than an artist. But at that moment that nothing else seemed as important.

Something else caught her eyes—a miniature green sculpture of a dragon, with gray eyes that blinked and moved around when it sensed movement. Ari had made it for him years before, after she'd read a book about dragons. The robot was easy enough to make. Reed had started a series of dragon cartoons after that gift. She couldn't believe he'd kept it.

"Here, let's get you changed," Reed said, taking her attention away from the dragon.

"I don't think you'd fit in my pants, but maybe Marco's." Reed handed her a long t-shirt.

"I'll grab some of Marco's sweats," Ari said. Marco was built more like Ari, thin and tall.

Reed offered to step out while she changed. Ari put on the dry shirt which reached down to her thighs. She laid her wet clothes over the back of Marco's chair and turned to dig through his dresser for sweats. Digging through the drawers, something black caught her eye.

Lifting a shirt, she found a gun. It couldn't be a real gun, those were illegal. Why would Marco need a gun at school? For a joke? She picked up the weapon, the cold metal heavy under her hand. It didn't feel like a joke.

"Are you done yet?" Reed stepped back in. "Man, my shirt is like a dress on you. Cute."

She ignored the comment, and instead turned around with the gun in her hand.

Reed's eyes widened. He stepped back into the dorm, shutting the door behind him. "What's the weapon for?"

"It's Marco's." A heavy weight pulled at her shoulders. Whatever her brother was mixed up in was big.

"Oh," Reed said, but not as surprised as Ari wanted him to be.

"Why does he have a gun? Did you know about this? He's going to be expelled if anyone finds out."

Reed walked towards Ari with his hands up. "Hold on. Let's put it away while we talk about it."

More than happy to get rid of the gun, she placed it back in his drawer. Maybe if it was out of sight, then it wouldn't seem as real. Her hands, now empty, shook uncontrollably. Reed had her sit on Marco's bed. She tugged the hem of his shirt down to cover the top of her thighs.

Reed pulled a chair and sat across from her. "Marco's been getting mixed up with some sketchy guys lately."

Anger rose up, hot and fast. "Why didn't you tell me?"

He let a long breath out. "I've talked to him about it and was hoping things had gotten better. But today he asked for money again. I've lent him some, but he wanted more."

"You should have told me." Anger burned the back of her eyes, frustrated by being left in the dark.

"I know."

She tried to push aside the fury building inside and focus on how to help her brother. "You don't think he's stealing."

"No, Marco wouldn't do that."

"Wouldn't do what?" Marco asked in a jovial voice as he walked through the door but froze when he saw Ari.

The color drained from Marco's face, and she raised her defenses. This was Marco. She had fought with him enough as a kid. Unfortunately, now, the stakes were much higher now.

"Reed, I'll only ask this once." Marco slowly shut the door. "Why are you on my bed with my sister, and where are her pants?"

Ari stood, determined not to let him turn this situation around. "Marco, why do you have a gun? Do you think it makes you a man?"

Ari took after her mother and grandmother and could yield a hot Spanish tongue. They both stood for a moment starring at each other. Finally, Marco caved. He headed to his drawer to make sure it was there.

"You don't know, okay. I need it for protection."

"Who do you need protection from?"

"None of your business!" Marco spit back at her.

"It *is* my business and Mom's if you wind up dead."

"Is it Mom's business that you're sleeping around like some slutty freshman?" He glared at her with more contempt than Ari had ever seen. They had fought over the years, like most siblings, but there was a line of how far they would go and he'd just crossed it.

Ari's words stuck in her throat. In her frustration and rage she lunged for him. She punched him in the shoulder and tried next for his face. Marco grabbed her hands. Reed had both hands around her waist hoisting her away from her brother. She fought against his hold. How dare he stop her? Did Reed not hear what Marco had just said?

"You don't want to do this," Reed said.

Blood rushed in her ears. "Yes, I do."

"Give me a minute, and then you can kill him." Reed turned back to Marco, keeping Ari behind him.

"Look, Marco. I didn't sleep with your sister. We've kissed a bit and that's it. She came over soaking wet. She was looking for a pair of sweatpants when she found the gun."

Marco lowered his gaze, a red mark blossoming on his cheek. He nodded and bit his lower lip. "Okay." Then he reached inside his drawer to grab the gun and put it in the back of his jeans.

"We're worried about you, Marco," Reed said. "I don't want to see you hurt, or your future destroyed."

Ari's temper continued to boil. She didn't want to care about her brother. How could he talk to her like that? He knew her better than anyone, or so she thought.

"It's my future." Marco looked at his face in the mirror above his dresser and ran a hand through his hair. "I gotta go. Don't wait up."

"Can't we talk about this?" Reed asked again.

"Don't worry. You have my blessing, Reed." Marco motioned to Ari with weary disgust. "You can have her."

Ari growled and reached for the closest thing she could find, a cup of water, and threw it at Marco. It missed his head and crashed against the wall as he shut the door.

As he left, he'd sucked out all the energy and fight from the room. A bot beeped and emerged from under the bed to begin cleaning up the mess. Ari stumbled back and sank onto Reed's bed.

Reed approached, hesitantly. "You okay?"

Ari stared at the tears that fell into her hands. Suddenly aware that she was partially naked and sitting in Reed's room with tears pouring down her face, embarrassment burned her face.

"I better go. It's getting late." Ari hurried to put on her wet jeans while avoiding Reed's glance. "Turn around so I can change my shirt."

Reed reached for her arm. "Hey." He steadied her and waited for Ari to meet his eyes.

"Keep the shirt. I like it on you." Reed pushed a wet strand of hair out of her face. "Let me walk you back, and we can grab a drink from the student center."

"I don't think I can." Ari's voice wavered.

Reed pulled her in close. She fought back the tears as she relaxed in his hold.

"You're not alone in this, okay?"

Ari nodded.

"You sure you don't want a hot chocolate or something?"

Ari shook her head. She didn't feel like hot chocolate but tightened her hold on Reed. Her world was unraveling around her and the only thing she had to grab onto was him.

CHAPTER 20

After a couple days, Ari's anger at her brother gradually turned to fear. She had tried messaging him several times, but he didn't answer. She wanted to tell their mother but decided to give him a few more days to respond, a week max. Besides, what could her mother do?

Throwing herself into her schoolwork, she hoped to ignore the mess that was her brother, and the unanswered questions about her abilities in the VR. The routine helped, but the worry and ache remained. After hours of work in Programming, her grade climbed to a B+. She found art a nice distraction, and even Dr. Coleman's VR class was easier, although her cuticles might have disagreed with that last part as they received the brunt force of her anxiety from the VRs.

Thursday night, Ari and Tessa were knee deep in homework when a knock sounded. Not surprisingly, Tessa ignored it. Ari jumped up to answer it. They didn't have many visitors, other than other students wanting to borrow notes or something lame.

When she opened the door, Reed stood there. His dirty blond hair was styled up in front and his shirt looked crisp and clean.

"What's up?" She tried not to be too obvious as she checked out his cute jeans that hung just right on his slender hips.

"I wanted to ask you something." He glanced down at his shoes and nervously kicked at the carpet.

"Okay ..." She wondered why he didn't just message her.

"Do you want to go out this weekend, like on a date?" He glanced up, his cheeks flushed.

Her lips curled up in a smile. She had never seen Reed nervous before. Her stomach did happy flips. "Sure. You could have just messaged me."

He shook his head. "My mom gave me some rules about girls. I never bothered following them before, but they sounded like a good idea."

"I'm interested in hearing about these rules."

He glanced into her room where her computer was up and running. "Another time when you're not busy." He stepped towards her and planted a light kiss on her cheek. "I'll see you soon."

She stayed in the doorway watching him walk away. Her cheek tingled where his lips touched her skin, and her heart pooled in a puddle at her feet.

By the time the weekend came, even the mountains of homework couldn't ruin her mood. Reed had asked Ari on a date, an official date. Their school sat on the edge of a small town with only a few restaurants and stores, but Ari didn't care if he took her to a swamp. To spend time alone with Reed, outside of school, sounded amazing.

Ari changed into a pair of black pants and a green top. She was straightening her long black hair when Tessa walked in.

"Getting ready for your date, I see. Don't do anything I wouldn't do." Tessa grinned.

"We're going into town to eat or something."

"Cool." Tessa settled into her chair, drink in hand.

"What are you doing tonight?"

"You're looking at it. I'll maybe order some pizza and crush some guys online whose egos have been getting too big." Tessa pushed back a stray of long hair and turned to her computer.

"Okay. I'm heading out then. Smash some egos for me." Ari grabbed her bag. She was supposed to meet Reed downstairs.

Tessa put on her headset and the look of determination that often accompanied it. "Will do."

By the time Ari made it down to the lobby, Reed was already there by the front door, watching the sky. With one hand in his pocket, he stared outside. The falling sun cast a gold glow to his hair and outlined his features. He looked ... beautiful. And not just in the "I want to kiss your face off" kind of way, but truly beautiful. She hated to disturb him.

As she approached, he turned to greet her. His face lit up in a smile. "Ready?"

Unable to help herself, she just stared.

"You okay?"

"Yeah." Ari took his hand, shaking herself out of her stupor. This was Reed who she had known forever. *Get a hold of yourself, Ari.* "This is a bit surreal. You and me, going on a date together."

"I know what you mean." He reached for her hand, and they left her dorm. "I feel like I should be asking your mother's permission or something."

"Don't worry. I actually talked to her about it."

"Really?"

"Yes, last night. She says she couldn't think of a better boy she could trust me with. I'm glad that I never told her about Garrett."

"Don't remind me," he growled. "When I saw you two together—"

Thankfully, security interrupted him. Several guards stood by the gate. Ari and Reed approached the officer at the gate and scanned their identity bracelets. Several others walked back and forth along the fence. The electric fence wasn't enough? Extra guards have been stationed since the intruders.

"Curfew is at ten tonight. No exceptions," said a tall, pale officer that Ari didn't recognize.

"Really?" At the beginning of the year it was midnight on the weekends.

"The gates are closing early due to Monday's incident. If you want to stay out later, you have to sign out an extended pass." The officer's pressed lips didn't offer any room to debate.

"We'll be back." Reed pulled Ari along.

Ari was used to guards at her old school, but they were friendly and more relaxed. These men weren't security guards but soldiers. "How often do things like Monday happen?"

"Not that often, but there are enough attempts that security is kept pretty tight. Some fanatics think the VR and the computer age are detrimental to evolution or something."

"Some days I wonder that myself," Ari replied. She had witnessed the ill effects of VR first hand.

"Come on." Reed grasped her hand tighter. "We're supposed to be having fun. Forget about the guards."

Alone with Reed, it was easy for Ari to forget about everything else. He took her to a small restaurant with fresh food that tasted of home. She got lost in his eyes more than once, and he had to remind her to keep eating. Over hot salsa and spicy meat, they talked of home and even of the future. Reed was in his last year of school. After finals he would be assigned as an intern, anywhere in the country. He'd requested to stay in the Southwest, close to his mother and Ari.

"Want dessert?" He scanned the small screen that

displayed the menu.

"I'm actually stuffed." Ari hadn't eaten that much in a while, but it was so worth it.

He paid on the screen and then turned back to Ari. "Okay, well I have another surprise for you."

"Surprise?" She raised a brow as her lips pulled up in a smile.

"It's nothing too exciting, but I thought you'd like it." He reached for her hand as they left the restaurant.

As they walked by various outdoor restaurants, stores, and VR bars, she relished having Reed at her side. They held hands or lightly touched, both of them like magnets, constantly drawn back to each other. Ari wondered if this feeling of wanting to touch him or be next to him would ever fade.

At the next block, an older store sat squished in the corner. Large green letters flashed overhead that spelled "GAMING" and then underneath it read "BUY, SELL, TRADE." Reed headed towards the store.

"This is it?" Ari worried for a moment that he was taking her to a VR, a popular date for most people. And while she could stomach a VR date, she would much rather have Reed in reality next to her.

"Trust me." Reed continued through the automatic door.

From a screen on their right a mechanical voice welcomed them to the store and offered to locate specific products for them. Reed ignored the prompt and continued inside. "Hey, Pete."

"Good to see ya." Pete was a slim man with brown hair pulled back into a short ponytail.

They didn't stop to chat, but instead headed to the back. The store held a random array of multi-dimensional games, sensory games, and even some VRs. Ari noticed a sign for screening rooms in the back. The store wasn't packed but had several people browsing the merchandise.

Tucked away in one little corner, there were some

books, real physical books. She hadn't held a book since her part-time job cataloging and scanning old novels. It had been the only time she had touched books. Books you knew didn't change with a slight tap of your finger.

She picked up a yellowed book with a cowboy on the front. Though paperback, the cover was coated with some sort of plastic. As she opened the book, the smell of mothballs and old paper wafted up. The fragile paper had browned on the edges. It was the epitome of the older generation, when stories were only one-dimensional.

"You like them?" Reed leaned over, resting his chin on her shoulder, and wrapping his arms around her waist. "How much is it?"

"Probably worth more than I am." Ari looked for a price on the back.

"Doubt it. Pete is trying to sell off all his books. These antiques don't sell as well as they used to."

She turned the book over but didn't see anything.

"Here." He reached for the book. "I'll go ask him. Stay and check out the others."

She picked up another book, this one a cheesy romance of some kind. Another customer approached to peruse the books. The man was older, but with strong, broad shoulders. His friendly smile and goatee softened his muscular features. "Do you happen to know much about these antiques?"

"Some, but not much." Ari shrugged, not able to shake the feeling that she had seen him before somewhere.

His caramel eyes blended well with his tanned skin. "Do you study ancient text in school?"

"No, I'm in the VR program here."

"Very cool. I work in VRs. I'm Dave, by the way." He reached out a hand to shake.

Ari hesitated for a moment, assuming he must work at the VR bar they passed. This was a busy store, though, and he appeared friendly enough. She returned the handshake. "Ari."

The man glanced briefly at the front desk to where Reed was, and Ari followed his gaze. Reed was talking to his friend, engrossed in conversation.

"Ari, have you ever thought about going into the corporate VR market?"

"No, not really. I'm just trying to make it through school. I have another year or so before I begin thinking about careers."

Dave's face fell a bit, his eyes looking older and more serious. "I'm sorry to say, you don't have that long."

"That long for what?" Instinctively, Ari took a step back.

"I work for VisionTech. We know about your trip in the game over break. We know what you can do."

Ari shook her head and started to walk away.

He set the book down but didn't try to follow her. "Changing a character in the middle of a busy game is not the way to stay discreet."

She froze, not out of fear but curiosity. How did he know about Garrett and the game? She was still trying to figure out what happened herself, and she wanted to know more despite this man being a stranger.

"Don't be afraid, Ari. We have no reason to let others know. They are our competition."

"Competition?" The word escaped Ari's lips, as her mind spun with what was happening.

"Recruiters. There are only so many warpers, and everyone wants one."

"I'm not a warper." Ari thought back to her lessons and the game with Garrett.

"You're telling me you don't see code inside the VR? And what about all those unexplainable incidences with Garrett or the glitches you see? There is a reason they happen, and the reason is you."

Ari swallowed and found her voice. "I'm not sure what's going on. I'm not whatever you think I am."

"We won't tell anyone, but it won't be long before the

government finds out through your school. I'm amazed you've lasted this long. You're definitely the oldest untrained warper there is." He let the last statement sit for a moment before continuing. "And let me tell you, of all the companies, VisionTech, is one of the best. Many places won't have any perks or spending accounts. If the government snatches you up first, you'll be working for the military torturing people, and training soldiers. Something a little girl should know nothing about."

"I'm not a little girl." She sounded absurd, like a three-year-old stomping their foot. Ari didn't care.

"True. But you're not a soldier either. Are you?"

She didn't answer him. The Never-Ending War had stretched into another decade. With so many countries involved, Ari couldn't even tell you who her country was fighting anymore. She wasn't a soldier and didn't want to become one.

The man slid a card into her hand and leaned in, his breath uncomfortably close. "Contact me if you have any questions or change your mind. Trust me. The pay alone can take your mother off the assembly line and into a private estate."

How does he know about my mother? Ari tensed at the idea that this man, this stranger, had researched her mother. What about the rest of her family?

"Hey," Reed said, walking up behind them.

Dave gave her one final look and walked away.

"Are you alright? I saw that old guy hitting on you, and I thought I better come to the rescue." Reed slid his arm around her. "Man, you're cold. Did he spook you?"

"No, no, I'm fine. Just creeped out a bit."

"I understand. There was this girl who graduated last year. She was on the strip with a guy that could have been my grandpa if he was still alive. Seriously. Sick."

"Yeah." Ari needed to leave, to find some fresh air and think. She didn't want to tell Reed anything until she knew for herself what was going on.

"Pete will give me a good deal on the book, if you still want it." Reed watched her, his brow tightening in concern.

Ari pasted on a smile. She never really did have a poker face. "Thanks, but I'm okay. I enjoyed looking at them though."

"You sure?"

"Yeah. I'm good."

"Okay. Up for dessert?"

"Sure." She slipped her hand into his.

"Great." Reed turned and led her towards the door. With her free hand, Ari tucked the card in her back pocket.

CHAPTER 21

A nother long week passed. A week full of sleepless nights. A week full of Ari telling herself lies, trying to convince herself that contacting Dave was a mistake. That if she kept everything to herself, nothing would change.

Saturday, Ari woke early to a dark and cloudy sky. Tessa snored softly, her rumpled purple hair strewn all over her pillow made her look like she'd had a wild night—even though Ari knew it was spent in front of her computer screen.

Ari headed out the door, hoping for an early start on studying. She grabbed a coffee from the vending machine and headed to the student VR lab on the sixth floor. She swiped her bracelet and the large metallic door slid open for her.

She checked in with the groggy aide who assigned a room for her to work in. "Call me if you need anything." He took another drink of his coffee.

"I got it." Sometimes Ari struggled hooking herself in, but she managed to do it by herself. It felt too intimate, too close for a stranger.

Ari walked down the maroon and silver corridor, with

large screens mounted on the walls flashing various announcements. "Tutoring help offered Saturday afternoons 12-5" one screen displayed. The screen flipped images then, "Career day January 18th." Ari paused at the monitor. She tapped on it and swiped her bracelet to send herself a reminder.

Her thoughts drifted back to the recruiter from VisionTech, Dave. Could she trust him? She didn't know. Ari wasn't sure if she was really a warper, but she could see the code. She wasn't sure what happened in the game with Garrett, but she needed to figure it out. Dave's promises about her mother lingered with her all morning.

For the first time in her life she wanted to go back in the VR. She wanted to see if she really was what Dave had said, a warper. She remembered his warning though and had second thoughts as she waited outside her assigned door. Her student card hung precariously over the scanner. Should she chance it? She didn't quite believe Dave. If he really was a recruiter, his only goal would be for her to sign a contract. There had to be other companies to work with. Maybe even working with the government wouldn't be that bad. The card shook in her hand, and her gut turned with unease.

Unsure of who to trust or what to do, she turned and left the lab. The student aide at the desk had nodded off next to a cup of coffee. Ari left her dorm and zipped up her jacket as the freezing wind cut against her face. She headed towards Reed's dorm thinking he might be able to sneak her into a virtual that wasn't being watched, but then remembered Reed handled security. He didn't have the keys for an offline VR. But Garrett did.

The pit of her stomach sank, and her pace slowed as she realized she had to ask Garrett for a favor, to face a conversation she had been avoiding for weeks. She walked into the tech center. The same place she had visited on the first day of school with the same trepidation rising but for different reasons.

Ari spun the ring on her finger, the one that Garrett had given her. Tessa had told her the real cost of the ring that turned into an earpiece along with other cool tricks. Ari couldn't afford another one of her own. Practicality won out. Besides, she didn't blame Garrett for what happened between them, not really. He was who he was. It was Ari who wasn't ready for that type of physical relationship with someone she'd just met.

With wide eyes, Garrett couldn't hide his surprise when Ari entered the room. Self-consciously Ari tugged at her messy ponytail. But she found solace in his wrinkly shirt and messy hair. His hair jet black looked a little shorter.

A condescending smile curled on his lips. "To what do I owe this great pleasure? Your HUB broke or something?"

"You got a haircut." Ari regretted the remark as soon as it left her lips.

"Huh? So that's how we're going to do this?" He played with a pen in his fingers. "Yes, I did get a haircut. How nice of you to notice." His tone was much sharper than his words.

"Can we talk? In private?"

He arched an eyebrow and turned back into that mischievous, cute little boy again. "Sure, let's go for a walk." He typed something into the computer and then hollered to the back. "Keyton, I'm going on break. Listen for the door."

He shoved something in his pocket and walked around the tall silver counter. After you, he motioned, and Ari led the way through the door. Ari headed towards the lake, hoping the shore would be empty this early. Garrett maintained a forced distance but kept up with Ari. She bit the inside of her lip trying to figure out a way to begin.

Once the lake was in sight, Garrett stopped walking. "So is this all about my grooming habits?"

"I'm sorry," Ari blurted out.

Garrett's face froze with no emotion, and then he continued on the path around the lake without a word.

Ari kept up next to him. "I had my reasons to leave, but I shouldn't have ignored you. You deserved more."

"And those reasons?"

Ari didn't reply at first. She watched the ripples on the lake as they curved alongside the rocky shore. She swallowed and continued, "I wasn't sure if I was ready for a relationship, and I heard about your reputation with the first-years. I didn't want to be another first-year. Not that way." She couldn't look at him. Her face burned.

He nodded and continued on the path. "You were right. If you weren't mature enough to talk to me, it was probably better that you left."

"Well," Ari stumbled over her words as he surprised and offended her in the same breath.

Garrett stopped and turned to her. "What do you need?"

"I was hoping you could get me into an unsupervised virtual."

He watched her, as if dissecting more than she said. "Is this about what happened in the game?"

Ari nodded.

"You freaked me out, Ari. After the game I went to complain about the glitch. Of course, they ignored my protest and gave me a discount for the next game, but they were worried about it for sure. I'm surprised they haven't contacted you yet."

"I signed into the game as Tessa's stepmother."

"Nice. I wonder if they contacted her?"

Ari remembered how angry Tessa's father was when he came over. "I think so."

"I'm surprised you've flown under the radar for so long, but most people don't have a fear of virtuals."

"Lucky me," Ari said sarcastically. "So, can you help me?"

He looked her up and down, making her skin crawl.

This was the part of him that Ari couldn't trust, the part of him she didn't like.

"We'll need Reed. Instead of changing the time, he'll have to find a way to get you off grid."

"I'll talk to him." Ari shifted slightly.

Garrett noticed her hesitation. "You mean you haven't told your boyfriend yet?" He guffawed at the idea. "Okay, I think watching this might be worth it."

"Whatever." Ari started to leave.

He caught Ari's hand. He seemed to be trying to make her uncomfortable and squirm under his grip. Instead, annoyance and anger grew in the pit of her stomach. She was done playing the scared little first-year. She tugged hard and he let go. "When can we do this?"

"My part is pretty easy, letting you in. You need to make sure you cover your trail if you don't want everyone to know. You won't be able to keep this quiet for too long, not in your program."

She ignored that last part. "I'll let you know after I talk to Reed." Ari walked away from the lake. A chill ran up her arms, and she wanted to leave.

"I'll miss having you around," Garrett said.

Ari paused for a moment, her back to him. In an alternate universe they could have been friends, but not in this one. Garrett pushed too many of her boundaries. She left, not bothering to answer.

Ari wrapped her hands around a peppermint hot chocolate as she sat across from Reed in his room. Marco had never come home the previous night. Reed convinced her that it wasn't unusual for her brother to sleep in another room for the night. Ari shouldn't be sidetracked with her brother. Instead she focused on telling Reed how she saw the code and about the recruiter on their date last week.

Reed's countenance fell at the news. "Why didn't you tell me this last Friday?"

"I didn't tell anyone. I don't think I was ready to believe it myself."

He set down his drink and leaned back. "Wow ... you're a warper. You're sure?"

"Well, no, that's why I want to go in one more time."

"And you can't use the VR lab because ...?"

"Because then the school will know I'm a warper, and who knows what will happen next." Ari sighed in exasperation. They'd already gone over that before.

"I'm stupid, I guess. When you first asked about scheduling a VR on-site, I thought you wanted an unsupervised VR to be with me."

The thought had never crossed her mind—even though it was common for most couples.

The next second Reed acted as if the words had never left his mouth. "I thought warpers were a myth. If they worked for the government we would have heard about it, just another specification in our schooling. Maybe that Dave guy was making it up."

"Maybe, but something is going on with me, and I need to figure it out." An uneasy feeling turned her stomach as she thought of her unusual abilities.

"I understand. Maybe we could ask someone?"

"Garrett once said he knew a warper that went missing. He's ready to let me in. I need you to make sure the VR trip isn't being watched."

Reed sat up, and Ari realized it was the wrong thing to say.

"You already talked to Garrett?"

"He was there in the game with me when it happened at the Strip. I knew I needed him to get me in."

"Still ..."

Guilt settled in. In retrospect, she should have talked to Reed first. Things were going so well between them. She wanted to figure this out before it messed things up between them. Guess it had anyway.

Reed turned to face the screen on his desk. "It will

take a little bit of work to run an off-grid VR. They have built-in program alerts when we go off grid. It's easier to change the time or date, but I might be able to work something out."

"Thanks." Awkwardness settled in between them. "Do you want to do anything tonight?"

"I'm working with Garrett. Marco hasn't been around much, so I get the late shift tonight."

Ari bit her tongue as she almost asked if he wanted her there. If he did, he would have asked her. Reed focused on his computer.

It hurt to leave things between them like this, but it didn't seem like there was anything she could say. "I'll see you around."

"See ya." Reed faced his screen. Ari walked down the hall in stunned silence. She hadn't realized Reed would be that mad. Garrett had been right. That idea frightened Ari in more ways than one.

CHAPTER 22

The days went by uneventfully with homework, virtuals, and the usually derisive comments from Wake. Studying proved difficult as her mind kept traveling back to Reed and her supposed abilities. By the way Garrett acted, she felt like she might already know the answer about her being a warper. But what could she do about it? As much as she had initially hated the VR, she was slowly growing used to the idea of designing virtuals as a career. Dave's warnings rang in her ears though. She wanted a life on her terms, not anyone else's.

On Wednesday, Reed finally messaged her. He wanted to meet at the cafeteria for dinner. Ari agreed and went down early, thinking she could use the time to catch up on some reading.

She had her tablet out reading through an article with a drink in her hand when Reed slid into the chair beside her. His shoulder brushed against her, sending a chill down her spine. She had missed him.

"Hey." She smiled up at him.

"I think I found a way, but it will be tricky."

Ari swallowed. "I can work with tricky."

"We can try this Friday night. I'll work out some of

the details with Garrett."

He pushed his chair back as if to leave, but Ari caught his arm. She wasn't about to let the uneasiness between them grow.

"I'm sorry that I didn't tell you sooner. I was scared. I don't want things to—"

"It's Garrett," Reed spat out. "He's driven me crazy this year. I couldn't stand you being with him whether we were together or not. And you went to him before me." He turned his fiery stare at Ari. "I don't know what drives me crazier, that I'm actually jealous of him or that you are with him."

"Were," Ari corrected him. "It's been past tense for some time, and it'll stay that way. I needed his help. I know he was a jerk before—"

"Still is," Reed added. "Remember I work with him."

"Yes, but I need him, okay? This is sort of a big thing."

"I know." Reed reached across and grabbed Ari's hand.

His warm fingers tightened around hers. Her chest ached at the pain she caused him, and for the first time, she let herself acknowledge the fear that their relationship might end. Reed had been the one thing since coming to school that felt right, and she couldn't imagine a future without him.

"So, this Friday, you and me?" she asked hoping they could do this together.

"Yeah, this Friday. But I don't think I can wait for Friday for this." Reed leaned in to kiss Ari in a way that was probably inappropriate for public display, but neither of them cared.

Friday night there was another party starting later than usual, at one in the morning. They needed the party to be later for Reed, who was planning on deleting the footage in the system's weekly clean up. He also wanted several other students plugged in, just in case it didn't work. They were planning on switching the feeds, so it wouldn't track back to Ari even if they were caught.

Garrett told Ari he didn't like that part. He didn't like the chance that his whole business could be at stake. It had taken him two years to set up and some things he wasn't willing to sacrifice. Ari couldn't blame him.

Ari brought Tessa, because she could use the extra support, even if Tessa believed she was sneaking into another VR party. They walked off the trail, crunching over frozen grass. The bright moon helped to light their path.

"Sometimes I think these parties are all a big ruse," Tessa said as they approached the student center.

"Really?"

"Yeah, think about it. You really don't think the faculty notices twenty kids sneaking off to the virtuals every week or so?"

"We block our tracers though, and the bribe—"

"I know, I know. Truthfully, I think the faculty doesn't care. They want us to push the limits in the virtuals. Either way, I'm not complaining. But I don't think they are as naive as we think they are."

Ari hoped it wasn't true. She was counting on them being blind to what they were doing. She glanced at Tessa and wondered if she should tell her about being a warper. It's not like Tessa would say anything, heck she would probably give her advice. They arrived at the lab before Ari had a chance to talk to her. They went inside to find Garrett and Reed waiting at the door.

"Make it okay?" Reed placed an arm around her.

"Yeah."

A couple slid in behind them and went to pay Garrett. "Go ahead and pick your machines. The virtual is loaded if you want to start. Others will join you soon."

Tessa handed him a fifty.

"You don't have to—," Reed said, but Garrett interrupted him.

"Sorry, chap. I'm not really a good friend of your dear Ari anymore, and I've got bills to pay."

Ari rolled her eyes and before Reed could argue, Tessa cut them off.

"No worries. I got it," she said with a shrug and headed to a machine.

"You can plug in, Ari, but don't start getting freaky without me," Garrett said with a slight wink.

Ari knew he only made the comment to get a rise out of Reed.

"You aren't going in with her," Reed objected.

"You have to stay out here to wipe the files, and someone should be in there with Ari to make sure no one else notices."

"Tessa is in there," Reed pointed out.

"Does she know about Ari yet?"

They both looked at Ari, who shook her head.

"Sorry, dude. Don't worry. I'll take care of her."

"That's what makes me worried."

"I think I can take care of myself," Ari interrupted. "Don't you remember who ended up on top of our last fight?"

"Oh, yes, I remember." Garrett's smile grew as Ari realized what she had said might not have come across right.

"Whatever," she mumbled, trying to blow off his innuendo. She turned to Reed who didn't look happy. "I'll be fine, okay?"

He nodded slightly, unease obvious on his face. Ari leaned in and kissed him, ignoring Garrett's offhanded comment. Reed responded to her kiss with enthusiasm.

Ari reluctantly pulled back. "I'll be back soon."

Reed kissed her lightly on the lips. "Get in there and work your magic."

Her insides melted, and she didn't want to leave

reality. Knowing Reed was here for her meant the world. The fact that they were in a relationship made it even better.

Ari hadn't had the chance to talk to Marco or her mother about her problems yet. Marco was off busy doing whatever it was he did—which Ari worried would give her an ulcer. They texted back and forth several times, but their school schedules didn't offer a lot of free time, and messaging over the school's service made Ari nervous. But her mom? Well, Ari didn't want to have that conversation until she had a plan.

She hooked herself up. As the cold wire slipped into her port, the world around melted away.

She opened her eyes to a familiar ocean. It was the first VR that she took with Garrett. Although the moon was bright in the sky, unlike the last time she'd been here. She gritted her teeth, annoyed at him for picking this place.

Ari appeared in the same bikini and white sun dress as before. As she looked around, she noticed something new: a cabana and dance floor lit with tiki-torches. Other students were already ordering drinks and starting to fill the dance floor. She closed her eyes again and dressed herself in shorts and a shirt but kept her feet bare.

"I like the other outfit better," Garrett spoke close behind her, too close. "Let's go for a walk." Garrett headed towards the island away from the loud dance floor.

"Why this way?" Ari asked.

"So, no one catches you. They'll think we're looking for privacy for other reasons." He winked at Ari.

She gave him a dirty look. "I don't want them to think we're together."

"Don't worry. After that little exhibition kissing Reed, I'm sure they won't know what to think."

Ari kicked sand in his direction with her bare feet. "Very funny."

The vegetation thickened as the darkness settled in around them. The temperature dropped drastically, the cold seeping through her light shirt. Even the sand under their feet morphed into something new. Heavy palm branches littered the ground, cutting into her feet.

"Isn't this far enough? I can barely walk, let alone see where I'm going." Ari stopped, placing a hand on a nearby tree.

"Then why don't you do something about it?" he asked, his voice full of an arrogance that grated on Ari.

She had to remind herself he was doing her a favor. As she searched for code in the VR, the darkness covered anything she might see. "Why is this virtual so dark?"

"It was designed to keep you near the shore with the party. If we don't head back, we'll keep wandering and end up at the same spot." That made sense to Ari. These were called comeback loops in class. Every program had to have its limits.

She focused her attention on searching for the characters and numbers that lay beneath the surface of the VR. There they were, dark characters running all around her. As she focused on the code, it became clearer. The numbers and letters created the cold breeze blowing by, the shadows falling on the sand, and she could even read the branches under her feet.

The next task proved more difficult, since she wasn't sure how she'd done it before. A branch snapped nearby and broke her concentration. It was Garrett drawing near.

He lightly touched her arm. "Do you need help?"

Ari brushed his hand away. "Back off, Garrett."

"I remember last time we were in a slightly heated position when it happened."

Ari didn't need his help. "I remember you trying to kill me."

The warmth from his body radiated off him. His breath was a light breeze on her neck. "Only in a game, Ari. Not in real life. I think that's what you forget. Things you do here—they aren't real. They aren't the same. It's like a dream. There's no trouble with things that happen in a dream."

She closed her eyes, trying to ignore Garrett. The code still floated there in her mind, the sequence running faster than she ever thought possible to read. As her mind searched the code for the branches underfoot, it seemed to zoom in on what she needed. There it was. She mentally tore at the code, and it scattered. She found the code for the beach sand, and she copied and replaced it as if she had a computer screen in front of her.

Looking down, she wiggled her feet in the soft sand.

Garrett's feet appeared in front of her. "Nice."

"Stay put for a moment. I want to see what else I can do."

"Yes, ma'am," he said in mock salute.

Ari closed her eyes again, Garrett's presence still warm in front of her. The code for his warmth skittered across her vision, and then she remembered Garrett was plugged into a machine and really not that close to her. She started tearing down more code. It was as easy as deleting numbers on a screen. The hard part was putting something in its place. She brushed away some clouds, dismissed bush, and even took off Garrett's shoes.

"Hey, if that's how it's going to be, it's only fair if you undress yourself too," he said.

Ari ignored Garrett and kept searching the code. She had to know it well enough in her brain to add it into the sequence. The most she could do was put grass under their feet. She had completed that task countless times in school, so it was easy enough to recall.

When she opened her eyes, she found Garrett reclining shirtless.

"I didn't take off your shirt," Ari said.

He shrugged his shoulders and gave her a guilty smile.

"Whatever. We can leave. I think I have my answers."

Garrett stood up, shirt in hand, and they headed towards the party. "So how does it feel to be a super freak?"

"I don't know ... scary." Ari decided she needed to talk to her mother and figure out what was next. Maybe even Tessa would have some ideas. Ari had barely gotten used to school, and now this. The only silver lining would be the cash, and it sounded like a big lining.

As they reached the group, Ari noticed Tessa dancing with a guy. When the song ended, Tessa headed over.

Her eyes fell on Ari then Garrett, his shirt in his hands.

"Have fun?" Tessa's sarcasm spooned on extra heavy.

"Nothing happened. I promise," Ari snapped.

Garrett nudged her with his shoulder. "You can't say it was nothing."

"Shut up," Ari replied.

"Whatever. You're not the only fish in the sea." He started to leave but made it only two steps before he dissolved right before their eyes—something Ari had never seen before.

Ari turned to Tessa, whose eyes widened in surprise.

"Run, get out!" Tessa shouted as she closed her eyes and disappeared.

Ari opened her eyes to the darkness of the lab. People were unhooking and rushing out of the room. Before she could reach her cable, swift hands unplugged her.

"Hurry." Reed pulled her out of the chair. By the time she stood, bright lights filled the room.

A stern voice carried throughout the room. "Please stop or you will be restrained."

Ari froze, her grip tightening on Reed's hand, while several armed security guards filled the lab. Tessa stood next to the door with a guard at her side. Several other students were scattered throughout the room. Ari felt like she was falling, though her feet remained glued to the floor, and all she could think was: *What did they see?*

CHAPTER 23

A ri stood in front of the large wooden door that she remembered from her first day. Even then, she knew she never wanted to come here again. She stared at the brass knocker in the middle, knowing he was watching her. All the students captured had to speak to their advisors to receive their punishment, even if it was two in the morning.

"Come in," Advisor Williams's voice boomed from a speaker in the door.

Ari entered and eased into the old leather chair farthest from him, the same chair as last time. Even though it was the middle of the night, Advisor Williams was wide awake and impeccably dressed. He continued to work on his computer for a minute while Ari waited in silence, studying his painting. Golden wheat swayed in the wind as an old house made of wood stood in the corner. Back when they made houses of wood. The falling sun cast shadows of golds and purples on the landscape. When the advisor finally spoke, it made her jump.

"Do you know why I have an antique door?" His lips pressed in a grim line.

The question startled Ari, who held back what she

really thought that he was vain and old. Given her silence, he continued.

"It's to remember, Ms. Mendez. To remember. Before this age of automation, wireless living, and virtual reality, we had to open doors, usually with keys. They didn't slide open with a scan of your finger.

"This age has made many lazy. Why open doors when they fly open? Why read a book when you can watch one? Why work hard when you can go into a VR to reap all the benefits you never have earned? Why work hard at school when you don't have to pay for it?" He leaned forward, palms pressed together. "But you will have to pay for it, Ms. Mendez. Trust me, you will pay for it."

Pushing back the anger at his insults, the fear of her skills, and tired emotions, she responded. "I do work hard, very hard."

"Really?"

He turned back to his computer. With a click of a button, video filled one wall. Screens bigger than Ari flashed up with a video of the VR lab. There she was with Reed, kissing him goodbye before plugging in. Garrett seethed in the corner, watching them. Ari's stomach tightened, angry at Williams for watching this, watching them. If there was a camera in the lab without the students' knowledge, where else had cameras been placed? She couldn't help but wonder if he'd seen everything that had happened in the virtual.

"Sneaking out at one in the morning for this," he motioned to the screen, where Reed gave her one last kiss, "Isn't what I'd call working hard, Ms. Mendez. I will put a demerit in your file, and I will increase security in your dorm as well to prevent future occurrences. Remember, more than one demerit and I can submit your name to the review board for expulsion. You are dismissed."

Ari stood to leave, part of her grateful he didn't see her inside the VR and part of her angry at how he had treated her. Yes, she deserved to be punished. She'd snuck out, and broken the rules. She understood that she had to pay for that decision, but he didn't have to treat her like a third-rate citizen, watching her and Reed like a peeping Tom. Her fatigue loosened her tongue as she turned back.

"By the way, I work hard, harder than you know." She left his office not waiting for a response and hoped she didn't regret that later.

By the time Tessa and Ari were released the sun was on the rise. Ari couldn't remember the last time she watched a sun rise and wasn't too excited to see that one. Before reaching the dorm, Tessa motioned with her head and turned onto the path towards the lake. Ari let out a sigh. Her body was not in the mood for a walk at that time of the morning, but the guilt from the previous night hung over her. She shouldn't have invited Tessa, especially with what was at stake.

Tessa's dark wrinkled clothes looked out of place in the morning light as she sat down in the grass near the lake. Tessa crossed her legs in front of her, putting one large multi-colored boot on top of the other. The freezing morning wind pushed at Ari and she zipped up her jacket. Sitting next to her friend, Ari pulled at a stray bit of fake grass, playing with the plastic perfection.

"We need to talk in private." Tessa glanced around as if checking for others. "Who knows where they put recording devices."

Ari shivered, thinking back to the video she watched in Advisor Williams's office, and the key logger on her computer. She knew her roommate was right to be paranoid.

"What happened last night?" Tessa shoved an angry hand through her purple hair. "I thought something was wrong when you walked off with Garrett while Reed stayed out of the program. But I never thought it was bad enough to get us all caught."

Tessa had a right to be mad. Ari shouldn't have invited her. "I'm sorry you're in trouble. I didn't know that would happen."

"I don't care about the demerit. What happened with you?"

Ari swallowed realizing she needed to tell Tessa the truth. "I'm a warper."

Tessa froze for a moment and then narrowed her eyes. "What are you talking about?"

Ari struggled to find the words to explain. "I see code. Everywhere in the VR, running behind the optical illusions they present. Even the smell, though those are harder to nail down as they float everywhere."

"You see code?" Tessa spoke slowly.

"Yes. I first noticed it at the Grid. I met Garrett in the game and stripped his powers from him. That's probably why your dad was mad at you. Sorry." Ari glimpsed at Tessa's expression of disbelief, and then turned back to the lake. "I went in last night to confirm what I thought. Not only do I see code, but I can manipulate it as well. I'm able to change it at will, though I'm still working on that."

"You can change code from inside the program? It's true? Warpers are real?"

"I guess so. I'm not sure what I am." Ari threw the fake piece of grass into the lake. "I had someone approach me after our game on the strip. Someone must have seen what happened in the game."

Tessa gave a hearty laugh from deep within her belly. "No wonder my dad was so pissed. Random people have been questioning my stepmom. That's a good one."

"Glad to help you out. Problem is, now what do I do? The school is watching my every key stroke. Do I wait until they find out? What happens next?"

Tessa's face fell, all laughter gone. "I'm not sure. I'd lie low. I think there is a reason we don't know about warpers."

"I agree." Ari planned on talking to her mom over

Christmas break since she didn't trust her computer. She prayed the recruiter was wrong, and she could lie low for long enough.

CHAPTER 24

Ari welcomed Monday's classes along with the homework that kept her busy all week. It gave her mind a break from worrying about the future. Unfortunately, after tests were completed on Friday, the thoughts that had been lurking in the back of her mind returned with full force.

She couldn't get out of school, and she was required to work for the government after her three years of schooling in whatever position she was assigned. It could be at the North Pole. And there was no declining a government position. If she quit her schooling, her wages would be garnished at any other position she took. If she defaulted on payment, her mother's wages would be garnished, which her mother couldn't afford.

On the other hand, if she informed Advisor Williams of her gift or used her abilities in class, then she would be immediately transferred, leaving her friends and family. There was a reason no one really knew any warpers. Her other choice was to ignore her abilities in the VR. Not just for her schooling, but possibly for the rest of her life. And while it might not be the smartest choice, denial was the easiest choice.

If she didn't change, nothing else did either. She could stay at school with Reed and ignore the recruiter.

By Friday she was exhausted. The teachers gave them extra assignments to prepare for their end of term final before winter break. She was laying on her bed, reading her tablet, and trying to keep her eyes open, when she heard someone at the door. With headphones on and absorbed in her game, Tessa didn't hear their AI announce the visitor.

Ari answered, surprised to find Reed holding a flower. They had texted a lot throughout the week but hadn't talked since the night they got busted. Before he could speak, Ari wrapped her arms around him, breathing him in. She thought he had to study tonight, but she welcomed the surprise.

"I'll take that to mean you're happy to see me," Reed said.

"Definitely." She pulled him inside. Next to him, the stress and uneasiness of the past week melted away. All that mattered right now was the present.

Reed laid the flower on Ari's desk and then turned to her roommate. "Hi, Tessa."

Tessa pulled her headphones off one ear. "Hey, Reed. What are you up to?"

"Nothing, sick of studying. We all don't get to play games for class."

"I wish," Ari said. Marco and Reed often teased her for getting a placement that allowed her to be in VRs most of the time. Ari had never realized that playing was so much work.

Tessa stood up and stretched her legs, covered in silver jeans today. "I'm going to grab more caffeine. Want me to get you anything?"

"No thanks," Ari said shaking her head. Tessa was being polite, giving her space with Reed, and she appreciated it.

As soon as the door closed, Reed playfully tackled Ari

right onto her bed. After a few minutes of doing her new favorite thing in the world—kissing Reed—he pulled back to lie next to her. Reed's lips pressed together as if he had something to say.

"What is it?" She placed a hand on his face, loving the touch of his skin.

He leaned in and nuzzled her neck. "Have you decided what you're going to do?" he whispered, knowing that there was probably an audio bug on Ari's computer as well.

She kept him close, wishing they didn't have to have this conversation. "You mean besides pretending that it's not real and hoping it will all go away?"

"I was talking to some people about what the recruiter told you."

"Who?"

"Some friends that I've met online, gamers that I've known for years. It was untraceable."

"And?" She had a feeling he would be a lot happier if the news was better.

"They only had rumors, nothing too concrete. But they agreed that warpers are never acknowledged because they are too valuable. Companies and governments will kill to have a warper. They said if you have an outside offer, you should take it."

"But I can't." Her body tightened in frustration and she struggled to keep her voice down. "I have to pay back my loan, and I can't leave it for my family. I don't really have a choice, do I?"

When Reed didn't answer right away, Ari pushed him to tell her what he'd discovered.

"Most warpers drop off the grid in various ways, but it appears that those that go into government work are erased off the grid—permanently."

Ari stared blankly for a moment trying to understand what he meant. The government wouldn't kill warpers. They were worth too much. "Maybe they don't stay in touch with old nerdy gamers anymore," she reasoned.

"Maybe. It's the not knowing that is driving me crazy."

"Me too."

He tightened his hold on her, his body pressing against hers. His firm grasp grounded her.

She leaned into his chest. "I'll be careful in the VRs. We have time."

"Maybe we could talk to that guy again? You never know what he could work out."

"Maybe." Ari didn't want to think about it. Reed was acting more like a big brother than her actual brother who she hadn't heard from all week.

He tried to object, but Ari silenced him with her lips. At first, he resisted her attempt at distraction, but then surrendered and kissed her back with gusto. Her belly burned with desire. Every touch, every kiss ignited her senses, making her want more. It must be what a junkie felt like, never getting enough.

In between kisses, Reed mumbled, "We have time." Ari prayed they were right.

Over the next couple of weeks, she realized how difficult it was going to be to hide her gift for the rest of the year, much less for the years to come. In the VRs, she didn't have to search for the code anymore, it stood out plain as day, and the actual virtual easily faded in the background. When she spotted errors, she had to resist the urge to fix them right away and then remember to fix them in the program.

Her favorite class turned out to be art design with Ms. Mienka. Ari didn't have to create the drawing, but just manipulate the images. She thought of all of the drawings and sketches Reed had hanging in his room, and how amazing it would be to see those drawings brought to life. Her thoughts of Reed were interrupted by a message on her HUB asking her to go to the wellness clinic after class.

Wellness clinic? Ari had never needed to go there before and wasn't sure what they wanted with her.

Professor Mienka continued to lecture while Ari's thoughts raced. Ari checked her HUB again and messaged Reed.

Wellness clinic asked me to come by after class. Any ideas?

Her foot tapped nervously against the floor. It was probably an annual checkup, she told herself. Her HUB flashed Reed's reply.

Girl stuff???

Ari rolled her eyes, even though he might be right. Maybe it was to check her implant for mandatory birth control—required for all underage girls and boys. Embarrassed, she wished she hadn't brought it up to Reed.

After class, she made her way to the student center amid the noisy and hungry students fighting their way to the cafeteria. Soft flakes fluttered around her. The first snow of the season seemed to add to the excitement. Ari smiled as she turned heavenward to the white chaotic sky. At home, snow was rare. It was more ice and sludge, lining the sidewalks early in the winter and hung around like a muddy border outlining everything during the cold bleak months. But here, the grounds were always kept immaculate. It might turn into a beautiful winter.

The snow distracted her from her curiosity about the appointment. As she walked through the entrance to the wellness center, she was caught off guard when greeted by Advisor Williams.

"Enjoying yourself?" His lips curled up into a cruel smile, while his eyes remained fierce.

"It's snowing," Ari answered, a bit thrown off. *What was he doing here?*

"I'm glad you noticed. Have you spoken to your brother recently?"

"No." Ari shook her head, trying to think back to their last conversation. They'd messaged several times back and forth since the weekend they were busted in the virtual.

He'd given her a hard time about turning into a rebel. They'd even talked about going home over break. She tried to tie him down for dinner to tell him about being a warper, but he was always too busy. Ari assumed it was another girl, or just hoped it was.

"Follow me." Williams turned briskly and headed down a hall.

Her stomach tightened in fear as she plodded after him. Where was Marco? Was he hurt? He was always the one to be reckless.

Williams wasn't giving anything else away as he stepped inside the room and waited for Ari. When she walked in, there was Marco, lying peacefully on a bed as if he was asleep.

Ari bit her lip and blinked back a burning feeling in her eyes. She stood there not wanting to move closer. If she touched him, reality would slap her in the face.

"He's in a virtual dependent coma."

Ari knew, deep down she already knew, that this would happen one day, but as Advisor Williams said those words, her heart broke. Her family was shattering into pieces, and she stood helpless. Darkness crept in, and it wasn't until strong hands touched her that she remembered her surroundings.

"Advisor Williams, grab that chair." A stout nurse helped Ari sit down. "You really could have been a bit more tactful when telling her." The nurse spoke over her head to Advisor Williams.

"We have treated these children with white gloves for long enough. They are expected to be adults and need to start acting like it."

"Even an adult wouldn't handle this well."

"Her father has been hooked for years. This is familiar territory for her."

The nurse's voice was softer than before. "It may be familiar, but it doesn't make it easy." The nurse turned to Ari. "Ms. Mendez?"

It took a few moments, but she blinked and turned her head towards the nurse. She had an older face, a kinder face, with bright pink lips.

"Your brother was at a VR bar in the city. They called us when they couldn't wake him. He's resting but still hasn't woken up."

"Are you going to feed him?" Fear coursed through Ari. Her brother could starve to death and neither Ari nor her mother had the money to feed him. They would have to find money somewhere.

The nurse placed a heavy hand on her shoulder. "Of course, we will."

Ari searched for the tubes, the plastic lines that Marco would need to survive. When she was unable to find them, the nurse showed her the tubes tucked neatly under his blanket.

"Ms. Mendez," Advisor William's harsh voice spoke behind them. "I have been unable to contact your mother, and we have some information to go over now that his placement is in question."

The nurse stood straight with her hand on her hip. "Really, Advisor Williams? She is in no state to go over any of that. And there is a chance he could wake up in the morning."

Of course, Ari knew this. Seventy percent of people that didn't wake up after being unplugged would wake up after their body went through its normal sleep rhythm. It had happened often with Ari's father, until one day it didn't. Like her father, some people subconsciously created their own VR, not willing to come back to reality.

"Fine," Advisor William said with an indignant huff. "But with this sort, things never work out in the long run." And with those uplifting words, he left.

Ari moved closer, sitting on Marco's bed. She grasped his hand through the light blankets, as if she could pull him back to reality. But she knew all too well that it didn't work that way.

CHAPTER 25

Ari woke to someone shaking her shoulder. She'd fallen asleep sitting in a chair with her head on Marco's bed. She blinked several times, clearing her vision of the scratchy code that filled her dream. With all the studying and stress, she wouldn't be surprised if she bled in code.

"Ariana, dear, it's your mother," said Nurse Carey.

Ari wiped the sleep from her eyes. For a few blissful moments of unconsciousness, she had forgotten about Marco being stuck in a virtual. Reality lay heavily on her shoulders as she stood and headed towards the nurse's station.

Nurse Carey led her to her desk. Ari's mother was on the screen, eyes red and puffy.

"I told your mother the situation," Nurse Carey said softly. "I'll leave you two alone for a moment." Her shoes squeaked against the floor and with the whoosh of the door, a silence entered the room, threatening Ari's sanity.

Ari swallowed. There was so much she wanted to say—wanted to scream really—but she held it in. If she opened the flood gates, they might never close.

Her mother broke the silence first. "They are going to

send Marco home if he isn't awake by the end of the week."

"How?" Ari said. "You can't afford to pay for both Marco and Dad."

"Nurse Carey told me I can take a loan out against your education. You'll have to pay it back once you graduate."

Ari bit her lip and nodded. "Okay." She would do whatever it took to save Marco, which sparked her next decision. "I'm going in." Often when people were in VR comas, loved ones would go in to help convince them to return to reality. It didn't work with their father, but it might with Marco.

Ari's mother shoulders sagged. "I hoped you would. It might even be free compared to doing it in the clinic. But be prepared, Ari, that he might not want out."

"I don't care. I'll drag his lazy—"

"That won't help. Remember you play by Marco's rules in there not yours. I've tried enough times with your father, God knows, to no avail."

Ari knew that was true, and it cost more than a normal VR since they had to pay the medical staff to hook her father up to a VR. After missing Christmas for a couple years, her mother finally decided to spend the money on the living.

The hatred she had for her father resurfaced like a wave of heat through her body. She wanted to punch something, or someone. Something to make this fair. But that was the wish of a child. Life was never fair.

"I'll see if they can let me do it today." Ari glanced at the time and realized it was six in the morning.

"Call me after, okay? You can wake me. I don't think I'll be sleeping much anyway."

"I'll call or message you soon."

"Thanks, Ari. For being there and taking care of this. I can't leave work."

"I know." Ari clicked off the screen before the sob

stuck in her throat escaped.

Her HUB soon vibrated with another message. There were several from Reed and one from Tessa. She started to message them back, but her fingers hovered over the keyboard, unsure of what to say. *My brother is hooked just like my loser dad?* Reed might not care, but it wasn't any less embarrassing. She finally settled on messaging Reed: *Marco's sick. I'll be with him for a while.*

A heaviness settled into her bones as Nurse Carey changed out his feeding bag. Ari wondered if the nurse had slept at all. Her short brown hair was perfectly curled, and her lips colored pink. Her hands were quick and experienced as she hooked up the new feeding tube before she turned to Ari. "Now that he is fed, how about getting something for you?"

"I want to be hooked up with my brother."

If Nurse Carey was surprised she didn't show it. "That may be a possibility, but it won't happen until after breakfast. You already missed dinner. What kind of medical personnel would I be if I let you starve?"

"Can I go in if I eat?"

Before Nurse Carey could answer, Advisor Williams walked in the door.

"Go in where?"

"I want to go in the VR with my brother."

"Why would the school do that? It's a waste of precious time and resources."

"To wake him up, of course." Ari's hands clenched at her side. She couldn't believe this man's indifference. She was grateful Nurse Carey interrupted before she really told him how she felt.

"It would save on costs in the long run, Advisor. I'm willing to set it up in here."

"Has his mother signed the paperwork?"

"I sent it over. She will sign it before she leaves for work in a few hours."

Irritation was written all over his face as he knew

Nurse Carey had the upper hand. "Fine, but only after we receive the paperwork. And after Ari's classes."

"What? I'm not going to class."

"We pay for them, so yes you are. Only medically excused absences will not be marked as demerits in your record. Or are you more like your brother than we thought? He didn't care much for attendance either."

Nurse Carey put a hand on Ari's shoulder, her touch steady and warm. "She will be fed first, and then she'll go to her class. It will take me a bit to get a VR unit in here, anyway."

Advisor Williams gave a curt nod then left the room.

Ari wasn't sure if she wanted to hit him or scream. Instead she sunk down on the foot of Marco's bed in exhaustion.

"Ignore that old crow, dear, and let me get you some coffee."

"I wish I could," Ari said. Williams held the key to her future in more ways than one. He would find her placement after her schooling was done. And so far, it wasn't looking good. He also had the power to kick her out and make her life a mountain of student debt with no way of getting out of it. Schooling was free as long as you finished with a passing grade and worked at a government assigned position afterwards.

She could only focus on Marco. He had to be okay. She needed him. And somehow, she would find a way to let him know.

The nurse pushed a warm cup of coffee into her hands. "Drink up. You have a long day ahead of you."

Ari nodded, numbly. She savored the bitter taste of the coffee warming her. "Do you think he will wake up?"

"Probably. He's young with a lot to live for. Though you may have to remind him of that."

"That's what I worry about." Ari stared into Marco's innocent face with his hair sticking up all over. She hoped she could offer enough of the real world to lure him out of

DeAnna Browne

his virtual one. As much as Ari detested it, maybe living in a virtual was easier, a carefree escape she almost wished she could enjoy.

"Take the coffee with you so you can make it to breakfast. You have to have something besides caffeine."

Ari didn't want to eat, but she needed out of there, especially if she had to go to class. She picked up her bag with her tablet that had been periodically beeping inside since she had silenced the HUB on her wrist hours ago. Not ready to talk to anyone, she silenced the noise, swung the bag over her shoulder, and headed to the door.

As the door swooshed open, Nurse Carey said, "Answer your interface, Ariana. Your friends are worried about you."

Ari just kept walking.

She grabbed a breakfast shake and headed to her dorm room in hopes of a shower before her first class at eight.

"Are you going to ignore me all day?" Reed's biting words came from behind. She wasn't exactly sure why she'd ignored his other messages. Embarrassment, maybe. Denial and the hope her brother would wake up this morning was more likely.

"So, you know?" Ari turned around, and once she glimpsed his hurt face, guilt punched her in the gut. "I'm sorry."

"Nurse Carey told me." His eyes, dark and heavy, spoke of his own restless night. "Why didn't you tell me?"

"I ..." She dropped her gaze. She was tired, and not ready to answer. Anger, guilt, and hurt overflowed, and she couldn't keep it in any longer. "What was I supposed to say? My loser brother got hooked like my deadbeat dad. Who knows, maybe I'll be next?" Ari yelled, not caring who heard.

Reed paused for a moment, shock perhaps. His face softened, and he stepped forward closing the distance

196

between them. His presence warmed away her frustration—a relief that she didn't deserve.

"Do you honestly believe I would think that? Because my dad took off and yours is in a VR coma, does that make any difference? I have lived for the past two years with Marco. He's like a brother to me."

Tears pooled in her eyes. She dabbed at her eyes, knowing he was right. He understood in a way no one else would. She kicked herself for doubting him, again. She lifted her chin. "So, what does that make us?"

A grin slowly crept on Reed's face. "A very twisted family?" He encompassed her with his arms, and she melted into them.

She didn't realize how tired and alone she had felt until he held her.

"Don't worry, though, I never thought of you as a sister," Reed whispered into her neck.

She reluctantly stepped back. "I better shower and get ready for class."

"Are you going?"

"Williams didn't give me much of a choice."

"That guy's a moron." Reed grabbed her hand, and they walked to her dorm.

"It's okay. Hopefully it will keep my mind off things. I can't go in until this afternoon."

Reed stopped, abruptly pulling Ari back to face him. "You're going in?"

"Of course. They'll let me do it here for free before they send him to a center where my mom will have to pay."

"Why doesn't your mom come and do it?"

"She can't get off work." Ari lowered her eyes only briefly. She wasn't sure why her family situation bothered her. Reed had been to her house enough to know, and it's wasn't like his family was a whole lot better off. But his mom only had to work one job, and it was enough so that they didn't ever go hungry.

"Then I'll do it," Reed offered.

"Williams barely approved of me going in. Why does it matter?" Being tired, it took Ari a minute to connect the dots.

"I'm worried with your new abilities, that you'll be tempted."

"If you're telling me to hide my abilities and leave my brother in there, I can't do it." Ari had to admit she was thankful Reed had suggested it. She hated to tell him that she hadn't thought of it before. Maybe there was some way to change Marco's virtual to help him come out.

Reed must have sensed her thoughts. "Can you help him when he gets out if you get shipped out of here?"

"We're not even sure if changing the VR will help him."

"I mean it, Ari. I don't think Marco or I want to finish the year without you. Please don't."

"It'll be fine," Ari said and placed another quick peck on his lips.

"You don't know that," he said. "I have a lab today during your lunch, but I'll meet you in the wellness clinic after classes."

"You don't have to—"

"I'll meet you there." Reed cut her off before she could finish and then headed to class.

She watched his tall, slim frame walk away through the crowd. A cold breeze made Ari shiver, sending her inside.

Ari made it to her dorm to find Tessa pulling her purple hair into a high pony tail. She threw her bag on a chair and headed to the closet. She probably should at least change before she headed to class.

"Where have you been?" Tessa turned to face Ari. "I thought if you had a wild night you'd be in a better mood."

"No wild night."

Tessa grabbed her hand and made Ari sit down on her bed. "What happened? You're still in the same clothes, and you look like a walking zombie."

"Thanks," Ari said, sarcastically.

Tessa shrugged.

"It's Marco," Ari said. She swallowed, not sure the words wanted to come out of her mouth. But after the episode with Reed, she realized she didn't need to do this alone. "He's in a virtual coma."

Tessa pulled back for a moment, surprise painted her face. "Really? I'm sorry."

"Thanks." Ari rubbed a hand over her face, wishing she could wake up from the nightmare. "I'm going in this afternoon, to try to get him out."

Tessa's brows rose, acknowledging what exactly that meant without saying it. They both knew their room wasn't secure. "You sure?"

Ari nodded.

Tessa paused for a moment before continuing. "I can ask around and see if anyone knows anything, even do some research for the project we talked about."

Ari read between the lines and realized Tessa referred to Ari using her newfound abilities in the VR. "Aren't you worried about people listening in?"

"We've had our own code for communicating in games," Tessa said with a wink. "I gotta head out, but I'll let you know what I find."

"Thanks."

With no time for a shower, she grabbed a new shirt and noticed something sticking out, Dave's business card. Someone who knew more about her abilities than she did. Calling him might not be a great idea, but she'd passed great ideas hours ago.

She called Garrett on the way to class to ask him about a safe way to call Dave. She would have asked Reed, but he hadn't wanted her to use her abilities in the VR. Garrett didn't answer, so she clicked off her ear piece and wrapped it around her finger.

Ari made it to class as the last bell rang. Her teacher, who Ari and Tessa secretly referred to as Dr. Toadstool, was at his podium, already lecturing with the notes projecting behind him.

She opened her tablet and started recording her professor's lecture. Her concentration was shot, and she knew she needed a backup. Still thinking about her brother, she messaged Garrett.

I need to talk to you on break.

She struggled to follow the lecture on plotting with multiple story lines. She was surprised that she received a return message so soon.

Last time we talked I ended up getting a demerit on my transcript.

Reed and Garrett had gotten into a lot of trouble when the school busted their VR party. It would probably affect their placement at graduation the following year. Reed said they both knew what they were getting into, but that was Reed. She didn't think Garrett had taken it as well, and she hadn't talked to him since. Determined to save her brother, she refused to feel guilty, and messaged Garrett.

I wouldn't ask if it wasn't important. Marco is in a VR coma.

And I should care why?

Ari bit her lip in frustration. *I'll owe you.*

You already owe me.

He was right. She did owe him already and didn't have any way to pay him back. She pulled her hair into a pony tail, trying to figure out her next move. She would call Dave at lunch. Maybe Tessa would let her use her phone. The school couldn't be watching every student's phone, could they?

Before she could close her messaging interface, another message flew across her screen.

Meet me for lunch. I'll figure out some way you can pay me.

Ari wasn't sure if she should worry but figured anything Garrett could come up with couldn't be as bad as things were already. She hoped at least.

Before class was done, Tessa texted that she'd hit a dead end with her research on warpers and VR comas. As Ari exited her class for their lunch break, she realized that moment would be her only chance to talk to Dave. Wrapped in her jacket, she made her way to the student center to meet Garrett. Waiting near a bench, she pulled out the card. Maybe if she called Dave they could talk without giving too much away. She turned the ring around her finger, considering it.

With her distracted thoughts, she didn't see Garrett approach, soda in hand. "You wanted to talk?" Annoyance and disdain colored every word. "This better be good. I'm dreaming up complex and morally reprehensible ways you can pay me for this favor."

This so wasn't worth it. Ari would just borrow someone else's phone. "I can't play your games anymore."

"My game? Really?" He stepped closer. "You dump me, then hook up with a friend and continue calling me for help. Remind me, whose game is this?"

"That's not how I meant for this to happen." Ari had to admit, it looked bad.

"But here we are." He gave her a condescending smile. Ari wondered how she'd ever found that cute.

"I don't need your help anymore. It's not worth it." Ari turned to leave, but Garrett grabbed her arm.

"It is. Trust me." His voice was softer, and the sneer left his lips. This was the Garrett Ari remembered on the first day of school—too bad he was so often covered in layers of supercilious slime.

With a sigh, she sat on the bench. "I need to make a call, an untraceable call."

He nodded and sat next to her. "There's an Internet number you can dial into that will distort your signal. The site changes its IP address frequently to avoid detection.

But if you know how to find it, you're gold."

"Really?" Ari wasn't sure whether to believe him.

"Yeah. If they trace you, they will be going all around the world." He grabbed her HUB and dialed in the digits. Ari slipped in her ear piece and waited for Garrett to push send. "Payment first."

Ari huffed in exasperation, "Okay. What is it?"

"Sleep with me."

"What?" Ari's jaw dropped, and it must have looked ridiculous, judging by the laughter erupting from Garrett. "Get lost." She pushed him lightly, and he laughed harder.

"Sorry, I couldn't resist." He ran a hand through his messy hair.

"Glad I could give you a good laugh."

Once his laughter died, he straightened up, his face serious. "I want a favor once you're out of here."

"What kind?" Ari asked with hesitation, not wanting to leave it open to anything.

"Remember, you're going to be worth a lot. I want to be able to contact you, maybe ask for an in with a job or something."

"I'll do whatever I can." That sounded easy compared to the other things she had facing her. Thinking of Garrett though, she wanted to make sure she covered herself. "But I'm not doing any weird sexual VR stuff, okay?"

"Don't worry, you wouldn't be any good at it anyway." Ari wasn't sure if she should be insulted or not.

Garrett hit call and stood to leave. "Good luck," he said as he strolled off towards the student center.

Ari's hands shook from cold, or maybe nerves, as the phone buzzed in her ear. She nervously scanned for people who might eavesdrop on her conversation. One couple huddled nearby at a table, but, otherwise, the courtyard was empty. The weather must have chased everyone indoors.

"Hello?" a man's voice answered.

"Is this Dave?"

"And this is?"

"Ari. We met before over antique books."

"Where are you calling from, Ari? Is this line secure?"

"My friend dialed through a line that is supposed to be untraceable."

His voice noticeably relaxed. "Good girl. Are you ready to go to work?"

Ari bristled against being treated like a canine, but she needed help. "Can a warper manipulate a VR to help people in VR induced comas?"

There was a pause in the line. Fear struck Ari for a moment. She had assumed Dave would help. It had never crossed her mind that he would refuse, especially given that he hoped for her employment.

He spoke deliberately, like a father whose child has been caught in over her head. "You better start from the beginning."

"I don't have time to explain," Ari said, which was partially true as lunch ended in twenty minutes. She really didn't want to go into the details of her family's horrid past with a stranger.

"Then the answer is maybe."

Ari straightened up. She could work with maybe.

"See the thing is, people that are hooked are in a sensitive condition and there isn't any research in the area."

"But you said maybe—"

"I know. As a warper, you have a special ability to change their surroundings, especially if you know them. This helps you motivate them to realize they are still in the program. The problem is if you push them too hard they might retreat to their own world. Sometimes even if they are hooked in a program with you, they don't see it. They see what they want to see, and live in the world they want to live in. They don't want out, Ari."

It wasn't a lot, but it was enough. "Thanks for your help, Dave. I really appreciate it." Ari reached up to end the call.

"Wait, Ari," Dave's voice sounded urgent.

Ari's hand paused over her ear piece.

"Is the medical VR you're going into secure?"

The pause in Ari's voice told him the answer.

"Then don't do it. If you're caught, this will probably be the last conversation we ever have. If you join our company, you will be in a better position to help your friend."

"It's not a friend. It's my brother, and I can't wait. The longer he's in there the more likely he won't come out. It's been over twenty-four hours as it is. I'm sorry but I have to go."

"Please call me again—"

Ari clicked off the phone in the middle of Dave's reply. For the first time she wished she could run away. Find a job and forget the responsibilities of her family, money, and everything else. That daydream didn't last more than a second because she had to get to class. Advisor Williams would be keeping a close eye on her.

Ari made it through the rest of her classes, though she thought she would go mad. During class she searched through the electronic library archives about gifted programmers without typing in the name warper. She only found a few excerpts about warpers, even though they weren't called that. One old text referred to a gifted student using cerebral programming. It didn't tell her anything she didn't already know. She was surprised to find they even called the practice 'unsupported' and 'lacking enough empirical data to prove it productive'.

After class, Ari hurried to the wellness center. The wind cut straight to her core, and she wished she'd brought a heated coat. The clouds overhead made promises of snow and Ari felt homesick. On chilly days, she would eat popcorn and cuddle under a heated blanket with a book. Even Marco used to join in, acting out the characters in absurd dialects.

She missed Marco and hated herself for letting this happen. While she was off making out with Reed, Marco was hooked up to a machine wishing it was his real life. She found Reed outside the wellness center, holding a bag.

"Hi, I thought you might need something." He offered her the small bag and a cup.

Ari knew she should eat, but she wanted to see her brother. "I don't think I could stomach anything,"

"At least try the tea. Nurse Carey said she is finishing up some paperwork and will get us when she's done."

Ari took the cup. "Thanks. Is Advisor Williams here yet?"

"No. Should he be?"

"I hope not. I got enough of his pleasantries this morning."

"I would think so."

They sat in orange metal chairs outside the doorway of the wellness center. She drank the warm tea while Reed nervously picked at his jeans.

She could tell he wanted to talk. "What is it?"

"I don't want you to go in there. I can do it for you. I spoke to Nurse Carey already."

Ari didn't want to fight. She was too exhausted. "You know I have to do it right?"

"You think you do." His stubborn gaze bore into hers.

Yes, she would rather not do this, and before starting school, she would have taken Reed up on his offer. But she could do things Reed couldn't, and despite the unknown consequences, she had to try.

Ari leaned into Reed and wrapped her arms around him, his familiar musky scent enveloping her. She leaned her head into his neck as she whispered, "You know I do."

CHAPTER 26

O nce inside the VR, the smell of alcohol and the soft drone of conversation greeted Ari. A mass of people littered the shiny VR bar. It was Reed's idea, actually. When you plug in a comatose person, the virtual needed to be something that seemed plausible for the patient's brain to accept. Otherwise, they rejected the scenario and continued in their own made-up world, unable to let others in.

Reed knew that Marco had been to this VR before. The dark bar glittered with tiny white lights hanging from the ceiling. When Ari looked closely, the binary code ran down each light. Eerie shadows scattered on the faces of the people in the bar. It took only a moment to realize the first fallacy, as Dr. Coleman called it. Every one of the programmed people was extremely attractive. All could pass for models, even those that dressed down a bit.

No offense to her brother's looks, but he easily stood out in the crowd. He sat perched on a stool at the end of a long bar, looking a touch befuddled. Ari took a deep breath then headed towards him.

"A couple more of those," Ari told the bartender motioning to the colored drinks that a couple of nearby girls were holding. "Even though you don't look like you need it," Ari said to Marco.

"I guess." He shook his head slightly. "Hey, Ari. When did you get here?"

"A few minutes ago. I was held up at school."

"School?"

"Of course. You go on vacation and already forget about it?" It surprised Ari at how easily the lies came pouring out of her mouth.

"I guess I'm more drunk than I thought." Despite his statement, when his drink arrived he gulped most of it down.

"Yeah, do you want to head back to campus?" Ari asked kindly as she stifled her desire to hug him and drag him out by his ear.

"Hell, no. I should at least hit another VR before they shut down." He scanned the crowd. His gaze lingered on a pair of girls.

"Hey, why don't we do one together?"

Marco cocked an eyebrow.

"I thought it would be nice to hang out. We never spend time together anymore." With the way Marco looked, Ari was sure going in a VR to talk was not what Marco had in mind.

"You gonna pay? Because I usually find some needy girl to pay for me."

Ari couldn't restrain herself and smacked him on the arm. "Don't be a pig."

"What? They want company. I'm low on cash. Nobody complains."

Ari remembered the missing money from her account. "You're the one who took my money."

He rubbed an invisible spot on the table. "I planned on paying you back. I swear." Lifting his eyes, they held guilt and regret.

Unable to muster the energy to be mad, Ari welcomed the drink from the bartender and took a sip. "Yes, yes you will."

Ari pushed back the urge to hit him and focused at the job on hand. "If you walk me home, I'll invite you to Tessa's condo next weekend."

"Really?" Marco's brow creased as if doubtful at first, but then after a moment shrugged and stood up straightening his jeans. Dark, heavy circles hung under his eyes. Despite wearing sharp clothes and hair, he appeared drawn and tired. Ari was surprised that would show in a virtual when in the real world his body was healthy.

"Thanks." Ari fell in step with him as they headed towards the exit. They cleared the bar and started back towards the school, the empty sidewalks lined with animated advertisements.

"You look like hell, Marco," Ari stated as she watched him closely.

He shrugged. "Thanks for the love."

"What's going on?" Ari bit back her real question of why he wanted to run away from life to some artificial version of it.

He stopped and stared at her. "I don't feel like a lecture from my little sister. Okay? So, if that's what this is, then walk yourself home."

"Sorry. I'll stop." As Marco stared at her, Ari searched for something, anything she could say that wouldn't push her brother away. "It's Reed."

"What about Reed?"

"I wanted to make sure you were okay with us going out together."

Finally, Marco started walking again, and Ari let out a heavy breath.

"I was a little shocked at first," Marco said. "But he's Reed. He's a great guy from our old neighborhood. Better than shacking up with one of these geeks."

"Thanks, Marco." Ari had never asked for his blessing or permission, but it was nice to know he approved.

"Don't end up making out in our room, okay? I don't

think I can handle walking in on that."

"Don't worry, my bed is fine," Ari joked, prompting an appalled look from Marco.

"Better watch it. I'm not past calling Mom."

"Yeah, that'll be the day. *You* actually ratting me out." Growing up it was always Marco getting into trouble and getting called into the principal's office. Marco was always the wild one and Ari the scared one, according to the neighbors.

They finally crossed through campus security and headed onto the pristine campus as the lights flickered on.

Ari slowed as they approached her dorm. "You know you have to go back to school, right?"

"We're already at school."

"I mean *really* be at school."

His gaze lowered with a heaviness that made Ari realize that reality was slowly setting in for him.

"I know," he said with a pained expression that soon turned angry. "I have to graduate and get a job that I hate for the rest of my life to support my poor mom and crazy dad."

"Would you rather stay hooked and let your sister and mom take care of your withered body?" It hurt Ari to imagine Marco becoming like her father.

"At least I'd be happy—blissfully happy—not in a career, doing a job I never wanted to do in the first place." His eyes filled with tears. Tears Ari hadn't seen since him cry since he'd broken his arm when he was ten.

"Are you happy?" she asked. "You know you're still in here, right? Hooked to a program and still feeling the guilt from it all."

Marco remained silent, unable to answer. His lips formed a strong crease as if he could hold everything in.

"You have to leave here. Mom needs you. I need you." The fear grew in her. She would change this whole virtual into a living inferno that even the devil would be impressed with, if she had to. Anything to get Marco back.

He wouldn't speak to her. He turned his back, and for a moment Ari thought she was going to lose him. She watched as his shoulders heaved with a burden Ari couldn't see. Then he slowly disappeared before her eyes.

Ari thought she would be happy that she'd been able to pull him out without using any of her warper abilities. Instead, a hollow ache grew in her stomach after seeing her brother so depressed and discontented with his own life. He was supposed to be fun and crazy Marco. She willed herself out of the VR and wondered what kind of Marco would be there when she returned.

He didn't have much to say when Ari went to his bedside. Reed tried to joke with him, but Marco ignored his attempts. Nurse Carey kept the atmosphere in the room positive as she buzzed around taking his vitals and ordering his meal.

"Hey, why don't I go grab some dinner, and we can eat here with you?" Ari offered.

Reed stood. "I can get it."

"No," Marco said firmly, avoiding their gazes.

"It wouldn't be much trouble. We can be back in a bit," Ari said, a bit confused at Marco's new attitude.

Nurse Carey interrupted, "Why don't we let our patient rest for a while? You two can come back in the morning."

Ari looked to Marco again to see if that was really what he wanted. He lowered his eyes, starting at his hand, the one with a needle attached.

"We'll check in with you later, bro," said Reed. "You have your HUB in case you need us. Call, okay?"

"Sure." Marco kept his eyes lowered. Reed had to pull Ari's arm to exit the room. She wanted to stay, to fix him somehow. She thought getting him out would be the hardest part, but now she wondered if that was true.

"I'll get your dinner and be back in a minute, sweetie."

Nurse Carey followed Reed and Ari out of the room.

Ari stopped her once they were out of the wellness center. "What's wrong with him?"

The woman took a deep breath and adjusted a curl in her hair. "Hon, why do you think people get hooked in the first place?"

Ari tried not to resent being spoken to as a child. "Because they don't want to live in the real world."

"Yes. And even if they come back, it doesn't mean they want to be here anymore. It's usually because of guilt that they return."

Ari flashed back to her conversation with Marco, knowing what the nurse said was true.

Nurse Carey continued, "He's depressed, which is a common symptom of what he has been through. He will need counseling and will probably be suspended for a period of time."

"Suspended? But he did nothing wrong."

"He abused the VR systems. And being here with an open VR facility for students like him isn't good. Advisor Williams will inform your mother of the specifics and advise her if there is a chance of his re-admittance."

Ari took a step backwards, not wanting to believe what the nurse was saying. Marco was getting kicked out of school?

Nurse Carey put a hand on her arm. "It's like a lot of other addictions. They are not cured in a day."

Ari knew Nurse Carey was right. She'd watched her father for years as a little girl, but she couldn't believe it was happening with Marco. She couldn't watch another family member slowly deteriorate into a life that wasn't even living.

CHAPTER 27

The next morning, Marco was quiet over breakfast, finding his eggs more interesting than talking to either Ari or Reed. His friend started to give him a hard time, but Ari silenced him with a hand. Marco didn't know what Ari almost risked, and he didn't need to. Not then.

Ari leaned down to hug him goodbye, a gesture he weakly returned. "Give a hug to Mom for me."

"Sure," Marco mumbled. It killed Ari to watch her brother like this. The life he always had in him, the joking, the love, was gone. Was it even real?

He barely looked Reed in the eyes as he patted his arm. "See you soon at Christmas break."

"Okay."

They left with Nurse Carey's reassurances that this post-VR depression was normal, and he should be feeling better by Christmas.

"Want to meet up for dinner?" Reed asked, once they exited the wellness center. "I have my study group at lunch again. Everyone's stressed about end of term exams." He was finishing his third year, and Ari knew how important his scores were. The tests determined where he would be placed for his internship, and eventually how much money he could make.

"Sure, okay," Ari said, distracted by worries of Marco.

"I've got to go to class." He grabbed Ari's hand. "He's going to be okay."

"You don't know that."

Reed was silent for a moment before agreeing. "You're right, but even if he's not, we'll deal with it."

Ari nodded. "I can't be late to class." Reed let go of her hand, and Ari hurried towards her dorm that held so much of what she hated: virtuals.

No wonder we have lock-downs, she thought. *This place might be worth blowing up.*

By the next week, Marco headed home, and Mom said he was doing well, whatever that meant. Ari focused on school, spending time with Reed whenever possible. Saturday night, Reed came over to watch a movie on Tessa's over-sized screen. They cuddled up on Ari's bed, while Tessa sprawled out on hers. They passed around cartons of ice cream, trying to convince each other which one was the best.

"Everyone knows chocolate is practically a food group by itself," Ari argued.

"If you're like every other girl in world. Peanut butter and cherries? Now that's a tasty variety," Tessa replied.

Tessa had been kinder since Ari told her that her brother had been sent home. Tessa had never brought it up again, even though Ari often heard the gossip around campus. She appreciated her roommate. Sometimes friends didn't have to talk, they could just be.

Reed set his spoon down and silently traced Ari's arm, leaving it with a tingling sensation Ari loved. As they watched a fantasy movie with vampires tearing each other to shreds, Ari's thoughts kept returning to Reed, his body wrapped around hers. Ari would love nothing more than to have his arms around her all night.

Soon the movie faded, and Ari squinted against the bright lights that Tessa flipped on. "Ari, you are the only person I know that can fall asleep during a horror movie."

"I haven't been sleeping great."

"Wait till finals come," Tessa retorted.

Ari moaned, and Reed pulled her tighter against him.

"Let me get on my game before you two start." Tessa grabbed a drink out of the mini-fridge and sat down in front of her large screen. Within seconds, she had her headset on and the screen full of different shots of her game in action.

"I should probably let you go to sleep. I know we both have projects to work on for school," Reed said reluctantly.

"Not yet. That was a nap." Ari held onto his arm, not ready to let him go. She'd dreamed of being with him for too long. It felt surreal some days, and she didn't want it to end.

His body relaxed underneath her.

She won. "Just a little longer." If she was a cat, she would be purring.

He tucked a strand of hair behind her ear, then his hand traced down her neck, resting on her collarbone. "Are we going to catch the same tram home? I was hoping we could spend more time together over break."

"Sounds great. About break ..." Ari said and then hesitated. She didn't know if she wanted to bring it up, but it wouldn't get easier with time.

"What? Have you not told your mom about us?"

"That's not it. My mom was actually excited about us." Her mom had even said she couldn't do much better, but there was no reason to give Reed a big head.

He kissed the top of her head. "Good. My mom said it was about time."

"Really?" Ari turned back to face him, wondering how long Reed had thought of her romantically.

Reed smiled at her, bigger than usual, which made Ari close the distance and meet his lips. She melted into his soft lips, lost in the taste of Reed with a touch of chocolate. Finally, she pushed back. Tessa was still in the room, despite being absorbed in her game.

"You wanted to talk about break?" Reed held onto to her waist as Ari faced him. His hand touched her bare skin, sending a warm current throughout her body.

"You're very distracting." Ari pushed his hands away.

"Alright, alright." Reed raised his hands in surrender as he leaned back against the metallic head board.

"I want to go see my dad."

Reed's brow creased, then the lines deepened. What a way to kill the mood. Not that she expected Reed to be pleased, but she'd hoped he would be understanding and willing to help.

"You mean ..." He couldn't say it.

"Yes, I want to go into the VR with him. Maybe try to help him leave like I did for Marco." What Ari didn't say, what she was too scared to articulate, was that she was willing to use her skills as a warper to help convince her father to leave.

Reed pushed himself up to a seated position and stared at Ari with disbelief.

"Please try to understand." Ari sat up as well and placed a hand on top of his, but Reed was cold and angry.

"I think I understand all right. You're going to give away your life for a man that has already thrown his away more than once." Reed's voice grew, no longer the hushed whispers.

Ari turned to see if Tessa was still playing. Her hands were a little slower than usual on her keyboard, as if she was trying to ignore them.

"He is my father, Reed. You, more than anybody, should realize that."

"Don't talk to me about fathers." Reed climbed off her bed. "Sometimes it's better if they're gone rather than having them around to screw up our lives."

"I was hoping you could help me." Ari needed him to cover her tracks, but she didn't even know if that was possible in a hospital.

He ran a hand over his short hair. "Of course, I'll help you, but I'm not sure if that will be enough or if I can keep you safe."

She wanted him to be okay with it, but she had to do it with or without him. "I have to."

"No, you don't. Does your mom know? Because I'm pretty sure she would say no. It's too dangerous."

"I need to do it while I can. You're leaving at the end of the school year as it is." Every day was more of a struggle for Ari to conceal her abilities. She planned to finish the school year with Reed. At the end of the year, he would move on to his career assignment, and she could take Dave's position or something. It hurt to watch Reed's pain.

"Why do I have the feeling you're checking out of this relationship early? You could wait until I graduate." Reed picked up his bag and swung it over his shoulder.

"I can't."

He nodded, his jaw tightening. Then without another word, he turned and walked out.

Ari stared at the door as it shut, shocked at how fast things had turned sour. Maybe she hadn't made the right choice, but she wasn't sure what she could have said to make it any easier.

Tessa continued playing her game, commenting between keystrokes. "Boys suck."

The following week was quiet for Ari. She found herself constantly checking for a message and even stalked Reed's social network for any updates he cared to post—which were none. She started to message him several times, wanting to explain but there was nothing left to explain.

He knew her better than anyone else. He knew she had to do it. He just didn't want to accept it.

So, she threw herself into her midterm project virtual which all her teachers would be grading. It would be the first virtual the students were required to create, and each teacher had different criteria they expected, from the storyboard, to art design, to complex code and procedure. Tessa helped a lot as she was at the top of the class, though she didn't always agree.

"I could name a couple guys that are a lot better than me," Tessa said before taking another bite of their pizza covered in ham and pineapple—another one of Ari's new favorites.

"Maybe in complex coding, but you have moxie no one else has."

Tessa pulled back slightly, acting surprised. "Moxie?"

"Something my grandfather used to say about someone with gumption, spark." Ari bit into another piece of pizza.

"Huh, moxie," Tessa said the word again, her latest lip ring giving her a slight lisp. She turned back to Ari. "So, where's your moxie?"

Ari stared at her for a second, confused.

"Reed." Tessa's eyes narrowed at her. "Come on. You've been moping around all week after that fight. What's the deal?"

Ari picked off a pineapple. She struggled to talk about her home life or anything personal. Tessa had no problem sharing, including her dad's sex life, which often turned Ari a couple of shades redder.

"It's my dad." Ari proceeded to tell Tessa the whole story. "Reed doesn't want me to see him on Christmas Break. He thinks it's too dangerous." She left out using her abilities to help her father.

Tessa set down her slice of pizza and stood. "Let's go to the bathroom."

"What?" Ari knew Tessa was not the type of girl to go

to the bathroom in groups.

"Come on."

Ari followed her into their small private bathroom. White tile and silver fixtures gleamed. Tessa waved a hand in front of a sensor and turned on the shower.

Once the water was pounding against the tiles, she turned to face Ari. "I get why you have to go see your dad. I do. But I don't see why you feel like going into the government program is your only choice."

"Because once they know, there will be no other options."

Tessa gave a short laugh. "You have to stop acting like some poor little girl. You have skills people would kill for, literally. And you're bright and smart enough to figure another way out of this."

Ari bristled at the remark. How could Tessa so smoothly compliment and insult her at the same time?

"I say we start with that agent that contacted you. Dave, right?" Tessa grinned and the ring on her lip curled her lip, making her look bit mischievous and frightening at the same time.

The next day Tessa scheduled an appointment with Dave for the following Friday after school. She wasn't as worried about what was on her call log as she often spoke to agents or people in the industry. Thankfully, Tessa was going with Ari. Between Tessa's father's business and her own gaming experience, she had expertise Ari desperately needed.

Ari focused on her project while she waited for the meeting. She'd been inspired by a picture she'd once glimpsed online and decided to recreate a fantasy world based on it. She was in way over her head but loved the challenge.

Ari worked in the VR library on Wednesday night. They had systems where she could visualize a 3D version of her program while working on the code on a nearby screen. It made work easier, even if she had to do it in the lab instead of her dorm room in her pajamas. The lab was empty, except for the lab techs and Wake, the jerk from class, who sat at the next station. Ari had no problem ignoring him. She focused on her program, needing to pull at least an A from Dr. Coleman on the project.

Thinking about a troublesome spot, she stared off in the distance for a moment. Out of the corner of her eyes, she noticed Wake's gaze, but turned her attention back to the images in front of her. Ari tried to block him out. He might be great at programming, but his features reminded Ari of a chubby rodent.

Her HUB vibrated with a new message from Reed. Unfortunately, it seemed as short and cold as he had been for the last week.

Can we talk this weekend?

Ari typed back. *Sure. Saturday night?*

Tessa and Ari were meeting with Dave on Friday night.

Sounds good. I'll pick you up at 5pm.

She tapped her fingers on the table, excited for her date with Reed. He was worried about her, but she also knew he would come around. He sucked at holding a grudge. Otherwise he'd never have been friends with Marco.

She hurried to throw her stuff in her bag before rushing out the door. She'd made it to the elevator before she realized she'd left her drive for her VR hooked in the system. Swearing silently, she walked back to the library. Thankfully, it was right where she left it.

On the way to her VR class, Ari nervously picked at a nail. Dr. Coleman planned to give each student feedback about their project, so they could finish up any changes by the end of the week, which was the last day of classes as well as finals. Walking into the classroom, the snowy landscape outside stole Ari's attention. Gray skies hung heavy, dropping snowflakes in perfected chaos. She didn't believe anyone would ever be able to recreate that in the virtual world.

As students filed into the room, someone ran into her from behind, knocking her bag off her shoulder and spilling its contents to the floor. When she reached down to collect her stuff, she looked back up to find Wake chuckling with his buddies. Ari thought of a plethora of names to call him, but caught sight of Advisor Williams, watching everything and not making a single move. Stifling her anger, she finished gathering her bag and took her seat.

Dr. Coleman stood at the front of the class ready to begin. "Please come in and take a seat. We have a lot to do today so we need everyone to please go quickly into their programs."

Ari pulled her long hair into a messy bun on top of her head and thought briefly about Tessa's hair, shaved underneath for easier access to her port. It was tempting. Like her mother, though, Ari had long wavy hair that she wasn't eager to part with.

She slid down in the seat, plugged in the drive that held her program, then inserted the cable in the back on her head.

Walking around the classroom, Mica stopped by Ari, "Good luck."

Ari hoped she wouldn't need it.

Before she could even open her eyes in the program, Ari knew something was wrong. Darkness surrounded her, a void that had no end. A blinding pain went through her mind as she struggled to see her program. The lush landscape highlighted with purples and blues that she'd spent hours creating was all gone. She couldn't even see the code. Where had it all gone? Despite the intense pain, she tried to concentrate on the background and bring into focus the picture she had worked on for so many hours.

She couldn't lose everything, not when she had worked so hard all semester. Her efforts resulted in a stabbing sensation in the back of her eyes.

Ignoring the nails pounding into her temple, she focused on codes she'd spent hours typing and re-typing. She pulled some of it from memory and pushed it into the program. She hoped to have something there, light even, before Coleman showed up. Green grass and a basic light flickered on and off for a couple seconds before it all went black. Pain exploded in her mind, and she screamed out in agony.

Then it ended.

As Ari struggled to open her eyes against the blinding light, she found a worried Mica hovering over her. "You okay?"

"Not really." She had a piercing headache. Her hand blocked out the florescent lights in the room as they seemed to only amplify the pain. It was only a few seconds before Ari recognized Dr. Coleman standing next to her. Ari struggled to sit up and Mica grabbed her arm to help. Advisor Williams stood several feet behind Coleman but kept his gaze locked on her.

"What happened in there, Ms. Mendez?" Dr. Coleman asked.

"My program ... it's destroyed," she said between pained gasps.

Mica turned to the computer. "It looks like the one you downloaded to our server is empty. Maybe a virus wiped it."

"Really?" Coleman's impatience at this delay was obvious. "Just what I needed. Shut down her computer."

"Do you have your backup?" Mica asked.

Ari nodded. "In my bag."

Dr. Coleman motioned for Mica to retrieve it, and she obliged. When she had it in hand, he told her to check it out on his protected computer and upload it to the network.

He then turned his attention back to Ari, pulling up a nearby chair. For a moment he actually appeared concerned, but maybe Ari was reading him wrong.

"What happened in there?"

She froze, unsure of where he was going but knowing he was asking more than his words said.

"It was dark. I was searching for my program and this pain took over."

"Was there anything else? Any changes to the program?"

Ari remembered the code she tried to push into the program to no avail. He didn't need to know that. "No, sir."

"It could have been a virus or something else. I will run a diagnostic to see what I can find."

Mica approached them, shaking her head slightly. "It's empty. Totally wiped. I checked our school backup network and can't seem to find anything stored there either."

Ari's mouth hung open as unintelligent gasps came from it. All of her projects, homework, and notes were on that drive. Her mind flew through the possibilities of what could have happened. She had been in the library last night, less than twenty-four hours ago.

Then Wake popped into her mind—annoying, evil, beady-eyed Wake.

"It was Wake." The words came out as a whisper.

"What?" Dr. Coleman leaned forward.

She straightened in the chair and looked her professor in the eye. "It was Wake. He was in the library last night when I forgot my drive."

"That is a serious accusation, Ms. Mendez." His face tightened, questioning her.

It was the only explanation. Wake had been out for her since day one. "It's the truth."

"Okay then." Dr. Coleman stood, smoothing out the wrinkles in his pants. "I'll send a report to your advisor and the ethics board and see what happens. In the meantime, I would start on your project."

"What? That took hours to complete. There's no way it will be good enough in time."

"It will be quicker the second time. Better get started." He strode off, obviously not willing to discuss it further.

Ari bit the inside of her lip. Her emotions coiled tight inside of her—any leak and she wouldn't be able to stop the flow. Ditching her last class and praying she wouldn't get another demerit for it, she spent the afternoon in the library re-creating her program with triple backups. She didn't finish as much as she wanted before she received a message, or more like a command, telling her she had a meeting with Advisor Williams at 3:30pm.

Not willing to waste any time, she hurried to his office. As much as she hated meeting with that man, she had a tiny hope that he'd found her original program. She wanted to squeeze it out of Wake's little throat.

"Ms. Mendez," Advisor Williams greeted her, seated behind his large antiqued desk. "Take a seat."

She lowered herself into the leather chair and placed her bag on her lap. The familiarity of this office officially bothered her.

"I've been reviewing your complaint and the incident in your class today."

"Did you find my program?"

Williams shook his head. "There was no evidence of the accusations you made against your fellow student."

Ari's mouth opened, but she had nothing to say. She closed it and lowered her head, struggling to keep her gut-wrenching disappointment tucked away until she was alone and could afford a meltdown.

Advisor Williams ignored her silent pain. "We searched Wake's system, and nothing was to be found. The accusation will stay on his record in case this happens again. But reviewing your hacked drive, I discovered something else."

Her eyes flashed up, as her self-pitying turned into fear.

He glanced to the screen on his computer. "You never finished your VR evaluation before coming to our program. How is that?"

"I have, I mean, I've a great fear of VRs ever since I was ten."

"Due to the business with your father, no doubt. No wonder about your brother. With your exceptional scores on all of your written tests, your phobia may have done you a favor. Yet, this unfinished virtual needs to be completed as soon as possible. I'll schedule it for tomorrow." He turned to his computer.

"No," Ari blurted out before she could stop herself. She couldn't think of a reason why she couldn't take the test, but there was a problem. She was a warper. Maybe could just not use her power? But the government tests went way beyond normal, and no one was exactly sure how they worked.

Advisor Williams peered over his sharp nose. "Excuse me?"

"Sorry, I just meant that I have to finish my project first. All my work for finals is wiped, and I have to finish, or I will fail. If I'm kicked out, I won't need the eval anyway."

He paused a moment. "You can complete the evaluation on Monday."

She released a shaky breath. "Okay."

"It is procedure mostly. But looking over the recording of your time in Dr. Coleman's class, I think it would benefit everyone to make sure you are in the right assignment."

"The right assignment? You mean they can change my assignment."

"Not usually, but it is a possibility. We all have to

serve our government where needed." For the first time, Advisor Williams smiled. And the freak smile unnerved Ari more than his usually grim expression. "Please schedule the exam with my assistant. Good day."

Without another look, Ari was excused. After scheduling the test, she left the building. The sidewalks were already cleared from the previous snowfall, piled up on the lawns with icy perfection. Light snowflakes continued to drift down. She felt like one of those swirling flakes; despite her best intentions she had no clue where she would land.

Ari could almost relate to Marco and his desire to escape from the reality of others wanting to make choices for you. Maybe the control of a virtual world could give something that the real world couldn't. Choice.

Continuing towards the student center in a bit of a daze, it took her a moment before she realized someone was calling to her. Garrett was wrapped up in a green down jacket and a blue striped beanie.

"Oh, hi." She turned to face him, huddling down deeper into her own jacket.

"So, you'll still acknowledge me on campus? How very gracious of you." He gave a mock bow. His movements were theatrical, but his face remained sober.

"Sorry, I've had a lot on my mind." Ari's blue scarf escaped the confines of her jacket, one side flying in the wind and heading to freedom. She reached up to tuck it back in and her bag slid down her arm. She dropped the bag on the sidewalk and ripped off the stupid scarf, balling it into a wad. Her frustration from class, the jerk Wake, Advisor Williams, and everything else boiled inside of her. She wanted to scream into the wind but, instead, threw her scarf on the ground.

Garrett hesitantly bent down to pick it up. "Want me to carry that?"

Ari's breath came out in gasps, forming into clouds of mist in front of her. She needed to pull it together. If she lost it ... well, she couldn't think like that. She tucked a stray piece of hair behind her ear, embarrassed about her mini-meltdown. She picked up her bag and reached out to take the scarf. "Thanks, but I got it."

"Things can't be that bad for an up-and-coming star like yourself." He gave her a kind smile.

"Thanks." Her hair continued flying about her face, and she was forced to pull it back into a tight bun.

"You look like you could use a break," Garrett tucked a strand of hair she'd missed behind her ear. "I'd suggest a trip to the beach or something, but you have a boyfriend for that?"

His hand lingered a bit too long near her face as his eyes darted to someone behind her. Suddenly his expression turned haughty and patronizing, making Ari's stomach sink. She brushed his arm away roughly and turned around to find Reed.

Reed's eyes narrowed. "Keep your hands to yourself, Garrett."

Garrett stepped back. "Just helping."

"Help somewhere else."

"Don't worry, she's all yours. Have fun," Garrett scoffed and turned to leave.

Reed shoved his hands in his pockets, his body tight and angry.

Ari stepped towards him. "Nothing happened. He grabbed my scarf for me and was screwing around to make you mad."

"You didn't seem to object too much."

His comment put her on the defensive. "He caught me off guard. It was nothing."

"I know. Still doesn't mean I have to like him."

Ari leaned into him, hoping to lighten the mood. "I've seen some of the girls you've dated. They weren't all winners."

His body softened, and he wrapped an arm around her. "That is why I am no longer with them."

"Good."

He leaned down and kissed her lightly on the lips. Even with the cold whipping around her, a little kiss from Reed could warm her heart. She stood on her tiptoes to prolong the kiss for one more moment.

"I hate to stop." Reed pulled back, rubbing her arms. "But it's really cold, and you may need all ten fingers to finish the term."

A rock pummeled to the bottom of her stomach as he reminded her of all the work she needed to make up.

He must have noticed. "What's wrong?"

It was a long story, one she didn't really have time to go into. If she was going to survive the next few days, she would need some sustenance. "Let's grab something to drink and I'll catch you up."

CHAPTER 28

The night went by in a blur of homework. Despite constant temptation, Ari coded her program the painstakingly slow method. The next morning her HUB flashed a reminder of the meeting scheduled with Dave after classes. She should cancel. She didn't have the time to meet with him but talking it over with Reed the previous night had reminded her how important it was. Reed had agreed to come along for moral support.

"What is it?" Tessa asked from across their room.

Ari must have been staring off into space for a while.

"Just thinking about the meeting with Dave." She didn't think it hurt to say his name aloud.

Tessa ruffled her purple hair and put on her bracelet and rings. "I'll meet you at security after classes."

Ari started to tell Tessa she didn't have to, but her friend quieted her with a look. "I've worked on contracts since I could code. I'll be there."

Classes went by slowly, and she worked in the library through lunch. When Ari arrived at security, she was happy to see Reed and Tessa waiting for her. Tessa wore a bright blue shirt and tall buckled boots. Reed looked good as always in his dark jeans and a gray shirt.

"Hey." He reached for Ari's hand. A soothing touch that tethered her in place and helped her fight the chaotic emotions warring inside.

They passed through security and then continued on the path to a restaurant in town. The falling sun peeked out through the heavy clouds, giving a fabulous display in the sky, much better than the slushy mush on the streets that the snow left behind.

Outside the café, Tessa warned Ari, "Don't forget what you're worth. Ask for the world."

"I'm not quite sure what to ask for. Or if they can even help me." She had so many questions, she wasn't sure where to start.

"Nothing is too high, remember that," Tessa replied.

The sleek and modern café contained a variety of beautiful paintings projected on their computerized walls. The pieces looked expensive. Ari suddenly felt self-conscious in her faded jeans and self-designed shoes. *Guess I'm ordering water.* Reed squeezed her hand as if he sensed her discomfort.

A tall, sleek girl with platinum hair showed them to their seats. Their table was one big screen with menus and more. Not hungry, Ari folded her arms to keep her hands still.

"Relax, Ari. It's really not that big of a deal. If this company doesn't work out, there will be others." Tessa flipped through the menu.

Ari started to disagree, when a man approached. Ari recognized Dave from the gaming store. He had tanned skin, probably Hispanic like she was. She wondered if whoever sent him did that on purpose.

"Hello, Ari." He reached out to shake her hand and then reached out to Reed. "You must be Reed."

Hesitantly, Reed returned the hand shake.

"How did you know?" She shouldn't have been surprised in this digital age, but she still found that he knew her boyfriend's name disturbing.

"We research our candidates thoroughly. I know a lot, just like I know this must be your roommate—"

"Tessa." She cut him off. "Her roommate, best friend, and representation."

"Yes, I'm familiar with your father."

If Dave really had known Tessa, he wouldn't have brought up her father. She ran a hand through her purple bangs but didn't reply.

"Okay then. We better order something." Dave pulled up the menu on the table. "Please, it's on me."

Tessa entered her order.

"No, thanks," Reed said.

Ari wasn't interested in food either. She wanted information.

"Oh, please," Tessa huffed. "I'll order for the both of you."

"Thanks," Dave commented. "If nothing else, we need to keep up appearances."

Once orders were entered, he turned to Ari. "You're probably wondering what VisionTech can do for you?"

"For starters."

A wide smile spread on Dave's face. "We would love to offer you a job, with immediate on-site training."

"Terms," Tessa said before Ari could even respond.

"Okay then." He pulled out a small screen and uploaded a document. "This is our standard employee contract. Who wants it first?"

Tessa grabbed it. "Ari is not your standard employee so this better not be insulting."

She dove right into reading over the agreement.

Dave raised an eyebrow to Ari. She nodded. Dave appeared to be a regular guy, more like an uncle or neighbor, not someone who was trying to steal kids to work for his employer. Maybe "steal" was too harsh of a word, for if things were as bad as he'd told Ari, then he might use the word "rescue."

Ari coughed briefly to clear her throat. "There are

some ... umm ... complications also?"

Dave remained silent and waited for her to continue.

"I have a mom and brother that I will need to take care of."

"Many of our employees financially assist their families. We can assist in sending money without it being traced."

"So how often can I visit them or have them visit me?" Ari couldn't even consider never seeing them again.

"Our offices are a twelve-hour flight from here, and the location is not open knowledge to the public. Once you join our company, you cannot leave for vacations or trips. There are families there, but they all work if they are capable. We have the highest level of security available and go to great lengths to protect our employees."

Ari leaned back into her chair. Marco would never come live with her, and her mother would never leave Marco or her father. Her heart weighed heavily in her chest. It took effort to breathe. Was she exchanging one prison for another?

Despite her shocked reaction, he added, "I also can't guarantee contact with the outside world."

"I can't leave my family, my life." Ari couldn't help but feel the presence of Reed next to her. She wasn't sure she could walk away.

"You won't have a choice, Ari. Once the government knows what you can do, you will be moved to a secure facility. Foreign governments and dark companies will kidnap warpers if necessary. VisionTech believes that incentives work better than coercion. We like people to choose to work for us, and we pay then handsomely for it."

Ari reached for Reed's hand under the table. A large lump was stuck in her throat and she struggled to swallow. With her free hand, she reached for the water on the table. A waitress arrived with an assortment of exquisitely plated food and drinks. Ari didn't have an appetite. She stood on the top of a mountain, and any step might send her careening down.

Tessa set the electronic contract down and took a drink of the swirling peach and blue beverage in front of her.

"Of course, you won't want to sign until you read it all thoroughly, but it looks pretty standard." Tessa turned to Dave. "Ari will need triple the signing bonus to start as she is pretty broke and double the yearly salary. She wants it reviewed yearly as the market fluctuates and her skills increase."

Before Ari could get a word in, Tessa continued, "Also, she must have contact with the outside world. You reached us without getting caught, so figure something out. Her family, boyfriend, and of course myself, must remain in contact so we know she is safe and happy."

"Done," Dave didn't hesitate.

Tessa smiled and grabbed some sushi to eat. With some type of fish still in her hand, she turned to Ari, "Did I miss something?"

Miss? I'm still trying to figure out what you just said. Overwhelmed, Ari shook her head. Dave's serious, yet kind face, let her relax a bit.

"One question," Dave said. "How have you been able to hide what you do this long?"

"I never finished my school VR eval. I was terrified of VRs and couldn't last longer than a few minutes until the last couple months."

A look of doubt crossed over his face. "And they never finished your testing?"

"They never needed to," Reed said.

Ari coughed lightly, interrupting him. "Advisor Williams wants me to take the eval on Monday, before I leave on break."

Tessa spat chewed rice across the table before sputtering, "When did this happen?"

"Yesterday, after Wake stole my program, which I'm

supposed to have completed by the end of this week." Ari wondered if she would even make it to Christmas break. The project felt small in comparison to the rest of her problems.

"You can't take that test." Dave said. "We'll rush the contract and you can sign it on the plane. I can get transportation here within the hour."

Still in her chair, Ari pushed back from the table. "What are you talking about? I'm not getting on a plane in an hour going to who-knows-where with a man I just met. I'm sixteen, and you're asking me to make major life decisions in a couple minutes. I need more than dinner to digest this all."

"If you were my daughter, we would leave now." Gone was the carefree Dave, instead, a serious, almost anxious Dave sat in his place. "If you're worried about me or the company, contact Tessa's father. He's done work with our company, and they can verify I work for them. This isn't a joke. This is my job."

Tessa stuck her hand out. "Let me use your phone—I assume it's untraceable—and I'll confirm things with my father."

Dave handed over the phone, and Tessa stepped away from the table to make the call.

Ari glanced at Reed, knowing he wouldn't like the next part. "My dad is also in a VR coma. I have to try to get him out before I go."

Reed's grip tightened, but to his credit he remained silent.

"Remind me how long he's been in?" Dave asked as if he already knew the answer.

"Seven years."

"I'm sorry to tell you this, but he's gone. I've never known anyone past six months to make it out."

"I have to try."

"Would your parents want you to risk it? Because it would be a risk. You won't be able to continue with school once you take the evaluation or refuse it. And if you leave unexcused, they will send officers to come and retrieve you. You didn't think they had all of those armed guards only to keep the bad guys out, did you?"

Tessa sat back down at the table. "My dad knows the CEO of VisionTech. He says the company is reputable with off shore outreach teams. He'll look into Dave and message me if he pans out."

"Thanks," Ari said, though it didn't make her decision any easier. Everyone's gaze rested on Ari, waiting for her decision. Heat rose in her cheeks.

Reed spoke first. "Sounds like you need to go, Ari. You can't help him, and you can't risk staying." The resignation in his eyes hurt her. Reed had wanted her to hide her gift, so she could stay as long as possible, but even he recognized the reality of the situation.

"Okay." She would sign the contract, but she still had to try to help her dad. Not only for his sake, but for the sake of their family. She couldn't abandon her family without trying.

"Tomorrow night." Her words were hard and final. "I'm going home first, but then let me know where I need to meet you."

On the way back to school, Tessa's dad sent a message that Dave checked out. It reassured Ari to know she wouldn't be walking off to accidentally join a cult. It didn't make saying goodbye to her life any easier though. While Ari wanted to walk in silence, holding Reed's hand and preparing for the next couple days, Tessa had other ideas.

"Are you planning to ignore all of our advice and still try to save your dad? Some people don't want saving." Tessa didn't mince words. It was one of Ari's most and least favorite things about her.

Ari continued walking. "I know you guys don't agree with me, but I'm not asking you too." She kept her eyes forward, not ready for Reed's reaction. "I appreciate your help with Dave, but I think we all know I have to do the rest by myself."

Tessa pulled her to a stop. "Whoa, chica. While we don't think it's the smartest thing to go in after your dad, it doesn't mean we're abandoning you."

Ari wrapped Tessa into a tight hug. She couldn't have asked for a better roommate.

"Calm down." Tessa awkwardly patted her on the back. "I've had my share of stupid. We'll just remind you of that when we're all arrested."

Ari turned back and forth between her two best friends. "I don't want you to be arrested. I can do this alone."

Reed grabbed her hand again. "You don't have a choice. I'm staying with you Ari, as long as I can."

"Thanks." It came out in a whisper.

"It sounds like it's road trip time." Tessa began walking again, with Reed and Ari beside her. "Let's grab our stuff and head out tonight. We'll check out with campus security and stay at my condo for the rest of the weekend."

"Sounds good," Reed replied.

They didn't have time to make any more plans as they approached the security checkpoint.

Tessa spoke to guard as she went through. "Hey, we're going to head up to my condo tonight. I need clearance for one night."

The young guard was about as tall as Reed with thick arms that appeared out of place on his smooth childlike face. "Give me a minute, and I'll enter it in the system."

Reed walked through the scanner, his ID bracelet lighting up.

Tessa continue talking to the guard, standing closer than usual. "Yeah, we wanted some space to study for finals and my parents got their own VR link up."

"Impressive." The guard smiled at Tessa and then

turned to work on the computer.

Ari walked through the scanner and a beep sounded. She paused, unsure of what that meant. "I don't have any weapons."

"Not weapons, miss." The guard read something on his computer.

"Well, you two are welcome to leave tonight," the guard point at Tessa and Reed. "But your friend Ari is flagged to remain on campus for the time being."

"What does that mean?" Ari asked.

"It means you have to report to your student advisor for permission to leave campus."

Ari's mouth went dry as she stared at the guard's weapon on his hip, a stun gun on the lowest setting or, at its highest, a deadly killing machine. Reflexively, Ari stepped back, wondering how quick he was. Would he really shoot her? Even if she avoided him, there were others guarding the perimeter, and those guys had weapons as well. Was it too late for her?

"Ari, you must have forgotten another assignment," Reed teased, completely out of character for him. He reached for her arm, pulling her towards the entrance and away from any chance of escape.

Tessa jumped into the conversation, ignoring Ari who was frozen with fear. "Yeah, if I didn't live with her, I'd swear she was blonde. Let's hurry so we can be on our way." Tessa waved goodbye to the guard "Thanks."

Ari continued walking, one foot in front of the other. She wasn't going back to see Advisor Williams. She couldn't.

"Relax." Reed pulled her in closer. "There is more than one way to leave the school."

Ari's gaze flashed up to meet his. "Really?"

"Yeah. Tessa and I will have to leave through the front. The school won't realize you're missing by the time curfew gets into effect."

"Okay, then. We better leave right away." Tessa

glanced at her bracelet. "That will give us a six-hour head start."

"So how do I do it?" Ari asked. "How do I get out of here?"

"As much as I hate the idea of it, we'll need some help." Just as Ari got a sinking feeling of who he was talking about, Reed came out with it. "Garrett."

CHAPTER 29

A ri and Tessa hurried back to their dorm to pack. Tessa packed Ari's stuff in her large designer bags since it would be easier for Tessa to walk them out. Reed left them to go talk to Garrett. Ari hoped things went smoothly between them.

Reed messaged them.

Lucky break. Need to move fast. Meet me on the West side of the student union ASAP.

Ari hacked her bracelet, so it would keep playing the same loop of her reading on her bed. She prayed it still worked. Since they'd been caught at the VR party, the school had been tightening down, but it was worth trying. She slipped pliers into her bag, so she could take it off once she made it far enough away. Ari slung her father's old leather bag across her chest and left behind anything she didn't need. Tessa promised she'd send it to her mother.

They skirted the front entrance of the student union, avoiding people and sticking close to the trees and picnic benches. Garrett and Reed were waiting for them near a table, neither one smiling. Garrett was in the usual silver work uniform with an orange coat.

"You're running?" Garrett asked as they approached.

She set the large bag on the ground. "Sort of my only option."

"Why do your problems always seem to fall into my lap, like I have nothing better to do?" He raked a hand through his now short silver hair.

"You don't," Reed said bitterly. "And you owe me."

Ari briefly wondered what Reed was referring to, but since neither guy seemed forthcoming, she let it drop.

Reed approached, pulling her into his arms for a quick hug. "We have to leave now, if we're to meet up with you. We'll follow you and be ready at the scheduled stop. Okay?"

"Okay," Ari replied. It would take them some time to pick up Tessa's car and check out with security for the night. She squeezed Reed tighter, not wanting to let go.

Garrett cleared his throat. "We'd better get moving."

Reed leaned in and kissed Ari. It was rough and urgent and left Ari's lips tingling. He took her bag as he pulled away.

"Catch up with you soon," Tessa said.

Ari watched her closest friends walk off together. Garrett had better be true to his word and help her leave. She turned to look at him bundled in a thin orange coat as he stamped on the snow around him.

"Ready?" Ari asked.

"Waiting on you, princess." He turned and walked off through a narrow passage between the older buildings, leaving only snowy footprints to follow.

Ari hurried after him, not surprised by his coldness. She finally caught up in the passage way.

"What is this?" Ari asked, her breath coming out in short bursts.

"Walkway used before they remodeled." He kept it short and kept moving fast.

"So how is this going to work?"

He turned briefly, glaring over his shoulder. "Since I

239

got kicked out of the Tech Lab, I've been assigned to receivables. I take inventory for the technical supplies that come in and out of our school. You're going to catch a ride with a supply truck in a few minutes."

"And they are okay with it?"

He approached the door and, after he punched in a quick code, it opened. "Not planning on asking."

"I'm surprised they gave you this job after everything ..." Ari instantly regretted her words.

"Yeah, you mean after being put on suspension? Reed would never tell you, but we both got in more trouble than you know. I don't even think I got a 'thank you' out of it." Ari followed him through the door, trying not to let her guilt distract her. They entered a storage facility with lofty ceilings and filled with boxes and crates.

"I am grateful. I'm sorry—" Ari said.

"For what?" Garrett cut her off. "For getting me suspended, for taking off and never giving me a chance, or for using your boyfriend to get me to do your bidding? There is a lot to choose from."

His accusation struck her cold. He was right. He wasn't a saint, but she should have handled things better. Her face burned in response as she tried to sort out what to say next. He stood facing her, waiting expectantly.

"I'm sorry for everything that happened between us. I hoped we could just be friends, but I didn't know how to do that." Ari forced her gaze up, to look in his eyes. "I'll stay in contact and repay you one day."

Garrett approached, stepping into her space, which made her nerves jump as if hot-wired. He had a way of making her uncomfortable. She had to tell herself to hold still as he tucked a hair behind her ear.

"I hope you're right, but I won't hold my breath."

Ari would try, but she didn't know where she was going or what her situation would be. She owed him enough to try. And for that reason, she didn't slap his hand away as it lingered on her shoulder.

"We could have had fun." He kept her gaze as he stepped away from her. "You were more to me than just another freshman girl. But we'll never know. I wish you the best when karma finally comes your way. It always does."

His dark expression soon vanished, and he patted her shoulder with a smile before backing away. The haunting feeling was fleeting, and she brushed it off to focus on the task at hand.

"Now, let's pack you away." Garrett wandered between the stack of crates leaving Ari to trail behind.

CHAPTER 30

Fingers numb, Ari gripped the nearby crates as the storage truck jostled her down the road. She had only ridden on electric trams or cars. The massive truck with wheels up to her shoulder, bounced along the road with constant vibrations and no heat. The truck ran quietly enough, amplifying the noise of boxes shifting slightly against their restraints in the storage section of the trailer. She clutched a plastic crate nearby to avoid sliding down the aisle.

She had to be ready when the driver, a friend of Garrett's named Arman, made his stop. Garrett said Arman always stopped at a truck stop which had a good price on his brand of cigarettes. Putting this much faith in Garrett made her nervous. He had more than one reason not to help her.

Ari groped blindly in the dark for the large sliding door at the back of the trailer. It took her a few minutes, especially when her bag, slung over her chest and resting by her hip, kept snagging on boxes. Finally finding the door of the truck, she searched for release switch Garrett had pointed out earlier. No luck. It must be on the opposite side.

Stacks of boxes, like the old building blocks she and her brother played with as children, stood in her way. Finding a toehold on a lower box, she hoisted herself up and through a small space between boxes. Flashes of the traffic that surrounded her turned her thoughts to this huge box she was in becoming a dark coffin. A brief spout of claustrophobia motivated her to hurry. She crawled out the opposite end and found a small area to stand. The panel to open the truck was about the size of her hand and easy to find, even in the dark.

The panel manually opened the door. Arman reportedly had thrown more than one party in the trailer where they'd accidentally locked themselves in. Ari didn't want to think about what had happened in the trailer.

Now, I wait. His stop was only a couple miles away from school, so she should only have to wait a couple more minutes.

A blue light flickered on her finger, and she unwound her ring and placed it in her ear.

"You okay?" Reed's voice sounded a bit stressed on the other end.

"Besides being stuck in a moving tuna can, I am," Ari replied, already missing Reed, his voice, his touch. She mentally reminded herself to focus if she wanted out of said tuna can.

"Good. Tessa and I are sitting at the shop, waiting for you." Reed assured. "Well, it's just me right now. Tessa ran in to grab stuff, something about a road trip and an escaped convict."

Ari chuckled at the idea of her, an escaped convict. She had lived her life for so long as the perfect student, the perfect citizen, the perfect daughter. But she'd never had reason to rebel before. The thrill was actually a little exhilarating provided she didn't think about the consequences for too long.

The truck slowed as if at a stop light, and Ari adjusted her footing, gripping a shelf for support. An alarm sounded outside the truck, a little way off, but close enough for Ari to freeze.

"What's that?" Ari asked, not really expecting an answer from Reed.

"You hear that too? It's an ambulance driving by. That means you must be close. Wait." Movement sounded through the phone. "I see the silver truck ahead."

Ari sagged against the wall. "Good."

"Sort of ... but the truck's not stopping. It's continuing straight on the highway. He's not turning. I'm going to kill Garrett, that—"

"Kill him after I'm out of here."

"I'm coming. Damn." A horn blared nearby.

"Are you actually driving?" Most cars were self-driving, but in this case, Reed would have to manually drive. She doubted he had ever driven before. No one in their neighborhood even had a car.

"Yeah, I've done it in a VR before."

"I guess that's better than nothing." Ari tried to remain silent to let him concentrate.

A phone beeped. "It's Tessa. I'm going to have her join in the call."

Tessa's loud voice joined the call. "What the hell, Reed? You steal my car the second I leave you alone with it? If you really wanted to be left alone with Ari, you could have told me. Not that I would have lent you my car though."

"Tessa, quiet please." Reed snapped at her. "I'm following Ari. The truck didn't stop. It's the same one Garrett described to us."

"Ohhh," Tessa said.

"I'll come back to pick you up once I grab Ari."

"Grabbing Ari is going to be the tricky part," Ari said, referring to herself in third person.

"I'm actually only a few cars behind you."

"Really?" Ari lifted the cover off the panel, readying to flip the switch. "Want me to open the back?"

"No!" Reed yelled, making Ari reach up to grab the device in her ear. Tessa swore, and Reed continued talking. "Ari, wait until you won't get run over. Okay?"

"Okay," Ari said, letting time pass as she waited in darkness for his word. It took longer than she thought, with only faint static to fill the line.

Tessa was the one who finally broke the silence. "Reed, what's happening?"

The truck slowed.

"Okay. We're close to the freeway and I'm not sure when he's going to stop again. He's getting ready to turn. Ari, open the door. I'm right behind you."

She lifted the panel and flipped the switch. It hissed slowly. Ari jumped as an alarm rang loudly in the truck.

"Reed," she yelled over the noise, but she couldn't hear anything in response.

The back door lifted, and the truck pulled to the side of the road. Ari knelt on the floor as light seeped into the truck. In Tessa's car, Reed followed on the shoulder of the road a few car lengths behind her. The door continued to climb up, and Ari sat down on the edge with her legs dangling below in the open.

Her heart raced as she watched the dark road beneath her. Other cars flew past, some honking in warning. The alarm still blasted overhead, and the wind whipped her hair wildly around her face. Before the truck could come to a complete stop or common sense could catch up with her, she jumped.

She lost her footing in the jump and tumbled in a somersault along the rough gravel. She would have bruises to show for that tomorrow. By the time she got up, Reed was at her side, helping her up and rushing her to the car.

After a couple steps, Ari managed to steady herself. "I got it."

With a worried look, Reed let go and went to his side of the car. Before she even shut the door, Reed spun out into traffic. Cars honked, blaring their annoyance as he cut across traffic headed in the opposite direction.

"What in the world?" Ari gripped the edge of her seat.

"Sorry. You didn't see the size of the guy getting out of the truck." Reed's knuckles whitened as his eyes focused ahead. "Turn on the computer. I want to find the side streets in case that guy decides to follow us."

"Why would he do that? I don't think he even knew I was in there."

"Maybe not. But that might be Garrett's cruel idea of a joke to let that guy drive you to who-knows-where."

Ari didn't have a response as she wasn't quite ready to believe Garrett did that to her. "Let's find Tessa." Ari turned on the car's navigational system.

"And here I thought you'd forgotten about me." Tessa's voice amplified through the car.

Ari and Reed glanced at each other. A slightly guilty look crossed his face, mirroring how Ari felt.

She reached for his free hand and squeezed. "How could we ever forget about you, Tessa?"

"You better not." The sound of Tessa's voice, even if annoyed, made Ari smile.

With the help of the computer in Tessa's car, which Ari drooled over, they found themselves back at the mini-mart. Tessa's purple hair stood out amongst the older customers. Bags filled her hands, while she sported a large pair of obnoxious yellow sun glasses.

Tessa crawled into the back of the car. "Have the car drive for a bit while I go through my bags." Tessa's bags were filled with a wide array of clothes and food spilling out of them.

"I thought we were on the run," Ari said, turning back to face Tessa. "Who knew it was a vacation."

"Poor, Ari. You've probably never had a real vacation," Tessa said the words with a sarcastic edge Ari didn't like, but somehow expected from her. "I would feel bad for you if I hadn't seen your contract." Tessa stuck her tongue out, sporting an electronic ball studded in the middle of it.

"When did you get a that?"

Tessa shrugged her shoulders. "I got bored waiting for you. I did buy some stuff for you guys." She threw a bag of beef jerky to Reed.

He mumbled his thanks as he dug into the jerky. Darkness had fallen, and they hadn't eaten since their meeting with Dave which seemed like days ago.

Tessa popped a bottle and passed it up to Ari. "Here's some caffeine. We have a long drive."

"Thanks," Ari said, realizing how much Tessa had done for her. It would be hard to say goodbye.

"No problem."

"No, really," Ari continued, playing with the lid on her drink. "I wouldn't have been able to do any of this without you. You've helped with the agent, the car—"

"I love you too, now shut up. You're more exciting to hang out with than anyone else in school, even if you do suck at gaming."

"I don't suck." Ari protested, bringing up the ongoing debate.

"Hey, the fact that I hang out with you regardless says a lot."

"Thanks ... I guess."

"Wake up Izzy so we can listen to some tunes."

"Izzy?"

"My in-car computer," Tessa replied. "Or you can lose to me again. I have my game loaded on Izzy too."

"Bring it."

The trip flew by with gaming and never-ending cans of caffeine while Izzy drove. They joked, laughed, and slayed fictional monsters. While Ari enjoyed her friends, part of her knew it was the last time they would be together. It was hard to imagine leaving those two.

"Izzy," Tessa spoke to her computer, "I need a pit stop."

"Searching for the closest restrooms," Izzy replied in

an English accent.

"We only have thirty more minutes. Can you hold it?" Reed asked.

"Yeah, but my bladder can't."

Izzy pulled over at a public restroom stop. Neon orange lights lit the seedy parking lot in the middle of the night. Ari could tell home wasn't far away. She had to give Tessa credit though—Tessa didn't balk at the graffiti-lined block, or benches that looked like a bird's toilet.

Ari didn't like to think of Tessa going alone, and she did need to go to the bathroom too. "I think I'll go too."

Getting out of the car, the smell of rain hit her. They must have missed the storm, but the puddles still littered the road and sidewalk. She had a slight pang of homesickness, of popcorn on rainy days, and her mother who she hoped to see one more time.

"Might as well." Reed got out of the car and headed over to the men's restroom.

Tessa grabbed the old metal door and the stench hit Ari first.

"This is a dump," Tessa protested as they walked into the barely lit bathroom. "At least we only have to pee here."

The girls were careful to only touch what was necessary in the bathroom. Once back out, Ari wrapped her coat a little tighter around her. The dim orange lights guided them back to the car.

Turning a corner, Ari and Tessa stopped short, almost running into a large man dressed in dark clothing

"Hey, do you girls have a minute? I lost the charge on my car." He approached with one hand in his pocket.

"No, we don't," Tessa continued forward.

Knowing something was off, Ari reached for her but was too slow. The man pulled some sort of device from his pocket and struck out at Tessa. She fell instantly, twitching on the floor. Ari tried to help her friend, but the large man seized her arm, dragging her towards him. Tessa looked so helpless, alone on the damp sidewalk.

"Tessa!" Ari yelled for her friend.

The man covered Ari's mouth with a gloved hand and yanked her in close. His dank, smoky smell encompassed Ari as she struggled to free herself. He tightened his hold to the point of pain, and Ari cried into his thick hand.

He leaned down next to her ear, his voice sharp and serious. "Sorry, honey, but you are the one we want. You can come calmly, or I can hit your friend again with a voltage that may be permanent."

Ari's heart pounded as she stared at her friend on the ground. Ari wanted to fight, but she wouldn't. She couldn't let him hurt Tessa.

"Don't hurt her." Ari pressed down the fury building inside of her. She might be forced to go along now, but she wouldn't stop fighting once her friends were out of harm's way.

"Okay, then. Let's go." He pushed a device into her side, presumably the same one that knocked out Tessa. His free arm wrapped around her, keeping her close as he guided her back to the parking lot.

She kept her steps heavy and slow as she searched the parking lot for Reed or any other people.

"Don't try it," the man warned her in quiet tones.

A gunshot exploded nearby. Ari flinched, the loud noise ringing in her ears. Thoughts of her friends unarmed and alone flashed in her mind. She strained to find them, but couldn't see much in the dark, as her captor, apparently uninjured, tightened his grasp. He hurried his pace, pushing Ari along.

She continued, as if numb, along towards a dark van. Tessa and Reed—they couldn't be dead. If they were hurt, all bets were off. She had to know they were safe. Doing the only thing she could think of, she bit down on her captor's hand. He swore, but through the glove it wasn't enough to make him loosen his hold. She kicked and scratched and fought harder than she ever had before, adrenaline pounding through her body. It couldn't end this way.

Then a shock bit into her side, and Ari crumbled to the ground. Just like that, the fight was sucked out of her. It felt like an elephant had stepped on her chest as she struggled to suck in air. She stared at the tire of the van and wondered if she was going to die there.

The man dragged her upright. Her legs felt rubbery, unsteady. His rough hands pulled her close. "Stupid girl, guess we have to do this the hard way. Just so you know, that was only the low setting."

"Stop." Reed spoke from somewhere in the darkness. "I just shot your friend and I won't hesitate to do the same to you."

Her captor turned them both around, keeping her in front of him as a shield. "You don't want to play with me, kid."

One glimpse at Reed, and Ari could tell something was wrong. He was leaning to one side as he kept a gun firmly trained on them.

Reed focused his cold anger at her captor. "Not playing."

"As I see it, you're not such a good aim with a gun, and you won't chance shooting me if it means killing her."

With obvious effort, Reed took two steps closer. In the low neon lights, blood trailed down Reed's face from a cut on his brow. "You have no clue how many hours I've plugged."

The man behind her relaxed his stance a bit but kept his hold tight. "She's worth too much to stay with you, bud. That is reality."

Out of the corner of her eye, Ari glimpsed Tessa quietly walking towards them. Her feet shaky. Ari bit her lip, praying her friend was okay.

Ari pulled against her captor's grasp, to no avail. Thoughts flashed through her mind, but she worried any action she might take had consequences. "Careful, Reed."

"Listen to your girlfriend." The man pulled her back against the corner of the van, and someone swore behind them.

Without warning, a jolt of electricity raced through her body, stronger, deadlier than before. Her jaw clenched, and her arms and legs involuntarily contracted. Her face pressed into a cold, wet puddle, and she closed her eyes, wanting for it to all be over. Without giving her a chance to collect her thoughts, hands lifted her off the ground. She attempted to swat at them, pushing them back and squirming against their tight hold.

"Ari, it's me," Reed said in a hurried voice. "Come on. We've got to get out of here."

Confusion swarmed around Ari's already muddled brain. But it was Reed. His touch was sure and familiar. And if nothing else made sense, he always did.

Reed laid her down in the back seat of the car and sped out of the rest stop. He was talking, though most of the words flowed over Ari at first. She picked them out one at a time as if her brain was filled with alphabet soup.

"Ari, come on talk to me."

She struggled to respond. She turned her head, but it was a slow process. Forming words appeared to be just as difficult.

"Tessa, are you sure you didn't hit her?" His voice was heavy with worry.

"I hit him straight in the back. Hope that bastard wet himself," Tessa said from the front seat.

"Maybe it was the water on the ground. What did you hit him with?" Reed asked.

"A little toy my dad got for me when I turned twelve, an amped up stun gun."

Ari finally put all the right consonants and vowels together "Reed." The words came out in a whisper. She tried again, louder. "Reed, I'm fine."

He gave her a questioning look. "If you didn't sound like a ninety-year-old stroke victim, I might believe you.

But you're talking, so that's better."

Ari hummed an agreement. Glad to see the fear and anger leave Reed's face, she laid her head against the seat and stared at him from the back. Going over her last few conscious moments, she realized just how lucky they all were to have survived. She thought about the dirt bag saying that once she left she would never see Reed again.

She didn't want to leave Reed. She didn't want to leave his sweet smile, his soft lips, and his fingers that were rough and often ink-stained from his drawings. She loved every part of him. Maybe it was the near-death experience, but she didn't want to lose him. Ever.

"Come with me," Ari told Reed. Her own words sounded stilted in her ears.

He took his eyes from the road momentarily. "I am coming with you, Ari. Don't worry, I think maybe we should go to my house instead of yours. In case whoever that was gets your address. Your mom should be okay. She'll be at work. They'll probably watch her, but if we don't make contact, she should be fine."

Ari must have been tired, too tired to remember not to worry about all of that. She pushed herself up to a seated position. After a moment the spinning subsided. Glad to be reminded her mom was safe at work, she repeated her request. "I mean, come with me to work for VisionTech."

His brow crumpled slightly. "What? I still haven't graduated."

"Forget graduation and a job you hate. I'll make enough money to pay off our schooling. You can do whatever you want, do what you love. You could draw." Ari had been thinking about it for some time but felt too selfish, or maybe too scared, to mention it before. But after that night she didn't care anymore.

"What?" The surprise on his face would have made Ari shrink normally, but she couldn't seem to be bothered when she still couldn't feel her toes.

"You hate school. You want to do your art. So, do it."

"That isn't a job."

"You don't know that. Dave might hire you when he sees your work."

"There's my mom to think about and school ..." He faced the dark road ahead of them. "I just don't know."

A cold spread through her body as Ari turned to stare out the dark window, unsure if she'd said the right thing.

CHAPTER 31

When Reed opened the car door, the cold air woke Ari to her surroundings. Dawn was still several hours out, and the only light came from the car's interior lights. Ari slowly climbed out, and Reed pulled her into a hug. Her muscles ached as if she had been run over.

He kissed her forehead. "I was worried about you back there."

She drank up his touch before he pulled away a few seconds later. Turning around, she realized they were back in their own neighborhood, more specifically at Reed's apartment. The three-story brick building was painted brown with additions built on like an afterthought. It was chaotic, messy, and smelled like the cigarette butts littering the alleyway, but it was the closest to home she'd been in a while.

He motioned to Tessa, who was passed out in the front seat. "I guess we need to wake her up."

"Yeah," Ari agreed. "She saved our butts back there."

"Yes, she did." Reed stared for a moment as if he were somewhere else, momentarily lost in thought.

Ari leaned over and rapped at the window.

Tessa lifted her arm, covering her face to glare at Ari.

"Leave me here," she shouted through the closed window.

"Not in this neighborhood." Ari opened the door. "I like you too much."

Ari reached inside and pulled Tessa out, while Reed grabbed the bags.

Tessa was on her feet, rubbing the sleep from her eyes. "Are you sure my Izzy will be alright out here?"

"Do you have a good security system?"

"Yeah, she'll be fine." Tessa waved away her concern and headed to the building.

"Is your mom home?" Ari asked Reed as she held Tessa in one arm and her small bag in the other. As they approached his door on the bottom floor, Ari wondered if Reed's mother was about to be startled awake.

"No, she's been on the night shift for a while now. We can crash in my room." Reed used his code to open the door.

Ari wished Reed's mom was home, so she could hug her one more time. His mom was a staple in their neighborhood, one more person Ari wouldn't see for a long time.

Reed lugged up their bags. "Take Tessa to my room. She looks like she'll collapse any minute."

The two-bedroom apartment had a small kitchen, living space, and a single bathroom. It was similar to all the other buildings in the neighborhood. Ari lived in a building only two blocks away, except hers was a three-bedroom apartment, due to their family size.

The girls shuffled down the hall, while Reed moved to the kitchen. Ari glimpsed pictures of Reed as a child in frames on the wall. She loved the one from elementary school, back when she first remembered Reed. He was all knees and elbows, playing in the street with Marco and Ari.

Leaving the memories behind, she pushed open the first door and knew immediately it was his bedroom. It smelled like Reed, with a musky scent that could only be his. It smelled safe.

Without a word, Tessa threw herself down on the only bed in the room. She didn't bother pulling down the sheets or taking off her shoes, but face-planted into oblivion.

Ari had always wondered what his bedroom looked like, and it was sort of how she imagined it. Drawings littered the walls and a small sculpture rested on a nightstand. Ari thought about going back to the sofa in the entertainment room but, for some reason, it felt safer staying together.

She grabbed the blue pillow Tessa wasn't using and crashed on the floor. She didn't bother with her shoes either, just rolled over and, with a soft sigh, fell asleep.

When the sun peeked through Reed's window, Ari realized Reed's arm was wrapped protectively over her waist. His arm gave her a sense of security, like a blanket she wanted to cling to more than anything. She didn't want to move, but her mind started processing the previous night's events and dwelling on what she had to do that day. She squeezed his hand gently, not ready to let go of him yet.

Reed released a happy sigh at her touch and pulled her close to him. "Morning," he mumbled into her hair.

"Only if it has to be," Ari replied.

She glanced at the bed. Tessa slept heavily, her chest rising methodically and a slight wheezing sound escaping her lips. Ari's eyes darted around Reed's room, now that she could see better in the daylight. An over-organized, dusty feel permeated air. He hadn't been there for months. The only mess was the bags they'd brought with them. His walls were painted in swirling teals, like he couldn't decide whether to paint the sky or the ocean. It was beautiful, just like him.

Reed kept his hand around her waist and turned her to face him. "I could get used to this."

"Me too."

He didn't give her time to be self-conscious of morning breath or anything else as he leaned forward and kissed her. His firm lips rested against hers, sending a small spark down to her toes. That spark soon led to a burn within her, stronger than she'd imagined. While his hand kept a firm grip on her hips, her fingers rested on the soft spot on his neck, wishing she could pull him closer.

He brushed her thick hair back, and his lips traveled to her neck and ear. "Remember Tessa," he whispered into her neck.

Ari froze, mentally flying back to reality where Tessa slept mere feet away. With a disappointed sigh, she stared at his face. His sharp cheek bones led to soft and slightly swollen lips. Scruffy, dark facial hair sprinkled his cheeks, and she itched to kiss him again.

His smile pulled up to one side. "What's the saying? 'Think of the Queen'?"

She laughed into his chest, inhaling his scent and letting it envelope her. "Well, if anyone could be Queen, it's Tessa."

"True." He turned on his back and kept one arm around Ari.

"I can't leave this," she said as her hand rested on his chest. "I don't want to leave this."

"Oh, come on. I'm sure there will be other boys to kiss."

Ari hit his arm, but not hard. "It's not funny."

"You can make a program with me in it, and then you can visit me anytime."

Ari wished he could see her eyes rolling. "Please," she replied sarcastically then with a serious tone added. "I want you instead. Flesh and blood."

"I know." Reed's voice tightened. "You're off to do amazing things."

"It won't be the same without you. I really do—" Ari stopped herself before she could say those three words that surprised her as much as they would have surprised Reed. The L word had never escaped Ari's lips before, and she usually made fun of love struck teenagers who lusted all over the popular kids. Yet if she was going to be honest with herself, she did love him. She'd loved him before she knew what love was. He was the happy, sweet Reed, and no matter what happened in the future, part of her heart would always love him.

But she worried he didn't feel the same. She'd invited him to come with her, but she also knew how important his mom and his life was here—a life that she would no longer be a part of.

"What was that?" He turned towards her, his breath tickling her ear.

"Nothing. Just be glad we had one last night together."

"Don't talk like that."

Before she could reply, a beep sounded in the kitchen. Startled, she sat up.

"It's the coffee." He reached for her.

The sound of the machine dripping echoed throughout the small apartment. The smell of coffee soon permeated the room, and like a magical alarm, Tessa began to stir.

Ari left the unspoken words floating stagnant in the air.

Tessa eyed the makeshift bed the two of them had made on the floor. "I'm glad I passed out last night."

With a sly grin on his face, Reed ran a hand through his tousled hair. "Oh, this was from this morning."

"Spare me." Tessa flashed Ari a sarcastic grin.

Ari headed to the bathroom to clean up a bit. After the run in at the rest stop and sleeping in her clothes, not much was going to help. She ran a brush she'd found through her hair and braided it.

She returned to Reed's room to find him digging through his dresser. Tessa had barely moved.

"Ready to break into a hospital?" Ari faked a smile, hoping if she kept pretending that maybe it would be easier. She hadn't seen her father, talking or moving, for over six years, and the idea of going back into a virtual with him overwhelmed her.

Tessa pulled out a hair tie and shook her hair like a dog shaking off water. She sat up and tried to tame her hair down. "How about some coffee first?"

"Sounds good," Ari agreed.

As they headed out of Reed's bedroom, his mother came in the front door. She had on a gray uniform, dark hair wrapped up in a bun, and an inquisitive look on her face that quickly turned into a scowl. Tired eyes lined her face as she hung up her keys and waited for them to come into the kitchen.

"Hey, Mom," Reed appeared shortly behind them, in a new navy shirt and jeans.

"I don't know if I'm more tired than normal, or I'm getting old. Why are you not at school, but coming out of your bedroom with two girls and a flush on your face that tells me you've been up to no good?"

"Hey, I'm the innocent one in this." Tessa pulled up a chair to their small kitchen table. "I was just passed out the whole time."

"I don't think that helps anything," Ari said, trying to keep a guilty look off her face.

"Come here." Reed's mom pulled him into a hug, breathing in his scent. "You're going to give me gray hair."

She released him and ran a hand over his hair. "Have a seat, kiddos. I don't have much for breakfast since it's usually only me, but I'll fix something while you tell me the *whole* story." Her fiery gaze, focused on Reed, would have shot laser beams if possible.

"Thanks," Ari said.

"It's good to see you, Ari. Hope Reed has been

treating you right."

"Of course." If anything, she wished he was a little less gentleman-like, but she didn't think anyone would like to hear that, especially not his mother.

Reed made Ari sit down while he helped his mom pour coffee for everyone, and he told their story. Ari listened to the whole thing, adding pieces here and there, but pretty much let Reed tell the tale. Gratefully, he left out the part of being attacked at the rest stop. By the time he was done, Ari had finished her coffee. Tessa refilled her own cup and sat down again, holding her mug tightly.

Reed's mom took another drink. "So why are you guys here instead of at Ari's?"

She'd never missed much, and often had to keep Reed and Marco in line when they were younger. Reed had her same intelligent hazel eyes.

"Ms. Ramses," Ari started.

"Ari, you are too old for that anymore. Call me Monique," she told Ari.

Ari swallowed briefly and adjusted the foot tucked under her on the chair. "Well, you see—"

Reed broke in. "We think we're being followed. There is this guy at school, a real jerk. We're worried he might have said something to someone, so we came here instead. Since I have Dad's last name and you have yours, we were hoping they wouldn't be able to find us."

"While I don't love the circumstances, it's good to see you." Monique wrapped her son in a hug, holding tight. When she released him, she turned her attention to Tessa. "And how do you fit into this mess?"

"I'm the get-a-way car." Tessa grinned.

"Oh, that's yours? I was wondering about that. And you go to their school?"

"She's my roommate," Ari chipped in.

"No, more like her idol," Tessa added.

"I can see why," Monique added sarcastically, looking at Tessa's piercings.

"Tessa has helped me a lot," Ari said.

"Okay." Monique nodded as if coming to some sort of agreement within herself. "I'm glad you're a good friend."

Tessa never once moved her gaze from under Monique's inspection. "I do try." Of course, Tessa followed it with, "By the way, I'm not sure I'd call this coffee." Before Monique could respond, Tessa held up a hand and interrupted her. "Don't worry, I've had worse. Once in another country, I think."

Tessa smiled at Monique who pinched her mouth closed. Tessa was like that.

"Let me fix some toast for you guys before you head down to the center," Monique offered.

The care center where Ari's dad lay in his coma handled long-term medical and psychiatric care patients, a lame name for a place that changed a lot of tubes and bedding.

"Here, let me help with the toast." Ari stood as a ring sounded, signaling someone at the front door.

Everyone froze. Ari knew no one should be coming around at that time of the morning, at least not any neighbors.

Reed went to the door and looked at the small electronic screen. The way his hands clenched, Ari knew it wasn't good. *Williams,* he mouthed the words. Ari cringed, wondering how her Advisor knew where they were. He must have been tracking them. Reed motioned for them to all follow him out the back. Monique grabbed Reed briefly on his way, placing a kiss on his cheek. The front bell rang again.

"Ugh, let me get decent please," she said in a loud voice. She locked eyes with her son for a moment, communicating as only a mother and child could. Monique nodded briefly and then waved him off.

Ari grabbed her bags from his room. If they were running, she would have to dump them somewhere else so Monique wouldn't get in trouble. She headed towards the fire escape, but Reed caught her arm, pulling her into her mother's room.

"What?" Ari whispered.

Reed pointed up. Tessa's black boots dangled from a hole in the ceiling. Ari wanted to ask all sorts of questions, but Reed only offered his knee for her to climb aboard. There might be a time for questions later. But that moment wasn't it.

Monique spoke loudly from her spot at the front door. "What? My son? He's supposed to be at school. Are you saying you lost him?"

Ari pulled herself up into a cramped space with several long jackets. Tessa pulled her up and out through the maze of winter wear. They were in the bedroom of a completely different apartment.

"Hey," Tessa whispered and lifted her eyebrows in amusement.

Reed appeared next out of the closet. "We need to ditch our gear. They're tracking us."

Ari pulled off her ring and dropped it in her bag.

"I hope you know how painful this is." Tessa reluctantly emptied her pockets.

"I'll pay you back," Ari said.

"It's not the money, but the hours I spent setting it up to my specifications."

Once everything was stashed in the neighbor's closet, Reed left the bedroom with the two girls right behind him. They followed him running through an apartment almost exactly like his, with brown shag carpeting and faded white walls. Only the pictures and furnishings were different.

"Don't mind us, Charlie. Just passing through." Reed gave a quick wave to the man sitting at the kitchen table.

The balding man sat nursing a drink and gave a curt nod with no more surprise on his face than if it were an everyday occurrence. "And here I thought you outgrew your old antics. Be safe and be fast." The man shook his head and mumbled into his cup. "Kids."

CHAPTER 32

Ari's lungs burned as she followed Reed through the rundown buildings. She briefly thought back to her days as a child where they would race around the neighborhood for hours, playing hide-and-seek or tag. The joy of those days was replaced with fear as the three of them sprinted down a shady corridor. Adrenaline pushed them further and faster than any child's game ever would.

As they finally maneuvered out of the maze of old buildings, they found themselves within view of the tram entrance. The three of them stood in the shadows of a small convenience store, catching their breath. Tessa bent over, and Ari clutched a cramp in her side. Reed's face was flushed but showed no sign of fatigue. If anything, his face was more determined.

"It was Williams," Ari said once that her breath slowed, but the stitch in her side still ached. "He followed us here. Why?"

"Why not sooner? It doesn't take a genius, if they reviewed your VRs to figure out what you're capable of." Reed continued watching the street.

"He probably didn't think you'd escape school or

maybe he wanted to see who you'd run to." Tessa pulled back her wild strands of hair into a tight bun above her port.

"Time to go, now." Reed grabbed Ari's hand.

As the three of them walked down the street, she noticed Reed's fierce expression. "Let's try not to look like escaped convicts."

Tessa gave Ari a toothy smile. It was quite disturbing. Ari focused on the tram, hoping no one noticed them.

Morning commuters filled the platform, and Ari hoped to hide amongst the tired, bleary-eyed workers. They squeezed inside the crowded tram. The stench of sweat and dirt assaulted them as they found seats in the back.

"We might be a little early for Marco. He was supposed to meet us outside the center with your mom's visitor pass," Reed said quietly.

"What? When did you talk to him?"

"Last night when I was driving. You two were passed out. I caught him up on the situation. I thought it would raise too many flags if you went in as a student, not in school, asking for a visitor's pass."

Ari's gut tightened with worry, not for herself but for her friends and family. How much was she really risking for this? Her brother would be willing to bear the cost. "We'll need to be careful. Advisor Williams may be looking for Marco, possibly tracking him."

"Marco wouldn't keep his old school gear. He can get around on the streets better than anyone. He'll be okay," Reed said.

Ari squeezed his hand, turning her gaze to the window. Buildings, old homes, and cluttered lots passed by in a blur. She had taken this route several times with her mother to visit her father. Ari had hated seeing his weak, pale frame, barely clinging to life through the tubes and machines. But she'd rarely visited him in the VR despite her mother's requests. Marco went once but never spoke to her about it. Ari wanted to see her father, but part of her worried that if she went in, he might convince her to never leave either.

The last time she had seen him conscious was her eighth birthday. Her parents had been fighting that morning over money and VRs, the usual things they'd argued about. Both of her parents stopped when Ari entered the room.

"We're talking about some important things right now, sweetie. Go and play with your brother." Red rimmed her mother's heavy eyes.

"No." Ari straightened up, angry at her dad for using all their money on VR vacations, especially when she hadn't seen one birthday present anywhere in the house. "It's not fair. You take all the money. You make Mom cry. It's not fair. We don't need you." Tears streamed down her little face, but she stood strong, cutting her father with a few words. She'd never seen him conscious again.

That same summer, Ari surgically received her own port through school.

Eight years later, guilt and anger gnawed at Ari, but today she had a chance at redemption. She would convince him to leave or make that VR a living hell.

"Hey, you still here?" Reed squeezed her hand, pulling her back to reality.

"Yeah, just thinking," Ari murmured.

"Me too." He leaned over and briefly brushed her lips with a kiss.

Her stomach did that happy flip-flop dance that she associated with Reed.

"Get a room," Tessa added. "A room without me in it."

"Love you, too." Ari smiled. She turned back to the window and spent the rest of the ride imagining life without Reed, without her family, in a foreign land by herself. And she'd thought going away to school was bad.

They made it to their stop and found Marco drinking

coffee outside at a table.

"Good to see you." She wrapped her brother into a hug. Stale smoke clung to him, like he now lived in a bar, but she didn't care.

"Glad to see you're causing more trouble than I am," he murmured into her hair.

She pushed him back. "Difference is this isn't my fault."

"If you say so." His eyes had that mischievous sparkle that he'd had as a child. Reaching into his pocket, he pulled out an old HUB and handed it to her. "This is linked to Mom's account, so you shouldn't have any problems getting into the facility. Good thing you look like her."

The small device didn't have a bracelet like most did, so she slipped the device into her pocket.

Tessa headed to the counter to buy drinks, mumbling something about decent coffee while the others waited at a table in the corner.

"I have something to give back to you too," Reed told Marco. Her brother reached a hand out, but Reed shook his head. "Not here. But as pissed as I was to have to bring it to you, I'm glad I had it on the way here."

The gun. As lucky as they were to have it, Marco could face ten years in prison for having one.

"Maybe you should toss it," Ari said, but Marco instantly rejected that idea.

"I can get good cash for that."

"It's not the cash I worry about." Ari watched her brother. She hoped he would be doing better at home, but somehow, he looked worse. His face had thinned, and his eyes had a haunted, dark look about them.

"Don't worry, sis. I always land on my feet," he said with a familiar smile that Ari had a hard time buying.

Tessa sat with a small drink in front of her. "So, what's the plan?"

"I'm going to go see my dad, then meet up with Dave.

He should be here in a couple hours."

"When are we heading back?" Tessa turned to Reed.

"After Ari leaves, I suppose. The sooner the better. I have a feeling Williams might be waiting for us."

Tessa nodded and took a sip of her coffee. "Probably, but I wonder if we took a detour by my father's condo we could claim we'd been there all along? It may require some hacking, but you could manage."

"What about your car?" Ari said.

"I let you borrow it," Tessa told Ari. "We can order a service to take us back. I can figure it out after I have some decent caffeine in my system."

"I wish I could take you all with me." Ari took time to look at each of them, trying to memorize their faces.

Marco scoffed. "And leave this great life? I've got too much going on."

"It's a single ticket, dear, but worth it. Even I'm jealous of your contract." Tessa took another drink of her large coffee.

"I'm with her, sis. I don't know why you fell into the pot at the end of the rainbow with our gene pool. I'd kill for that ability."

"I'd give it to you both in a heartbeat." And Ari meant it.

The plan was simple—well, simple enough. Reed was going to use Marco's visitor pass to get into the facility with Ari, while Tessa and Marco hacked the system from the outside. Marco was going to try to erase her trail, or the record of her being there. It wasn't a guarantee though. Neither Marco nor Reed could guess all the security measures the facility might have in place. Either way, time was of the essence.

Ari's heart raced as she walked through the large glass doors of the hospital's entrance. The middle-aged woman at the desk was focused on the screen in front of her. Ari

and Reed scanned their cards, and the cards' pictures
appeared on her screen. Reed looked nothing like her
brother, but Reed didn't care. He was going with her. The
women glanced at their pictures, gave them an annoyed
look, and waved them through. Maybe security wasn't too
tight here. It was only a hospital.

"I would like a private virtual visit," Ari said, hating
that her voice sounded so young and shaky.

The woman had already turned back to the screen.
"Fill out the request and pay on the screen."

Ari entered the required information, her fingers
shaking so bad she had to re-enter her father's name twice,
and then she paid with a card Tessa had given her. Ari had
only consented to let Tessa pay with the promise that she
would pay her back, and that if Ari was caught she would
say she had stolen the card from her roommate.

The monitor beeped, and the virtual was scheduled.
The woman, eyes still on her screen, pointed to the
scanners in front of the double doors. Ari steadied her
steps and remained calm though every fiber in her body
wanted to run.

Once through the scanners, Reed reached for her
hand. "It'll be okay."

As they walked through the doors, she wasn't sure she
believed him. The smell of bodies mixed with cleaner hit
them first. She'd been in health care centers before, but
this dying scent made her gag.

Rows and rows of beds filled one side of the room.
Unconscious people were laid out with white sheets
covering them. Tubes trailed out from under the sheets
into a metal device hanging off their beds. Fluorescent
lights shined down on their gaunt empty faces. The only
thing moving on these bodies were their eyes, flickering
with random disturbing movements.

The other side of the area contained private rooms
scheduled for virtual meetings. The metal doors had a
single control panel and a number etched inside. Farther

down the aisle, she watched an attendant push a bed into one of the private rooms. She assumed it was her father.

They walked down the hall and the tall male attendant greeted them at the door. "6G? For patient 26409?"

She nodded. Her father no longer had a name, but a number. A number she hated and could never forget.

"You ready?" Reed asked.

They both waited as her feet stalled, heavy like cement. "Okay." With a deep breath, she stepped into the room with Reed shutting the door behind them.

Her father's once bulky frame had shrunken, now frail and bony under the thin sheet. His gaze flicked back and forth behind his closed eyes. Silver littered his dark hair, especially filling out his beard. His hair fell down to his shoulders and was tucked behind his ears. He used to wear it in a ponytail tied at the nape of his neck. He never was one to worry about his hair. When she was little, he used to let her put it in ponytails with all the colorful clips she wanted.

She stepped towards him and tears blurred her vision. How could she hate and love one person so much in the same moment? Her chest ached as she strengthened her resolve.

"Are you ready?" Reed asked.

She ignored his question. She would never be ready. Hesitantly, she took a seat next to her father.

"It's okay if you change your mind."

Ari reached for her cable. "Go to the original program in his history. It should be the cruise on the Rhine River."

"If I get word from Marco, I'm pulling you out. You understand?" Reed had received an old HUB from Marco, so they could stay in touch.

"I'll be quick. Promise."

Ari bit down on her lip and slid the cable into her port. She closed her eyes, sensing the program was ready for her, and floated into a whole different world.

CHAPTER 33

Now familiar with the transition into the VRs, she wasn't surprised when the cool breeze off the water brushed against her face. The world around her had turned green and blue. A lush countryside lined the water, dotted with villas and even a small castle in the distance. As the sun set, it gave everything a beautiful golden hue.

Turning away from the water, she pushed off the railing in search for her father. With the size of the ship, it might be harder than she'd thought. Several stories tall and long, there was no end to the white railing winding around the length of the ship.

"Excuse me, miss. Would you care for a drink?" An exotic waiter with a heavy accent offered Ari a glass of what looked like champagne. The waiter's face with his crystal blue eyes and chiseled cheek bones was perfect, too perfect. The prison held enough beauty and luxury that was hard to leave, but it was still a prison.

"No, thank you." Ari replied. "But can you help me? I'm looking for Enrique Mendez."

"I'm not sure about him, but I know most people are upstairs dancing." He motioned to a set of stairs to her left. "There is a live band tonight."

"Thanks." Ari headed to the stairs. Looking down at her outfit of jeans and a t-shirt, she decided to go dancing. Her clothes morphed into a simple blue dress that her mother handed down to her years ago. What Ari used to struggle with in the program, now didn't take more than a second to fix. The music and laughter rose as she walked up the two flights of stairs.

Her hand trailed along the handrail made from dark wood lined with gold accents. The texture felt off, too smooth for the detailed engraving it showed. Dr. Coleman would be pleased with her observations, but there would be no more tests for her.

Stepping onto the dance floor, she noticed the clouds mingling in the background. High above the water, only the fading night sky surrounded them. The railing turned to soft white fabric laced with lights. Elegantly dressed couples floated by on the dance floor, spinning, smiling, and laughing. Maybe her father really thought he'd died and gone to heaven. She finally spotted his tall frame in the middle of the floor with a woman whose red dress exposed more skin than it covered.

Ari reached for the nearby railing. Despite her anger over the years, her heart leapt to see him so alive and happy. Granted after a minute of watching her father hold this woman tight against him, her joy fizzled. Vacation time was over.

Ari fought against her initial desire to strip this ship down to mere wreckage. It would just push him further away. She strode onto the dance floor, brushing off an approaching gentleman asking for a dance. He wasn't real. None of this was.

"Excuse me." She placed a hand on her father's shoulder, stopping them cold. "Can I have this dance?"

Her father kept his long black hair tied neatly in a ponytail at the nape of his neck. Without his beard, he looked younger. His hazel eyes peered out behind his heavy brow.

"Enrique?" The woman turned to her father.

Staring at Ari, he didn't hide the confusion that flashed on his face. Ari wasn't sure he would recognize her.

"Isabelle?" he asked, calling Ari her mother's name.

"Not quite." Ari remembered that he hadn't seen her for eight years. She had changed a lot since she was eight.

Her father dropped his hands, dismissing the woman he was with, or rather ignoring her. She strode away towards the bar. He then reached for Ari and drew her into his arms. The resentment of years past, constantly eroding Ari's soul, quieted, and she was back in her father's arms, like a little girl dancing on his feet in the kitchen. She had to fight the urge to get lost in this dream as well.

He reached into his pocket and handed Ari a simple white cloth. She noticed the tears that had been silently falling onto her cheeks. She gave an embarrassed smile and brushed them away.

"Are you going to tell me who you are? I thought you were Isabelle at first glance. But not quite. A relative, perhaps?" His lips pulled up into a big goofy smile, a favorite of Ari's and one she never thought she would see again.

She took a deep breath, needing the extra air to draw the words out. "I'm Ariana ... Ari, your daughter."

He stopped dancing. "No, you can't be." He pulled his hands away from her and stepped back. "That would mean ..."

"I'm sixteen. You've been gone for eight years."

Rubbing his jaw, he shook his head but kept his gaze locked on her. The music played on while the couples danced around them in an artificial state. The perfection of it all was absurd, especially with the tumult of emotions happening in the small little bubble that contained Ari and her father.

"It's time to come home, Dad."

He shook his head slowly. "I can't leave. Your mother and I must finish our vacation. It's not every day one can celebrate their tenth wedding anniversary."

She stepped towards him. If only she could reach him, hold onto him. "It's been more than ten years, Dad."

"How did you even arrive on the ship?" He spun in a circle now. "I know you say you're my Ari, but something's not right."

She concentrated for a moment, analyzing the code around her. People turned into streams of numbers and letters. The dancers vanished, music stopped, and a light shone overhead, like high noon in the summer. She kept the river and the basic frame of the boat. The bright light showed her father's worn and tired features, something he couldn't even hide in the VR.

"What in the world?" He squinted against the bright lights, blankly searching for the others.

For a moment Ari thought she'd gotten through to him. She held her breath, praying it had worked.

Then something odd happened. The world resumed to normal. Like a rubber band, everything she'd torn down snapped back to perfection. *What was happening?*

While she stood dumbfounded, he moved toward the staircase. "I think I drank too much tonight. I better head back to my room."

Ari rushed after him and grabbed his hand. "Please stop, it's me."

He turned back, his breath choppy and labored. Confusion creased his eyebrows, and she wished she could be that eight-year-old little girl again with two long braids down her back. Then the thought crossed her mind that she could change herself, or at least his perception of herself.

She closed her eyes and imagined a picture of herself at that age, specifically the one from her eighth birthday. She was blowing out the candles with her brother next to her, wearing her favorite purple shirt. It took longer than

Ari liked, and when she opened her eyes again, she realized she might have made the wrong choice.

His eyes bulged, and he stumbled back. "I need a drink." He turned to the bar.

In anger, she deleted the code again, wiping away the bar and the people.

Even though nothing stood there, he continued going through the motions, ordering a drink and mumbling thanks to the non-existent barkeep. With nothing there, he appeared like a child playing make-believe.

"Dad." Her voice cracked as silent tears fell heavy on her cheeks. "Mom wanted me to bring you home. She's worried about you."

He exhaled loudly, looking familiar with this argument. "Oh, I know. I'll be up to join her in our room shortly. She was never one for staying out late. It's okay, sweetie."

"She left her room. She's at home waiting for you." With emotion tightening her throat, the words came out small.

"How could she possibly leave? Just give me a minute." He tipped back a drink that only he could see.

"There was an emergency. She's hurt." Ari struggled to make up anything to convince him to go. "She's in bad shape, Dad. We have to go now."

She reached for his hand, trying to budge him, but he remained glued to the invisible bar. Even though he wasn't in his right mind, his brush off tore at her. She couldn't give up though.

"They would have come and got me. I spoke to her a while ago. She's fine."

Roughly wiping her tears away, she shoved those years of hurt into a box, the same box she had struggled to keep shut for years. Ari was no longer that little girl. An ocean breeze curled around her, and she focused on the code and what she could change.

She obliterated the ship, the sea and the surrounding lush landscape. Letters and numbers flew like a tornado around her head, breaking apart and morphing into something new. When she finished, Ari and her father stood on a plain dirt road, like the one that ran behind their apartment.

Turning in a circle, he stumbled over his words. "I gotta go back to our room. Maybe one more drink."

"There is no room, Dad. There is no cruise, no boat, no damn river. You are in a VR and your only way out is to leave with me, to go back home." She clenched her fists ignoring the pain in her palms. "You need to come home to me and Marco and Mom. Please, Dad. Come home."

Ari's words appeared to be lost in the air. He mumbled something about code and finding the loophole, but Ari couldn't make it out. She reached out and shook him by the shoulders, pain turning to frustration. "Dad?"

He didn't bother to even glimpse her way. He ripped his arm out of her grasp, and she fell backwards in the dirt. He walked away from her, stumbling towards an empty oblivion. Her whole life he had been walking away from her, and the pieces of her heart that he held, fragile and broken as they were, shattered.

The sick man, who was no longer her father, continued down the street to an old door, talking to people that were not there, and mumbling incoherently. A numbing sensation poured over her as she watched him in his own make-believe world, knowing she would never have her father back. Her father was dead. The only thing left was this VR recording, a shell of his former desires and wishes stuck on repeat.

Closing her eyes, she pinched the bridge of her nose, not able to look at him anymore. She morphed back into the older version of herself with jeans and a black shirt. It hurt too much to look at her childlike hands. Ari knew this could happen, but some part of her, that little girl with pig tails, wanted more. She had wanted a purpose for the past few months of her life. What would she tell her mother the next time they spoke?

Before she left the VR, a slow methodical clapping echoed in the program. It sounded nothing like her father, so she opened her eyes. In front of her stood Advisor Williams.

CHAPTER 34

How long had Advisor Williams been watching her from inside the VR? Standing there in his perfectly pressed gray suit and blue tie, his old blue eyes gave nothing away.

She stood, trying to keep her features calm as her blood raced. "Why are you here?"

"Oh dear, please don't waste our time with asinine questions. You children are all so predictable, skirting your responsibility to your country. The question you should ask is, what I'm going to do with you and your newfound abilities?" He stepped purposefully, careful not to dirty his shoes on the dusty road.

"I'll go back to school," Ari lied. "I just wanted to see my dad."

Williams gave a small sound of disapproval. "I've been watching you and your brother for a long time. Your brother is a waste of space, and at first, I worried you'd be just like him. I have to admit, I misjudged you. That was why it took so long for me to see what you really are."

"Really are?" Her gut clenched as she realized he knew about her abilities. She could only play stupid for so long as he closed the distance between them. This was a VR, she reminded herself. He couldn't hurt her in there. She was stronger than him.

"Don't get me wrong. The signs were all there for a warper, but it took me hours of combing through footage to see the truth." He stood mere feet away, watching her closely. "And even though you are gifted far above what you deserve, you still can't be trusted. You'll be taken immediately to a new facility, one that can help guide you through your true responsibilities. You can be shaped into the tool we need."

Her head snapped up, her body poised and ready to flee. Dave was right. She had never thought Advisor Williams was a saint, but deep down she hadn't believed the horror stories about warpers. How in the hell could she get out of this? *Reed!* If Williams was in here, they must have Reed already.

"You children think you're so special and deserve so much. You started from nothing and deserve nothing. Your only worth is what you can give your country." His tone turned dark, and disgust painted his face ugly.

"I've never asked for a handout." She stepped back, a bit frightened, never having seen so much emotion on Williams face before.

"Your *life* is a handout. Detain." The last word he said out loud as if talking to someone else.

Before she could respond, metal links tied her hands in front of her. "What the hell?" Her wrists hurt where the chains bit into her skin. It took her a second to remind herself it wasn't real. She blinked to find the code, and it took her several more seconds to remove the links binding her hands.

"You're too slow and untrained. Do you really want to play this with me? I'll give you nightmares you'll never forget." He pointed forward.

Fast, like lightening, pain erupted across her thigh, and she cried out. Red blossomed on her jeans. She couldn't figure out what Williams did, but it hurt like the devil. Why was this hurting so bad? VR programs were meant to dull pain receptors.

Williams spoke again, something she couldn't make out, and the pain in Ari's chest brought her to her knees.

Every breath she took was painful.

He stepped forward. "Do you like this little program? An addition I created when needed to motivate individuals."

Her eyes widened. She'd never thought anything like this was possible. With his next step forward, blinding pain erupted along her spine. She closed her eyes and dropped her head to the ground. She tried to force her way out of the program, but nothing happened. She tried again and again, screaming in frustration. Why couldn't she leave? A coppery taste of blood entered her mouth, and she thought she would die. No, she wanted to die.

"After several months at school, you still don't know your way around a VR. How disappointing." He crouched close to her prone form, his voice creeping inside her mind. "This is my little invention. It's modified to obey certain commands and protected by walls you've never seen."

The code. She searched deep into the program. Numbers and letters flew by and she recognized certain specifics, grass, sky, and more. But there was something she had never seen before. Totally unfamiliar, she tried to delete it, to wipe it out, but nothing happened.

"You're not the first warper I've had to drag in kicking and screaming."

He touched her temple and a blinding pain stabbed inside her mind. Past her screams, the pain reminded her of another time, the day in the VR, when someone had destroyed her drive. The blank file hurt like hell to try to navigate. There was nothing but pain. She still remembered the ringing in her ears and the migraine she'd had for hours. Before she could think too long about her decision, she erased everything she could see, all characters in the code. She hoped that by destroying all the data Williams's program needed to run, she would be free. Rage fueled her power, and she deleted everything. When her mind began to spin, she pulled out.

Unsure if she made it, she struggled for breath in the darkness. Snippets of light in the room she left flashed in front of her. She struggled to make things out as pools of black swam in her vision and code scattered across the darkness. Her wrists ached, restrained in front of her, and she realized she was back in reality. She glimpsed a guard as she tried to turn her head, the wires pinching her neck.

He reached for her neck to pull out her cable. He spoke, but the words were mumbled as if she were underwater. She wrestled under her restraints. It took another minute of panic until her vision came fully back.

Even though her wounds took place in the VR, her body ached, and her head throbbed. She ignored the pain and trying to search the room. "Reed!"

A soldier pushed her back down. "Quiet."

She fought as another man's rough hands pulled the cables out. "Reed," she screamed again, panicking as she tried to find him.

Reed called her name from somewhere afar but was cut off by the dry thud of a punch and responding moan.

Arching back, she continued struggling against their hold. "Let me go."

They ignored her, lifting her to her feet and hauling her out the door. Back in the main room, unconscious patients remained unmoved by the chaos in front of them. A few feet down the main corridor, Reed stood between two guards, a gash on the right side of his temple, and blood in the corner of his mouth. His gaze was frantic as he called for her.

"Reed!" Ari needed to know he was okay. He had to be okay.

"No need for theatrics." Williams appeared, his creased forehead the only sign that Ari might have gotten to him in the VR.

She strained against her captor's grasp, kicking behind her and twisting. She'd grown up wrestling with Marco, who never took it easy on her, and she knew how to fight. The guard hit her from behind, and her legs collapsed under her. Pain shot down her back, and she gritted her teeth.

"Stop!" Reed pulled forward.

"Don't injure her," Williams ordered, and her guard stilled. Williams's gaze traveled briefly between Reed and Ari, finally resting on Reed. "The boy, on the other hand, is disposable."

"No!" Ari shouted.

"Then behave."

She stopped struggling and the guard lugged her to her feet.

Reed's eyes were frantic and worried. "This isn't goodbye, Ari."

If it kept him safe, she would do whatever they asked. Even if that meant going with Williams. As they walked past the private rooms, her heart ached to see defeat written on Reed's face.

As she moved past him towards the exit, the world exploded around her. The blast knocked Ari to the ground as pieces of rubble rained down on her. An alarm blared above, cutting through any conscious thought. Pain radiated up her leg and the side of her face burned. For a moment she worried she was back in the VR with Williams. She struggled to open her eyes as smoke flooded the room.

"Get your ass moving," someone yelled in her face, someone with purple hair. Tessa.

Ari tried to speak, but started coughing instead, which sent her head spinning. Shouts sounded over the alarm. Sprinklers turned on overhead, water raining down over Ari.

A burly guard approached. A blast of light shot from

Tessa's hand, and the man fell to the ground, convulsing as if being electrocuted. Tessa pulled on Ari's good arm, and she focused on getting her legs to stand. Ari cried out when she put pressure on her leg. A large piece of plastic stuck out of her thigh.

"Don't look at it. Just move," Tessa ordered.

Ari obeyed. With Tessa's help, she could walk. Unfortunately, standing didn't help the world swimming around her. Ari searched for Reed but couldn't see anything through the smoke and chaos.

"Reed?" Ari yelled over the alarm.

"Up ahead. Just keep moving." Tessa pulled her through the maze of beds. The rain didn't bother the unconscious patients as it splattered their faces and soaked their white sheets.

Ari couldn't help but worry some of them might have been hurt by the explosion, even though it had come from on the opposite wall. "What happened?"

"Oh, your brother is now into black market toys. Sort of cool, if it doesn't kill him."

Ari moaned. If they all survived this, *she* was going to kill him.

Reed appeared on Ari's other side and a flush of relief coursed through Ari's body.

He glanced down at her injured leg and swore. "Let's get out of here."

They hurried to where Marco stood by an emergency exit. Marco's lip pulled up into a large smile, far too large for the trouble they were all in. "Hey, sis."

"Save it."

"Of course." He opened the emergency exit and they filed out into the alley.

A shot fired behind them, and Ari instinctively ducked. Williams hollered over the alarm. Marco turned back. He pulled the gun from the back of his pants and took aim.

"Marco," she yelled in protest.

Reed held her back. Ari knew most of the staff had already taken cover once the alarm had sounded. Armed guards stormed towards them. Marco got off several shots before the doors closed.

Out in the alley, they all ran, or as close to running as Ari could manage. Reed supported Ari's bad leg, helping her unsteady stride. A doorway appeared up ahead, and Marco motioned for them to take it. They were in the middle of an industrial park, filled with sky-rise buildings and offices. They continued down the alley, and it opened to a street. People cluttered the sidewalks, most dressed in business attire.

"One sec." Reed had Ari hold onto Tessa. He took off his button up flannel, leaving him in a black t-shirt.

"What are you doing?" Marco must have finally noticed Ari's wound. "Shit, sis. That's bad."

She sucked in a harsh breath as Reed pulled the piece of plastic out of her leg. He tied his shirt around her leg, covering the wound. "It's not close to a major artery, so hopefully that should hold for a little bit."

"That's a hell of a lot of blood for fine." Marco's eyes widened.

Ari tried not to look at her leg.

"I'm sorry—" Marco started.

"I'm just glad to be away from Williams, and I don't want to go back." She exhaled a big gust of air and focused on their next step. "We have to split up. They only want me."

"No," Reed and Tessa said in unison.

Reed continued, "You're getting on that plane first."

"What plane? I'm supposed to meet Dave several blocks from here." She briefly glimpsed the busy street. "We won't last out here for long. Every cop in the area is probably looking for us."

"I called Dave. He's meeting us on top." Tessa pointed up.

"There?" The sleek gray building next to them rose

high in the air.

"We aren't totally useless," Marco said. "Let's move."

They turned the corner onto the sidewalk. Ari stood in between Reed and Tessa, with Marco in front trying to block the view of her bloody leg.

"When we saw Williams enter the center, we improvised with the explosives," Tessa explained.

Reed tightened his hold around her waist. "Don't look now, but there's an officer across the street."

Ari turned her gaze down, knowing her face would be the first they would recognize. After a moment, she dared a glance. The officer, dressed in dark fatigues, was approaching them, talking to into his headset.

"Run," Reed yelled.

They hurried into the building and headed to the elevator. Their ragged appearance drew curious glances, and they ignored the receptionist's shouts.

"Sorry this one is full." Tessa pushed a man aside as they raced inside the empty elevator.

The door closed as a security officer sprinted towards them. Marco jabbed at the buttons for top floor and roof access. He pulled out a small device and hooked it into the system. It took mere seconds for him to override the system and grant them access.

Everyone was breathing hard inside the small elevator. Ari's leg throbbed, and black dots danced in her vision. She focused on staying upright and ignored her desire to sag to the floor. If she went down, she wasn't sure she could stand again. The bruises on Reed's face blossomed into a deep purple. Marco put his equipment in his bag and slung it on his back, sweat gathering on his brow.

Ari brushed back her hair. "Do we know if Dave is there yet?"

Tessa's face fell. "He said he'd hurry."

So that was a no. "And if there is nothing but officers up there?"

Nobody answered. Reed reached out and squeezed her

hand, saying everything they didn't have time to say. The elevator passed the top floor and arrived at the roof.

The doors binged opened, and the sun shone into the elevator. Reed held the door open with a hand and waited for a moment. The roof held random maintenance units, big silver boxes scattered along the roof. There was no sign of Advisor Williams or other security.

In the corner of the roof, a sleek pale blue aircraft was parked with its engine running. It had a modern oval shape with angular wings protruding from the sides.

"Look." Ari pointed to the aircraft. Relief coursed through her limbs. It had to be Dave.

"Run," Marco hollered, and they raced onto the roof.

With Reed at her side, she forced her heavy legs to run towards the plane. Even though every step was jarring and painful, she pushed on. Once in view, the rear side door opened in the aircraft. Dave sat in back with an armed guard and waved them in.

Shouts erupted. Coming from across the roof, Williams, disheveled and injured from the blast, shouted to the guards surrounding him. Two of Williams's armed men continued chasing them, while the guards dropped to a knee next to Williams.

She focused straight ahead. They were going to make it. They had to. The plane lifted a few feet off the ground, readying for takeoff. Gunfire exploded across the roof. Ari ducked her head but kept moving.

Tessa jumped inside first, and then Marco slid in right behind her.

Mere feet away, Ari and Reed fell to the ground. Pain shot down her leg from the impact. Pushing up, blood painted the ground in front of her, but it wasn't her blood. Reed. Blood pooled from his shoulder.

Two men in full protective gear jumped out of the plane, one returning fire and the other pulling her into the plane. Rough hands picked her up. "Reed!" she screamed. "Get Reed." Panic flared at the idea of what Williams would do to Reed bleeding out on the ground.

Deposited in the plane, she turned to the open door. Rapid gunfire and screams rang out as the plane lifted a foot or two in the air. A guard carried Reed under one arm, and they climbed on the readied plane. The door slammed shut behind them. Shots continued bouncing off the plane as it lifted in the sky.

Dave shouted orders to the pilot and grabbed a med kit. Reed moaned in pain and Ari placed a hand on his leg, wishing she could do more. One of the men pushed her out of the way as he worked on Reed's shoulder. She turned to look out the window, not able to shake the feeling that they were still being chased. She pulled back slightly, and then moved closer to the thick window. Numbers and letters raced around Williams, replacing the roof and the men, and running like code in a VR. Her pulse quickened. This couldn't be real, it couldn't be happening. Her heart raced as she glanced to the others in the plane. No one else was paying attention.

She blinked and turned back to the window. The code vanished as fast as it had appeared. Williams stood, surrounded by security, hollering at the nearby guards. Then in a brief moment, he turned to her. Not that he could see her as they lifted high above him, but somehow his hard gaze bore straight inside the plane with a threat of the future. He wouldn't forget about her.

CHAPTER 35

"**G**et that away from me." Reed pushed away Dave's hand, which held a very large needle. "Not unless you show me your degree."

"We already gave you a local, but it's not enough. You don't want to be awake for this."

"Trust me. I do."

Ari didn't blame Reed. They weren't quite safe yet. The plane was parked at Tessa's father's sky-rise. Tessa and Marco had headed inside to talk with her father, while Reed was treated on the plane. Ari's wound had already been taken care of, her one pant leg torn to shreds. Reed's shoulder looked worse, blood staining his arm and shirt. Dave had bandaged Reed's shoulder, saying the bullet went straight through, but Reed would need to go to a doctor to make sure there was no other permanent damage.

Sitting back against the chair, Dave ran a hand over his head. "I think you guys just aged me ten years. That was a close call."

"I know." Ari kept a firm grip on Reed's hand, not wanting to let him go for a moment. Looking at Reed

287

though, guilt ate at her. None of this would have happened if not for her. Now she was expected to just drop him and leave. It didn't sit well with her.

Ari trusted Dave. They had out maneuvered the government drones and easily stayed off radar as they travelled to Tessa's father's corporate office. Dave had saved them, and Ari planned on letting Tessa's dad and his attorneys deal with the authorities. But they weren't in the clear yet. Marco and Tessa were meeting with her father and his attorneys, planning their next step.

"Do you think Marco and Tessa will be okay?" she asked.

Dave turned to Ari. "Tessa and Marco weren't ever in custody, so with Tessa's father's connections they should be fine. We do keep tabs on family left behind."

But not Reed. Ari read into what Dave didn't say. Williams knew Reed was with her. There was no going back for him.

She glanced at Reed. She'd ruined his life and she worried he might not like the results. "Reed needs to come with us. It's not safe for him here." Ari was too chicken to watch Reed's reaction, so she kept her gaze on Dave.

"I know." Dave's eyes betrayed a touch of sympathy as he turned to Reed. "If you want to come with us, there is always a spot for data security support. You will be required to sign the same contract and be under the same restrictions."

Ari watched Reed's face, pale and drawn, and his silence worried her.

"Can you give us a minute?" she asked Dave.

"We're in private airspace, but it doesn't mean we're safe. You have two minutes, and then we're taking off." Dave stood and left the aircraft.

A cut on Reed's temple stood out, the clear bandage slowly sealing it. All because of her. And now his schooling and life there was over. How could he still care for her after everything she'd put him through?

"You don't have to come with me," she offered. "Maybe they can hide you somewhere. Take your mom to safety. If you want to bargain for something else, I will. Just let me know how to make this right." Her throat tightened with emotion. This goodbye had been coming for a while, but she'd never wanted to face it.

The plane's motor hummed as Reed reached for her. He traced down the side of her cheek. His touch sent a soft tingling sensation along her neck, and she blinked back tears.

"I'm not going with you because my schooling and career are over or because I may end up in jail. It's just not a good enough reason." He lifted his gaze, blinking thick lashes. "I'm going with you because I've loved you for as long as I can remember. I didn't know it was love at first. I thought I was just being a big brother, caring for you, and making sure you were happy and safe. At some point it turned into something more, something amazing that I don't want to end."

She let go of the breath she'd been holding. "So, you're coming with me?"

He leaned forward, resting his forehead against hers. "Just try to get rid of me."

Their moment of peace together didn't last long. Marco and Tessa appeared alongside Dave to say their final goodbyes.

Tessa gave Ari a hug. "Life is going to be so boring at school now."

Ari laughed as she pulled away. "I'll miss you, too. Thanks, Tessa." Thanks, wasn't enough for what Tessa had done for her, but it was all she had. Ari turned to her brother and hugged him.

"This isn't goodbye, little sis." He held onto her just as tight. "I will see you again, even if I have to hunt you down."

"Promise?" Her eyes burned as she held back the tears.

"Promise."

"Take care of yourself." She stepped back, though her heart ached to do it.

"You take care of my sister." Marco slapped Reed on his good shoulder.

Reed still winced in pain. "You know I will."

Dave approached. "We need to go now, before anyone knows we're here."

Ari nodded. She couldn't hold back the tears as she buckled into the aircraft. She watched Tessa and Marco until they shrunk into nothing. Wiping her eyes, she turned to the horizon. The sun set in a ball of gold as they headed to the ocean, the real ocean, a blue sheet of water traveling farther than she could see. Both Ari and Reed were on pain meds but refused to be put under. No, she needed to be awake. With Reed's steady frame beside her, she didn't want to miss a minute of the rest of her life.

HEAR FROM THE AUTHOR

You can find me at www.deannabrowne.com for upcoming projects and to sign up for my newsletter for free short stories and up to date releases. You can also track me down online on Facebook, Twitter, Amazon, and Goodreads. And I always appreciate your time in posting reviews. Thanks for reading and I hope you enjoyed it!

ALSO BY
DEANNA BROWNE

DEMON RISING (Dark Rising Trilogy #1)

Some sacrifices cost more than death.
Thirty years ago, dark magicians unleashed a new power
on the earth fueled by demons. Governments toppled,
millions died, and magicians seized control.
Twenty-four-year-old Becca survives these dangerous
times by relying on her wits, her fists, and the limited
goodwill of her boss, a local crime lord. When news comes
of a fire back home and the parents she left behind dead,
grief-stricken Becca realizes her dark past has finally
caught up to her.

On the hunt to save her missing sister, she must rely on
Darion, a treacherous ex-boyfriend with ties to the local
coven for back-up. Problem is he's a pyromancer that can't
be trusted, especially with her heart. Becca's forced to
navigate a sticky web of deceit and must decide what she's
willing to sacrifice to save her sister's soul.

AMAZON

UNHOLY SUNDERING, Dark Rising Trilogy #2
Out May 2018

ABOUT THE AUTHOR

DeAnna Browne graduated from Arizona State University with her BS in Psychology. She finds it helps to corral those voices in her mind and put them to paper. An avid reader and writer, she has a soft spot for fantasy with a touch of romance. Despite her love for food and traveling, she always finds her way back to Phoenix, Arizona with her husband, children, and pet dog.

ACKNOWLEDGEMENTS

Every book is a team effort, and this is no exception. I'm grateful for my tribe of writing group partners who listened to first chapters and were a great sounding board. A big thanks to my first readers that gave valuable feedback to make this a better story. I'm thankful for a great editor and cover artist.

Also, a never-ending thank you for my family, especially my spouse, Spencer, and my parents, Lynard and Eleanor. They help me manage my chaos, watch kiddos, and make meals. This book wouldn't have made it out into the world without their influence and support.